Fancy Meeting you Here

Also by Julie Tieu

The Donut Trap
Circling Back to You

Fancy Meeting you Here

A Novel

JULIE TIEU

AVON

An Imprint of HarperCollins*Publishers*

FANCY MEETING YOU HERE. Copyright © 2023 by Julie Tieu. All rights reserved. Printed in the United States of America. No part of this book may be used or reproduced in any manner whatsoever without written permission except in the case of brief quotations embodied in critical articles and reviews. For information, address HarperCollins Publishers, 195 Broadway, New York, NY 10007.

HarperCollins books may be purchased for educational, business, or sales promotional use. For information, please email the Special Markets Department at SPsales@harpercollins.com.

FIRST EDITION

Designed by Diahann Sturge

Crying emoji on page 262 © FOS_ICON/Shutterstock

Library of Congress Cataloging-in-Publication
Data has been applied for.

ISBN 978-0-06-324519-8

23 24 25 26 27 LBC 5 4 3 2 1

To Laura, Michelle, Vickie, and Grace—
from young girls to drama queens to amazing women,
thank you for your lifetime of friendship

Chapter One

Whenever I dreamt about my own wedding, I pictured a wedding dress like the one I was wearing. A simple, elegant gown with a train and long veil. The only difference would be that it be made of actual fabric and not this absorbent toilet paper.

"Stop moving." My best friend, Beth Chan, spiraled my arms with a roll of TP, covering my peony tattoos for my makeshift gloves. I looked like a mummy.

Jesse hung a "diamond necklace" around my neck to appeal to Rebecca's bougie tastes. "Ten seconds left," Jesse announced. I would say it was a shout, but Jesse Lo's voice boomed by default. It easily cut through the clamoring of twenty women channeling their inner Vera Wang in a small but classy tearoom in Pasadena.

I was unbothered and continued twisting roses out of quilted squares. As a wedding florist, it would be a shame if I didn't have my own bouquet and I needed to use every advantage. Rebecca's sorority sisters had somehow created a really convincing bodice with a complete mermaid gown. If this were *Project Runway*'s unconventional materials challenge, they would win.

"Time!" Rebecca clapped with delight as she judged her toilet paper brides. Even though Jesse, Beth, and I were her closest friends, Rebecca was not going to let best friendship sway her. She was going to use a discerning eye to determine her winner.

"Cheater," Rebecca said when she saw my bouquet. I knew she said that out of love. Rebecca made it down the line and made the clear choice. The prize went to her sorority sisters, whose names I'd forgotten. I only met them an hour ago.

"I really thought we had it," Beth said, consoling herself with a tiny cucumber tea sandwich. Beth didn't like being wrong, whether it was about tests or, in this instance, her toilet paper couture. It was a good thing she was better at the former. She was due to take her first set of tests for the United States Medical Licensing Examination in mid-July.

Jesse stole all the deviled eggs for herself. "Sorry, you know I can't eat carbs." Jesse appeared calm as she stared longingly at the display of scones and clotted cream, but stress radiated from her. Her own wedding was coming up, a month after Rebecca's, and with a CrossFit competition sandwiched in between. Everyone was having a busy summer this year.

Rebecca took a break from hosting her bridal shower and joined us at the end of the table, smoothing down her white Reformation dress as she sat. "Jess, slow down before you choke on a yolk."

Jesse mocked Rebecca's smug smile. "Thanks for your concern, Dr. Seuss," she said with a full mouth.

"Back to your corners," I joked. Emotions were running high now that we were counting down the weeks to Rebecca's extravagant wedding. Our group texts had become a dumping ground for wedding headaches. Rebecca complaining about how her mother, Assemblywoman Donna Yu, had taken over the guest list, inviting all her political allies. Jesse, ranting how she thought letting her parents plan a traditional wedding to save money created a bigger headache than she'd expected. There was enough anxiety going around that we didn't need to turn on each other when we needed each other the most. Since I had the double honor of being their bridesmaid and their florist, I really needed them to get along or else they were going to make my life more difficult than it already was.

People have asked how our group has lasted over the past ten years, assuming that our personalities clashed. Rebecca spoke her mind, the apple not falling far from her family's political tree, with the delivery of a well-intentioned meddling auntie. Jesse, in her natural state of Lycra and French braids, intimidated people with her brash brawn and beauty. But our group was balanced by Beth and me. Beth was smart and a natural helper, so it surprised no one when she got into med school at USC. She wasn't easily bothered except when it was crunch time for exams, when she basically went off the grid. Beth was only locatable by her chef boyfriend, Ethan, purely because they lived together. And me? I'd like to think that my penchant to avoid conflict made me a great mediator, even though my therapist suggested that I work on my communication skills.

But the real secret to our friendship was that we embraced each other's differences. We didn't expect each other to think the same way or agree all the time, even though it would have made our lives easier. This was how our friendship was able to evolve as we evolved individually and how it was able to outlast any of our romantic relationships. *Hoes before bros,* as Jesse would say.

Rebecca was unfazed. "Elise, are you sure you can't make it to my rehearsal dinner? Don't make me beg."

I would have loved to see Rebecca beg. She got her way with a bat of an eyelash and a *pretty please*. "You know I can't. I have a wedding booked that night." It was one of the few gigs I'd managed to secure this wedding season that didn't include a friends and family discount and I couldn't pass it up. "It was booked over a year ago." Before her fiancé, Mark, proposed, I should have reminded her.

Rebecca sniffed at my reply. "First my brother, now you. Who's next? The band?"

"I would if I could," I said with an apologetic smile. As for her younger brother, Ben, I wasn't in any position to speak for him. The guy had caused enough drama after he was MIA for the engagement party. I was the lucky lady to be paired up with him in the wedding party. Rebecca basically instructed me to be a human handcuff before he could go AWOL during the reception.

"You already bailed on the bachelorette party." It was unbecoming of Rebecca to guilt-trip me. She knew it would take more than that to convince me. She'd met my mother, who conveyed her "I left Vietnam for this?" look of disappointment after I dropped out of college and another when I quit my job at a renowned event planning company to start my own studio. My guilt quota was met for a few lifetimes.

"I had an event that weekend too." It was a small wedding at the Arboretum that required little setup, so I technically could have caught the flight with them to Miami if I'd had the money to spend. The irony of working in a multibillion-dollar wedding industry was that I didn't make enough money to participate in it as a guest.

"What about Sarah?"

"She's leaving." That wasn't exactly true. I had to let my assistant go. Just like I had to let Fernando, my delivery guy, go. It was my fault. The launch of my floral studio coincided with a dip in the economy and microweddings becoming trendy. Events scaled down along with my profit margin. Disregarding contractual obligations, I literally couldn't afford to cancel these events. Not even for one of my best friends. "Isn't it more important that I'm there for your actual wedding day?"

"Yes," Rebecca agreed with the enthusiasm of an angsty teenager.

Beth, noticing my discomfort, changed the subject to something everyone could get on board with. Everyone except me. "Elise, how come you haven't replied to my text about going on a blind date with Tom?"

I stalled by refilling my dainty teacup with raspberry rooibos tea. "You know I prefer to meet the love of my life the old-fashioned way—accidentally sending letters to my high school crushes or entering a marriage pact with my best friend in case we're both single at thirty, whichever comes first. So, what do you think, Beth? You and me in two years?"

Jesse palmed the bottom of her teacup, tossing it back with a loud slurp. "It's okay, E. I know you would have picked me if Steven hadn't gotten there first."

"Getting set up by friends and family *is* the old-fashioned way, Elise. It's the way of our ancestors," Beth insisted. "I like Tom. He makes a good pie."

Jesse snickered. "Does Ethan know that you've tasted Tom's pie?"

My face wrinkled at the setup and the innuendo. "I don't have time to date right now." It wasn't enough to placate Beth, who was determined to make this happen.

"He's nice," she said.

I shrugged. "So is my mailman, but you don't see me running off with him."

"Tom can cook."

I sipped my tea. I could cook too, if microwaving my mom's meals counted as cooking.

"He works hard," Beth added.

"I would hope so."

"He's cute."

I gave her a knowing look. Beth brought this up, but she hadn't produced a picture of him, claiming that Tom was shy about that stuff. This was all code that the man had to be ugly. This was the tax I had to pay as the only single person in our group. They probably thought I hated being the seventh wheel, but I was fine waiting for the right person to come along. After watching my parents fight their way to the bitter end of their marriage, I was in no rush to date.

I thought that their divorce would usher in a new chapter of harmony, but it had been two years since their marriage ended and our new normal didn't feel normal yet. My dad decided to spend most months back in Vietnam, so he wasn't really around. As for my mom, she would never say that she was depressed, but how else could I describe the way she used to hide in her room after work each night? We lived in the same house, but I rarely saw her. At least there were signs that she was coming out of it. She spent a lot of time with her Teochew association friends these days. The tides were turning, I hoped.

"I'll take a rain check," I said, but changed the subject. I read enough AITA posts on Reddit to know that keeping the attention away from the bride and groom was a surefire way to destroy friendships. "But we're here today to celebrate Rebecca's upcoming nuptials to Mark. Isn't it time to open gifts?"

Rebecca gasped as she jumped out of her seat. She was the only woman I knew who was excited to open lingerie in public.

"I know what you're doing," Beth said, twiddling her fingers as she picked up an Earl Grey macaron.

"I know what I'm doing too," I said. Maybe it was the optimist in me, but real love was worth waiting for. I believed that my dream man was out there and that was enough for me for now.

Chapter Two

Together with their families, your presence
is requested at the wedding of
Rebecca Yu and Mark Kim
Saturday, June 3rd
Five o'clock in the evening
Ellery Estate
Pasadena, California
Reception to follow

Whenever I was stressed, the easiest thing for me to do was to smile. I once heard that you could trick yourself into feeling happier by smiling. Most of the time, it worked. I'd done this for so long now that I didn't even think about it anymore. My perennial smile got me through every detour in my life. It wasn't a cure-all, of course. Not everything could be helped by an upturn in my lips, but it helped me tough things through until I made it to the other side. Which was why I fought to fix a smile to my face while I waffled about firing my cousins.

You're free to leave. Can you please leave the premises?
You're fired. Get out.
Professional decorum kept me from saying any of this out loud

after Tiffany and Kelvin snuck off to smoke while I was jamming the millionth rose into the backdrop behind the sweetheart table. They showed no remorse after arriving late to the Ellery Estate. I loved them and all, but they lacked the common sense to gently place my carefully crafted centerpieces on the tables. Tall, gold candelabras overflowing with soft pink English roses and fluffy white hydrangeas were plunked down on each table, disturbing the polished glasses and silverware and spilling petals everywhere.

I couldn't fire them though. How would I explain it to Aunt Mabel, who practically threw my teenage cousins at me after I stupidly, drunkenly whined about my overhead costs at our last family dinner? I couldn't refuse because they were poor college students willing to work under the table and Aunt Mabel wanted my dream to succeed as much as I did. She was the very reason why I fell in love with flowers.

Aunt Mabel hadn't planned on having a flower girl. It was a coincidence that seven-year-old me was dressed in the fluffiest, itchiest white tulle dress my mom could find. My grandmother and great-aunties thought I was Aunt Mabel's mini-me and thus decided that I should be part of the wedding party. Aunt Mabel easily agreed because it was impossible to argue with seven aunties. The pressure was real.

For my part, I took the role very seriously. How could I not, when my aunt, looking every bit a princess in her bell-sleeved white dress and sparkling tiara, gave me the special task of preceding her? I was to set the stage, laying rose petals along her path, making it worthy for her slippered feet. And I did, ever so gently sprinkling red rose petals to *ooh*s and *ahh*s from the crowd of guests, as if I were casting a spell on them.

In reality, I was the one entranced by the whole spectacle of the wedding. Everyone dressed in their finest, making declarations on a day painted in red. Red envelopes, red candles, red teacups, red qipao, red banquet hall. A joyous celebration so powerful that even my relatives with long-standing feuds could put aside their pettiness for one night to enjoy the joining of families and partake in courses and courses of delicious food. To this day, twenty-one years later, I remember it as the most perfect day. I could still recall the cheap musk that perfumed my aunt's Chinese wedding invitation.

Aunt Mabel and Uncle Leo's wedding was perfect. They had an eternal love that somehow spawned my stupid cousins.

Good god. Did they put out their cigarettes on the exterior wall? Had they no shame?

The Ellery Estate was the pinnacle of Art Deco elegance and the Grand Ballroom was no exception, with its draped ceilings, crystal chandeliers, and French doors providing sweeping views of the expansive garden. I jogged toward the courtyard before they defaced the property further.

"Hey, guys. Good work today," I said with a pleasant smile and a voice so sweet, it was a wonder birds hadn't landed on my shoulder to chirp along to my lie. I hated myself for taking the easy way out. If Rebecca were here, she'd tell me to stop being so nice and be direct. But in the back of my head, I heard Jesse's voice. That voice said that these fools had to go. "I got it from here. You can go home."

"Yes!" Kelvin's eyes lit up. "You're not going to tell my mom, though, right? I want to meet up with my friends."

"Me too," Tiffany chimed in, pleading with me with the biggest sparkling anime eyes.

I sighed. I didn't think Aunt Mabel cared if my cousins were out, but with me as their supposed boss for the day, they wouldn't have to rush home. Why the heck not? While they weren't great assistants, they weren't really the type to get into trouble. How much more damage could Kelvin do when he was wearing socks with his Adidas slides and Tiffany was distracted watching Tik-Toks? "Okay. Go have fun."

As soon as the words left my mouth, Kelvin and Tiffany texted their friends. They looked up after confirming their plans. So why were they still lingering? What else did they want? Oh right. "I don't have cash on me right now. I'll Venmo you later."

"A hundred bucks each, right?" Tiffany asked while I walked them out toward their car.

The worst money I'd ever spent. "Yeah. Drive safe!" I waved them off and once they drove away, disappearing down the long, tree-lined gravel driveway, I returned to the Grand Ballroom. Most of the work was done, though I'd have to clean up the mess Tiffany and Kelvin made later.

My phone rang, as it had every fifteen minutes. Rebecca had a detailed schedule for the day. If she wasn't one of my best friends, I would call her a bridezilla, but this was Rebecca doing Rebecca. According to my reminder, I had ten minutes to report to the bridal suite for hair and makeup. I stowed my phone away in my tool bag, ready to head upstairs, when I saw the empty gift table in the dark nook by the entryway. Damn it.

For most brides, the gift table only warranted a small vase of flowers, if at all. Rebecca, however, was not like most brides. She had specific instructions for this gift table. Rebecca and Mark hadn't set up a registry and instead asked guests to donate to the California Conservation Center, where Rebecca managed public affairs. A simple table would not suffice. Rebecca called for a display that was "like living in a coral reef but elevated. Less *Finding Nemo* and more Bali resort."

What the hell did my broke ass know about vacationing in Bali? Nothing.

Designing a seascape display with Rebecca was a useful exercise in learning what she didn't like. That list included seashells and starfish (too obvious), tropical flowers (it wouldn't go with the ivory and blush-pink wedding flowers), or any other décor that could inspire sea shanties. It didn't leave me with many ideas, but whenever I had a creative block, I went back to the drawing board.

What was the true purpose of this display?

Then it clicked. It wasn't to impress guests with my use of chrysanthemums as sea anemones. The floral arrangements had to center clean water in a way that would inspire guests to pony up for a generous tax-deductible donation. And save the environment, of course.

I came up with the perfect solution—towering cylindrical glass vases with green ferns submerged in water with a layer of white beach rocks at the base. With blue uplights, it would re-create the sense of awe that I felt whenever I visited the local aquarium. How small I'd feel as I tilted my head back to watch a school of fish disappear behind the giant, willowy kelp forest. Rebecca loved the concept and the execution seemed easy enough. Vase. Rocks. Water. Ferns. The only thing I didn't think through was where I'd get enough water to fill the damn things.

I loaded the vases on my flatbed dolly and then dumped a handful of white beach rocks and shoved ferns into each one. I backed myself across the dance floor and past the swinging doors to the kitchen. Maybe the manager would let me fill them by the sink.

"Excuse me," I said, trying to get somebody's—anybody's—attention. I raised my hand to make up for my height. Not a single person lifted an eye. Nobody heard me over the bustling kitchen noise. Sheet pans of vegetables were going into hot ovens. Prep cooks diligently julienned ribbons of mint, blended sauces, and filleted steak for four hundred guests at their respective stations. No one knew that I was there. Sometimes, I thought fading into the background was my superpower, but it was unhelpful in times like these.

I wheeled over to the vacant stainless steel sink. Normally, I would abide by the rules of the venue, but they would understand that the bride would have my ass if I failed both my jobs as florist and bridesmaid today. The bride gets what the bride wants. Besides, I'd set up the Ellery Estate like Gatsby's wet dream more times than I could count. I was practically an employee here. Using the spray nozzle, I filled each glass, watching the greenery dance as the water rose up to the top.

"Are you supposed to be here?"

The gruff voice came out of nowhere, startling me. I glanced up and found a man wearing a black, short-sleeved chef's coat, black pants, and the ugliest Cheetos-orange Crocs. It didn't look like the Ellery Estate kitchen staff uniform, so he must have been the caterer Rebecca hired to make Chinese appetizers for cocktail hour.

"I'll be done here soon, chef," I said politely even though this guy probably had no authority in this kitchen. There was something familiar about him that I couldn't put my finger on, but I didn't dwell on it too long. The wedding vendor circle was small and chances were that we had worked the same wedding or two. He did have a good face, though. It had a boy-next-door quality with a light stubble that accentuated his angled jaw. A face I surely would have remembered.

"Can I see your ID?" the caterer demanded.

Well, that wasn't neighborly of him. I spritzed the last bit of water to top off the last vase, eager to get on my merry way without causing a scene. "I don't have my ID," I said apologetically.

I'd left it up in the bridal suite. I didn't think I'd have to prove my identity when I was bundling bouquets and boutonnieres in the parking lot at dawn. That sort of thing had never posed a threat to anyone before. "Now if you'll excuse me"—I tugged my dolly toward the exit—"I have flowers to set up."

"You don't look like a florist to me." The caterer's eyes dragged on my undercut and my tattooed arm, bare from my white tank top. Then there was a cursory glance at my gray jeans and Doc Martens. I would have been flattered if it didn't feel like he was trying to pick me from a police lineup.

"Well, I am one." What did he suppose florists looked like? That we swooped in like fairies, flitting about in ball gowns, waving our wands until a garden appeared in the middle of a sterile hotel conference room? It didn't matter what I wore or what I looked like because part of the magic was to never be seen.

The caterer followed me out, intent on getting answers, and he was testing my patience. What else was there to say? I didn't have the time to explain myself to him. He didn't seem like he'd care or believe me that I'd created more elaborate floral installations at swankier places than Ellery Estate anyway.

"You're trying to tell me that *you* made all of this."

"I did have help," I replied as I pulled up to the gift table. I let his disbelief go because being on-site meant keeping my figurative hospitality hat on. I bent down to pick up the first vase.

"You look like you could use some help now," the caterer said, though he didn't make a move to assist in any way.

I resisted the urge to roll my eyes as I easily lifted the first vase and placed it on the gift table. Given my petite frame, most people assumed that I was as delicate as the flowers I handled. But I'd show him that I was stronger than I looked. I didn't need to go to the gym when I carried buckets of flowers every day in my shop and climbed up ladders to affix magnificent floral arrangements on top of gazebos, mandaps, arches, or wherever people wanted to declare their lifelong devotion nowadays. This vase was nothing.

I managed to set up the rest of the display without spilling a drop of water on the white linen tablecloth. Before I could throw my victory in the caterer's face, I spotted an intruder as I went to pick up the last vase.

A little white seashell chilling at the very bottom.

Maybe Rebecca won't notice. Who was I kidding? The woman once returned a brand-new pair of Louboutins over a little scratch on the bottom of her shoes, a perfectly normal place for scuffs to be.

"Fuck me," I complained under my breath, dropping down to the floor to get a better look at the seashell.

"*Excuse me?*" The caterer looked positively appalled, swinging his head around like he was waiting for someone to announce this was all an elaborate prank.

I choked on a laugh. Did I offend his delicate sensibilities? The cooks I knew sprinkled *fuck*s everywhere like parsley. The caterer did look a little too cute for the kitchen, like he'd faint from the heat. I didn't have time to deal with him, so I dropped the pretenses. I stuck my arm into cold water, stretching it as far down as it would go. "I need to get this seashell out."

"What's wrong with it?" The caterer sniffed. His feet shifted as he turned to scan the room, sensing the theme. "It looks fine to me. I doubt anyone would notice such an insignificant detail."

"Tell that to the bride," I muttered. The caterer's cough sounded like a laugh. "Are you just going to stand there or what? I'm in a hurry and you look like you have longer arms than me," I said desperately. "Do you think you can reach it?"

The caterer knelt, meeting me on the floor. His hair fell forward as he dipped his head lower to get a closer look at the object of my untimely demise. His eyes flicked up, meeting mine, considering his answer. I couldn't help but notice the contrast of his smooth skin against the scruff that framed his mouth. What a waste of a good face.

"Um." The caterer's eyes widened slightly. "I—" He cleared his throat and swallowed as he looked away. "I can try if you remove your arm."

My arm . . . was still in the vase. I slipped it out and without thinking, I swiped it across my white tank top. That was a mistake. I had let my boobs roam cage-free, knowing that later I would have to stuff myself like a sausage into a Spanx bodysuit. It was the only way I could fit into an unforgiving satin bridesmaid dress that I ordered a size too small, thinking it would motivate me to work out. Now, I looked like I was trying to win a spring break wet T-shirt contest and this man whom I just met was at direct eye level with my nipples.

This was much, much worse than dying from Rebecca's wrath. I avoided looking at the caterer's face while I untied my hoodie from my waist and put it on, zipping it all the way up. I held on to the vase as the caterer dunked his muscled arm into it with a sense of ease that made me think he'd done this before. The agile way his arm gracefully maneuvered around the greenery in his descent was art in motion.

"Argh, I almost had it." The caterer scratched his stubbled jaw. His immediate investment in this vase was appreciated. I wish I could stay to admire the way he stared at this pesky seashell, but my phone rang again in the distance from my tool bag. I was officially behind schedule.

"It's fine." I had to get ready for the wedding photo shoot. If I was lucky, I could swing a quick shower. "I have to go."

"Wait." The caterer reached into the pocket on his sleeve that I hadn't noticed before. "Aha," he said softly of the metal utensil in his hand.

"Chopsticks?"

"Plating tweezers," he corrected. "And the answer to your problem." In his arm went and the caterer picked up the seashell on his first try. He presented it to me almost as if he were offering me a bite of food.

"Thanks," I said, pocketing the seashell for safekeeping. I picked the vase off the floor. The caterer cleared the gift table for me, setting the guest book and engagement portrait of Rebecca and Mark to the side, so I could slide in the last vase to complete the display. "Thanks," I said again. He'd ended up being helpful after all.

"It was no problem," the caterer replied as he rearranged the gift table to its original setting, "seeing how much of a crisis this seashell would have incurred." Just when I thought I was a joke to him, he surprised me. "May I have your business card?"

I hesitated. While it was common practice for vendors to exchange business cards and offer referrals to each other's businesses, I wasn't sure what the deal was with this guy. Most vendors didn't question my identity or stare at me with their handsome faces in a way that made me feel like I was in a dreamy Wong Kar-wai film. Damn the blue mood lighting. It was playing tricks on me. I could not be lured by this tactless man, even though he smelled like a heavenly grilled cheese sandwich made with good butter and artisanal bread.

"I don't have any business cards on me," I said. A rookie move on my part. "I can add you on social media. It links to my website." It wouldn't hurt to make a new connection and once I knew his name, I could ask around to see what his deal was.

"I'm not on any social media platforms," he replied curtly, like the idea was beneath him. Geez. Okay.

"Well, not your personal social media handles. Your company's?" The caterer frowned, confused. Were we speaking two different languages or something? "Never mind. I can give you my number if you have referrals." I motioned the guy to give me his phone. "This is my cell."

"Do you usually give your number away so easily?"

Wow, this guy was going to make me regret this. "Yeah. I have to. I'm often on-site."

The caterer looked down at his phone as soon as I returned it. "Elise?"

"That's me." My eyebrows arched, registering the surprise in his voice. "Elise Ngo of Elise Ngo Floral Design. It's easy to remember." That's what I thought when I named my studio after myself, not thinking how often I would hear customers pause once they saw my last name. I didn't see what was so difficult about it. It's pronounced exactly as it's spelled. The *ng* was the same sound as any word that ended in *ng,* like *thing,* but with an *o* at the end. It was three letters and one syllable. Not the tongue twister people made it out to be.

I tried not to let the mispronunciation bother me. Naming the business after myself was to let the world know that this studio was all mine. After I resigned as a floral designer at Filigree Events, where I honed my craft arranging flowers for product launches and movie premieres, I started my own floral design studio to focus on weddings, my true calling. The designs and workmanship were all by me. Unfortunately, the loans and bills were also mine.

The caterer's entire demeanor relaxed, contrite almost, as he backed off. "You're—"

"I've been looking everywhere for you!"

The caterer and I turned to find Ethan Scott, one of the grooms-men, out of breath as he jogged into the room. Ethan had that slick, rockabilly hair that had everyone convinced that he carried a comb in his back pocket. It paired well with his black tuxedo. "Rebecca has us on a wild-goose chase looking for you. Why didn't you pick up your phone?"

"I just finished here. I'm coming," I replied.

Except Ethan was looking at the caterer and the caterer re-turned his gaze, working his jaw. At first, I thought the caterer was sizing Ethan up, but then he rolled his eyes as he clapped Ethan's hand, bringing him in for one of those shoulder-bump hug things. "Does Becks think it takes all day to put on a suit?"

Becks?

The only people who called Rebecca "Becks" were her family. It was only then I noticed how the caterer's eyes crinkled the same way Rebecca's did when she smiled. *How did I not see it sooner?*

"Ben?" I asked, though I knew the answer.

The caterer was Ben Yu, Rebecca's younger brother and fuck, he'd seen my nipples.

"It's nice to finally meet you," I said, putting more distance between us. I didn't intend to pass judgment in my greeting, but Ben had missed the engagement party and the wedding shower, leaving Rebecca and her parents to make up excuses for his absence. It brought unwarranted stress for Rebecca and if there's one thing Rebecca didn't need on her wedding day, it was stress.

"I came straight from breakfast service at Bistro Ynez," he ex-plained as if it mattered.

"I thought you finished your externship hours," Ethan said, butting into our conversation.

They were not doing themselves any favors by standing around and shooting the breeze. "I really should go now," I said, excusing myself. I grabbed my tool bag on the way out.

"See you soon," Ben called out before I exited into the hallway.

Aw, crap. He was referring to wedding party pictures that began in forty-five minutes. As I walked away, another realization hit me in the gut.

I'd have to spend the rest of the day with Ben.

Chapter Three

Ground zero for the bridal party was located in a private cottage on the other side of the garden where the ceremony would take place. It was over a hundred years old, outfitted with heavy mahogany furniture and porcelain vases adorning the original plaster fireplace. The suite was in constant motion, rife with pre-wedding anticipation. Mark's mother pushed past me in her blue hanbok to see her completed look in the full-length mirror. The hair and makeup team, donning all-black attire, were working on Rebecca. Jesse and Beth were fighting for counter space in the bathroom, both in their custom satin robes with "Yu Crew" emblazoned on the back. I took some comfort that none of the bridesmaids were dressed yet, but I wasn't in the clear because Rebecca had the hearing of a bat.

"Elise! You're late," Rebecca said, her eyes shut while a makeup artist affixed false lashes. She was showing restraint since there were other people present.

"There was a snafu with the gift table arrangement, but I took care of it." There was nowhere to undress, so I threw my Yu Crew bathrobe over my shoulders and removed my clothes away from others' view. Since Rebecca's eyes were still closed and everyone was running late, I tiptoed toward the bathroom before Rebecca could assign me a task. I darted past Jesse and Beth, throwing off my bathrobe as I jumped into the bathtub and drew the curtains closed.

"Saw your butt!" Jesse shouted as I turned on the water, which made Beth giggle. That was Jesse Lo for you. She didn't let refined environs or prim socialites keep her from expressing herself as immaturely as possible.

"You're welcome," I replied, slapping on hotel bodywash with my bare hands. "How come no one is ready?"

"Cut me some flack. I slept through my alarm," Beth mumbled, her sleepy voice trailing as she left the bathroom. She must have stayed up, burning the midnight oil. Beth had a tendency to mix up her words when she was in study mode. One semester, she showed up out of breath to a study session because the elevator was broken and she had to climb three "plights" of stairs. To be fair, going up three flights of stairs sounded more like a plight to me.

"And I only get up when Beth gets up," Jesse added, as if that were a reasonable explanation. Jesse led a six A.M. workout every morning at her gym, Lo's Health and Fitness. She'd let herself sleep in because she was dragging her feet through this snooty affair—her words, not mine—whereas Beth had a legitimate excuse.

I massaged a dollop of hotel shampoo into my hair. It had a musky scent that the bottle claimed derived from orange blossoms. "Rebecca didn't sic anyone to wake you guys up?"

"You know why," Jesse whispered quietly enough so that her voice wouldn't echo off the bathroom walls. "She felt bad." Rebecca feared Beth was a flight risk when she found out Beth had to study. Ever since college, where our friend group formed freshman year, Beth was notorious for going MIA when exams came around.

"No one's ever heard of a runaway bridesmaid," Beth had assured Rebecca when she asked Jesse, Beth, and me to be her bridesmaids last year. There was no way any of us would have said no. Our bond was forged through ten years of existential crises, breakups, and late-night karaoke. We could call on each other, no matter how inconvenient, like being a bridesmaid weeks before taking the most difficult exam of Beth's life thus far. But Rebecca must have noticed that Beth was looking worse for wear after two years of med school all-nighters.

After rinsing my hair, I toweled off and put on my bathrobe, cinching it tight around my waist. Jesse leaned in and whispered, "Don't tell Rebecca, but Beth forgot to write her speech. I had to help her." My eyebrow arched, a silent warning that Jesse received. "Don't worry. It's innocent and boring. No ratchet anecdotes, I promise."

I chose to believe Jesse for her sake. The guest list for this wedding was beyond our friends. There were Rebecca's and Mark's colleagues to consider. Not to mention Rebecca's parents' political connections. They weren't the right audience for our drunken escapades.

I took my seat in between Beth and Rebecca, when a makeup artist and a couple of hairstylists, armed with blow dryers and hot curling irons, swooped in.

"The photographer wants a picture of the three of you helping me into my dress, but no one is ready," Rebecca griped. This was normal pre-wedding anxiety talking. I placed my hand on her arm, hoping the warmth would melt her icy tone.

"Where is he now?" Jesse asked, unable to hide her grimace while the makeup artist contoured her face with a stiff brush. She should get used to this. It was a preview for her own wedding.

Rebecca carefully nudged a bobby pin back into her low, twisted chignon. "My mom asked him to take pictures of Mark and the groomsmen so he had something to do while he waited."

I scanned the room and saw no sign of Donna Yu. "Where *is* your mom?"

Before Rebecca, I had zero knowledge about local politics. It shocked Rebecca when I cluelessly reacted to the news that the venerable Donna Yu and Robert "Bob" Yu were her parents. How was I supposed to know that Donna Yu was a member of the California State Assembly? It wasn't like I spent my free time watching capitol committee hearings.

"She left to make some phone calls. The campaign doesn't stop on account of my wedding." Rebecca said this like she was used to it by now since Donna Yu had to get reelected every two years, but her jaw ticked as her mouth pulled into a tight smile.

"If it helps, Ethan texted saying that the guys are all dressed and ready to go," Beth offered. "Including Ben."

"Good. He made it," Rebecca replied, as she relaxed into her wingback chair.

"Was there ever any doubt?" I tried not to make any sudden movements while the hairstylist changed the part of my hair and twisted my locks into a low chignon. "He wouldn't have missed his own sister's wedding."

"You'd think so." Rebecca sighed. "When he quit his job for culinary school, everyone thought he'd give it up after a semester but look at him now. Slinging hash browns instead of coming to my engagement party."

"That's the thing about hospitality," Beth said. "Weekends and holidays are the busiest times." I nodded in agreement. Over the years, I'd declined several invitations for family gatherings and holiday parties to set up clients' family gatherings and holiday parties. "If school didn't keep me so busy," Beth continued, "I'd probably be annoyed with Ethan working so much. He has spent more time with Ben than he has with me."

"Ben?" I recalled how easily Ethan and Ben fell into conversation. I assumed they became quick friends from being in the wedding party together, but it sounded like they were closer than I thought. "How do they know each other?"

"Do you remember when Ethan worked at that bullshit fine dining restaurant on Wilshire?" Beth asked. "Ben was the dishwasher there and they're like BFFs now."

"How come this is the first time I'm hearing about this?" I asked. This kind of news would have come up in a group text.

Rebecca gripped the armrests. "Because they didn't know until yesterday! Ben had been going by his middle name, Tom."

Tom? I peered over at Beth. Her fox smile confirmed my horrible revelation. Ben was the Tom she wanted to set me up with. There was a 0.001 percent chance I would have agreed to the blind date, but it was a big fat zero now.

Rebecca continued to rant. "Can you believe it? It's like he's embarrassed by us!"

"Ben doesn't seem like the kind of guy who'd wash dishes," I said as the makeup artist hovered over me to beautify my face. Nothing about Ben made sense, but what did I know? The guy was a mystery. A ghost. He evaded every wedding event and was digitally nonexistent.

"That is an understatement," Rebecca replied. "Wait. When did you meet him?"

"Just now." I relayed how Ben helped me with the vase, intentionally leaving out the small detail about flashing him. If my friends knew, they would never let me live it down.

"I'm sorry, Elise. I didn't mind having an odd number of bridesmaids and groomsmen, but my parents were afraid of the optics if Ben wasn't included." Rebecca calmed herself by staring at her humongous, brilliant ring. "This wedding took on a life of its own once I let my parents invite their own guests. Suddenly, everyone had to be invited or else 'someone would get offended,' which was all code for their not throwing an endorsement behind my mom's campaign."

"We got you," Jesse said, shamelessly changing into her bridesmaid dress in front of everyone. "Give us the word and we'll pull you aside for some quote unquote 'wedding emergency.' Don't forget. We have a professional in the room here," Jesse said, referring to me.

"That's right." The makeup artist handed me a mirror when he was done. The natural makeup made my face feel naked. My eyes twitched for more eyeliner, but I let it go. *Whatever the bride wants, the bride gets.* "It's going to be perfect. Don't have anything but happy thoughts today."

"You guys are the best," Rebecca said, shutting her eyes with a touched expression. She clasped her hands around mine. "But please get dressed already so we can have a wedding today."

Beth and I exchanged a knowing glance before we stood up to get dressed. The more stressed Rebecca became, the crankier she was going to be, so Beth offered Rebecca a glass of champagne while I picked my bridesmaid dress off the hanger.

I took my last deep breath for the day and pulled on my beige Spanx bodysuit that resembled biker shorts with an attached elastic corset. It promised to push up my boobs and smooth my body into a naked Barbie doll because God forbid anyone see a hint of muffin top or belly button through my snug gold gown. The dress was a long slip that could pass for sleepwear except it had a slit on the side and it constricted my lung capacity. Beth, always the overachiever, went the extra mile and adhered a silicone chicken-cutlet strapless bra underneath her Spanx to fill up the cowl neckline.

There was a knock on the door. The photographer finally returned. "Is everyone decent?" He held up his camera. "Can I take pictures of the bridesmaids getting ready?"

Jesse, Beth, and I had already finished getting ready, but we were game. We pretended to zip each other's dresses and put on the matching drop earrings Rebecca gave us as bridesmaids gifts. We must have been doing a bad job acting naturally because he suggested that we have a drink and toast Rebecca. Jesse didn't need to be told twice and poured flutes for everyone.

"To the Yu Crew!" the photographer shouted in hopes of riling everyone up. We felt obligated to *whoo* so we did, sounding like an out of sync flock of owls as we cheered for our bride.

"To Rebecca," I said, lifting up my glass. Everyone looked expectantly at me like I was supposed to say more, but I hadn't prepared any remarks since I wasn't the maid of honor. I stammered a moment and said the first thing that came to mind. "The first of us to get married."

"Yeah, who woulda thought Mark would be the one?" Jesse said, clinking glasses carelessly before taking a sip. "What?" she said in reply to Rebecca's laser glare. "Mark's a douchebag—a lovable one—but still a douchebag," she stated, standing by her answer.

Jesse should know better. It was her lack of tact that pushed her out of the running for Rebecca's maid of honor. Beth and I looked away, not brave enough to face Rebecca. It was universally accepted that Mark was kind of a dick, but no one had said it so plainly among our group. Rebecca's sharp personality was the perfect counterpoint to his arrogance and it kept him from pissing people off (too much) when we all hung out together. That was how Mark ingratiated himself with our group and became one of the guys.

The champagne must have worked some magic because Rebecca laughed it off.

"He *is* an asshole, isn't he?" Rebecca lifted her glass in agreement. "But he's *my* asshole!"

"To you and your asshole!" Jesse shouted. The unexpected toast made Beth choke on her champagne, which in turn made Rebecca snort in the most unladylike way. Soon, everyone caught a case of the giggles.

"Caption that!" Jesse dared the photographer as he snapped away. "*In asshole-y matrimony!*"

He chuckled as he reviewed the photos on the camera's digital screen. "Not sure that'll fly with the editors of *Wedding Style*."

I stopped laughing. "Did you say *Wedding Style*?"

Published quarterly, *Wedding Style* was to wedding magazines what *Vogue* was to fashion magazines. It outranked *Martha Stewart Weddings* as the premier wedding resource for the latest trends in wedding fashion, décor, and destinations. I had seen my work grace the pages of *Wedding Style* when I worked for Filigree Events, but not since I struck off on my own and not under my own name. Excitement thrummed in my veins.

"Oh right," Rebecca said, suddenly remembering this like it was a minor detail and not the game changer it was for me. "Elise, have you ever met Russ?" The photographer nodded in acknowledgment at the introduction while I shook my head. "His pictures have been featured in several magazines, *Wedding Style* included. My mom's communications team thought it would be some nice PR to have my wedding photos published."

"It will appear on the website before it goes to print," Russ clarified. "That reminds me. Can I contact you to collect release forms for any of the individuals in the pictures?"

"You can contact my brother," Rebecca said as she reached for her dress. "He'll be working on the campaign."

The more I learned about Ben, the less I understood, but I didn't ask Rebecca about it. She was distracted by the insane number of buttons she had to unfasten on her fit-and-flare dress. I benched myself as Beth and Jesse helped Rebecca into her dress, knowing the delicate lace appliqué—designed to look like crawling ivy— would stick to my rough hands like Velcro. I looked on lovingly, oohing and aahing as Rebecca completed her look, but secretly, I was reviewing my arrangements in my head. I had rushed back to the bridal suite without cleaning up after my cousins. I had to find a way to do one final sweep before Russ had a chance to take pictures of the ballroom.

Before the bridal party left the suite for the pre-wedding photo session, I emptied out my clutch of the emergency bobby pins, oil blotting paper, and tissues and stuffed it with my essential floral tools and supplies. With *Wedding Style* on the line, everything had to be perfect.

Chapter Four

On the way to Rebecca and Mark's first look, I trailed behind the rest of the group as I pulled up *Wedding Style* on my phone, hoping to get some inspiration. Whenever I needed a hit of serotonin, I read the *Wedding Style* website. There were inspirational photos of destination weddings and helpful articles with headlines like "Twenty Easy DIY Wedding Favors," which was right up my alley, and "Crowd Pleasing Bridal Party Games," which could have been plagiarized from *The Onion*, if you asked me.

A pop-up appeared, interrupting my browsing, but it was one of the few instances where I was interested in what it had to say. Instead of a redundant message to sign up for their newsletter, a message shouted in big bold letters, CALLING ALL PROS. ENTER THE #SUMMEROFSTYLE CHALLENGE! I tapped the link underneath, which filled my screen with details.

#SummerOfStyle Challenge Rules

*Starting this June, *Wedding Style* will launch its inaugural #SummerOfStyle contest to find the best of the best wedding vendors and professionals across the

United States. Participants are invited to submit photos for a chance at different prize packages. Vendor categories include: photography, floral design, interior design, stationery design, and cakes. Each photo entry must include a short description to explain how it fits the theme. A panel of industry leaders and *Wedding Style* editors will judge entries. We want to see the latest interpretations of wedding traditions and inspiring creativity. Ten finalists in each category will win a feature on the *Wedding Style* website. All finalists will be entered into the grand prize drawing: a $20,000 cash prize and three-page spread in the next issue of *Wedding Style*. The contest is free to enter. By submitting photos, you must agree to the Terms and Conditions to allow Wedding Style/Mode Media Group to use them in their publications.

I skimmed the fine print that followed because I knew I was going to enter. My chances might be slim, but I had to try my shot at winning the money. It was enough to keep the studio going and give me some time to secure more clients. I'd worked so hard to strike off on my own and be my own boss. I'd hate to see it succumb to what I hoped was a temporary trend of small gatherings and elopements. If my studio closed, I wouldn't know what else to do. Winning the grand prize could very well be the thing to take my budding business into full bloom.

I cleaned up a few centerpieces. I hid some of the flowers that had bruised during transportation when Beth caught me.

"You'll have time later," she whispered.

"When?" I asked. Rebecca's schedule was tighter than my dress.

Jesse came and dragged me away from the ballroom. Fighting back against her ridiculous strength was futile. "You can sneak off when they're taking family photos."

I fiddled with my bridesmaid bouquet while I waited on the terrace. They probably thought I was being a perfectionist. I'd rather them think that than let them know how much keeping the studio afloat had taken over my life. I didn't want to let them down, not when they'd done so much for me. The studio had their fingerprints on it too. Rebecca was the one who'd helped me negotiate a better lease with my landlord and Jesse had come after work to help me paint the walls so it didn't resemble the shady cell phone store it used to be. They'd always been the first to support me and today, of all days, I had to be just as good of a friend to them.

"Let me see yours," I said, swapping my bouquet with Beth's. I opened up some of the smaller pink roses, curling their velvety petals by pressing them through my thumb and index finger like a slow snap.

"You're gonna miss it, Elise," Jesse warned, waving me to join her up front. I switched bouquets back with Beth and took my place at the end of the bridesmaid line, just as Russ instructed, to capture our reactions for the first look.

Traditionalists didn't like "first looks" because grooms weren't supposed to see their bride until she walked down the aisle. But Rebecca and Mark took the opportunity to share this moment semiprivately, with only the wedding party present. The three of us leaned over to see Rebecca standing in the center of the terrace, facing the rose garden. Moments passed until hushed tipsy laughter came from the opposite end. It was Mark and the groomsmen.

"Make sure to get my good side," Mark said, clicking his tongue while he pointed at Russ. As Mark approached Rebecca, his usual smirk disappeared and his steps slowed. This was what I loved about weddings. A cynical person would say that weddings were just parties that celebrated a union between two people, but what else could facilitate intimate glimpses between a couple? When else would I see an ass like Mark release a nervous breath before tapping on Rebecca's shoulder? Watching their faces brighten, rivaling the May afternoon sun, stirred the romantic in me. My eyes misted as Mark and Rebecca leaned their foreheads together, exchanging hushed words with each other.

Oh no. I didn't want to be The Cryer of the wedding. I glanced around, making sure nobody saw me dabbing my eyes when I found Ben looking at me. His shoulders hunched as he stood with his hands in his pockets. There was a restlessness about him, like an indifferent cashier taking orders at a fast-food restaurant. As our eyes locked, his face relaxed. I hoped that meant he didn't consider me suspicious anymore.

"Everyone! Look over here," Russ announced, his camera shuttering in quick succession. "Now look at the couple. Smile!" he reminded the group. I turned away and grinned at the camera. "Now can I have the bridesmaids and groomsmen pair up?" Russ waved the wedding party to one side of the horseshoe staircase, which led down to the lush garden where the ceremony would take place. "Let's have Rebecca and Mark at the foot of the stairs and . . ." Russ's voice trailed off while everyone followed him down the stairs, coupling off as they broke away from the group. Beth with Ethan. Jesse with Steven. I was the only one paired with a stranger.

Speaking of whom, Ben extended his hand like a gentleman, waiting for me so that we could descend the stairs together. I paused for a moment. Clients jolted with surprise whenever they felt my calloused palm against their skin. I didn't want to relive that with Ben.

I hid my hands behind me. "I think I can handle a few stairs."

"I didn't say you couldn't." Ben dropped his hand to his side and stood stiffly as he waited for me. I didn't want to hold up the group, so I weaved my arm into the crook of his. It was the best alternative.

"Stay right there," Russ shouted at Ben and me before we took another step down. He staggered each couple two stairs apart.

Russ held up his hand, signaling that he needed to get a different lens. Everyone chatted among themselves, but I couldn't hear from the top of the stairs. It was hard not to feel envious when all my friends had their significant other to pass the time while I stood idly by, waiting for instructions to pose with a guy who'd followed me as if I were a shoplifter.

As if he heard me thinking about him, Ben lowered his head and whispered, "I'm sorry." His breath warm on my bare shoulder. "I should've properly introduced myself. I'm Ben."

It sounded sincere enough. "Hello, Ben. I'm Elise."

"Nice to meet you. I'm glad we could put this morning behind us." This was a better start. It gave me some confidence that we could be cordial for the rest of the day. Then, he said, "And this is where you apologize to me."

I angled my face to look at Ben over my shoulder, not expecting that his face would still be right there. Close enough to know that his former grilled cheese scent was replaced by a clean aftershave. I leaned back. "For what?"

"For being rude to me this morning."

"I was not—" I gaped at him. "You were the one being rude, questioning me."

"I was taking precautions because there was an un-uniformed person loitering around the kitchen of a high-profile event. But now that I know you don't pose a threat, I apologize. However, if you had been more forthcoming, it would have been resolved quicker."

I narrowed my eyes at him, wishing I had a good comeback. Instead, I said nothing. We were going to be paired together for the rest of the day, so the mature thing to do would be to set aside any ill feelings for the sake of the wedding. For Rebecca. For *Wedding Style*. My eyes dipped toward his boutonniere. The green floral tape that bound his creamy white rose didn't wrap the entire stem. It was a small imperfection, but an imperfection that I couldn't ignore.

"Let me fix that." Ben didn't understand what I was talking about, his expression growing increasingly alarmed when I produced my pocketknife, which I'd hid in my bouquet. "You're not the only one who carries tools."

"Are you planning to kill me in broad daylight?" he asked. There was a hint of a smile on his lips, like he was trying not to laugh at me. Little did he know. Jesse made Beth, Rebecca, and me take her self-defense class months ago. I might not be able to kill Ben, but I had a gnarly groin kick in my arsenal.

"Give me some credit. There are way too many witnesses here." I removed the pearled pin from his lapel and slipped it between my lips. I unraveled the green tape half an inch. I pressed the stem against the blade of my knife with my thumb, trimming the end, and bound the tape once again.

Ben watched my every movement, from the second I removed the pin from my mouth to the moment I replaced the boutonniere onto his lapel. He probably wanted to make sure I didn't poke him. "I don't understand all the fuss. Nobody would have noticed."

Ben's offhand comment annoyed me, made worse by the heady ocean scent of his cologne. We were standing too close.

"*I* noticed," I said, putting more space between the two of us, keeping my tone as amicable as I could. "And if I noticed, then the camera would have been less forgiving. I need it to look perfect if I want to be featured in *Wedding Style*."

"Ah, so that's what this is about?"

"Not that you would care but making it into *Wedding Style* is like my Olympics. It's the highest honor I could strive for and I need the exposure."

"Exposure is overrated." Ben scoffed. He tugged on his sleeves and double-checked his cuff links. "Is that why you agreed to take Rebecca as a client when you're a bridesmaid?"

The audacity of Ben to insinuate such a thing, especially when I was in possession of a weapon. "I agreed because Rebecca asked and she's my best friend. I'll have you know that I didn't even charge Rebecca for my labor. That was my gift to her." It didn't feel right to charge my own friend. Not to mention, I was cash poor these days.

Ben nodded like he approved. "That's nice of you. Flowers are overpriced anyway. How much does it really cost to put some flowers in a vase?"

My eyes twitched. Ben sounded like he genuinely wanted to know the answer, but the question was asinine and unoriginal. I should have stabbed him with his boutonniere pin while I had the chance.

"Okay! We're back in business," Russ shouted, corralling the wedding party back to their places. He instructed the groomsmen to rest one arm against the staircase to their right while wrapping their free arm around their bridesmaid on the left. Mark placed his free hand on the small of Rebecca's back. Like a ripple, Steven's hand landed right above Jesse's butt and Ethan weaved his arm around Beth's waist. I straightened as I saw Ben's arm move from the corner of my eye, anticipating his touch, but it never came. His hand hovered over the center of my back. It was unexpected, how the indirect warmth of his palm pricked my skin.

The rest of the photo session was like this. Ben maintained a closed-mouthed half smile, hardly touching whether we posed standing or seated next to each other. When we made any sort of contact, Ben put space between us so it would be brief. It made things awkward, but I respected his personal space. I didn't want to make him uncomfortable. But when we posed for our last photo, which had the entire wedding party sitting in front of a small water fountain, I thought Ben was going to expire from our arms and thighs pressed together. He was so rigid, sitting stick straight, hands clasped together on his lap. The ceremony was more of the same.

After Rebecca and Mark tied the knot, guests dispersed under the canopy in the rose garden for cocktail hour. While Rebecca and Mark were preoccupied taking pictures with guests, and others with their scotch and wine, I snuck away into the ballroom to touch up my centerpieces. I weaved through each table, making sure the flowers were holding up. It appeared I had worried for nothing because the servers were cleaning up any fallen petals as they placed table numbers and dropped off butter dishes.

I was about to rejoin my friends at the bar, where they were sipping Rebecca and Mark's signature drink, blood orange margaritas, when stern voices entered the ballroom. A tall man with salt-and-pepper hair stormed past me like I didn't exist, griping about something under his breath. Rebecca's mom walked in soon after, gently sweeping her hair away from her face. It was different to see her trade in her power suit for a mother of the bride dress. The one she had on was a tasteful platinum column gown with a conservative portrait collar.

"Mrs. Yu," I said to alert her to my presence. "Is everything okay?"

"Elise," she replied. The concern that had graced her face seconds ago practically melted away at the snap of a finger. "I told you to call me Donna."

"Donna," I corrected. It was a novelty not to use an honorific for someone I considered an elder. The elders I grew up with spoke Teochew, Vietnamese, or Mandarin and they would be offended if I didn't address them by the correct term. I felt more comfortable calling her Assemblywoman Yu, to be honest. Technically, I was her constituent since I lived in Arcadia, smack dab in District 49, which covered the west San Gabriel Valley. I learned this tidbit from the Donna Yu email newsletter that seemed to pop up in my inbox every day.

"Do you need me to call security?" I inquired. The disgruntled man had huffed and puffed his way to the open bar and threw back a shot of dark liquor.

"Oh, nothing for you to be concerned about. Emilio works for me. He gets this way during elections."

"Are you sure? I've watched every season of *Scandal* and I know how ugly politics can get." I said this as a joke and it paid off.

Donna laughed a real laugh, not the staged one for photo ops. "Don't believe everything you see on TV. In politics, we may not all be friends, but we try not to make enemies either. Most of us, anyway." There were so many ways that could have been interpreted and I wasn't sure if I should be scared. Donna, realizing this, added, "We learned that the person running against me isn't someone to be underestimated, but I'm not too worried. I'm not going to lose sleep over it."

"That's good. Sleep is very important," I said, sounding like the auntie in the conversation. Honestly, I didn't know what to say. It was true that anything I knew about politics was from *Scandal* and I wasn't gladiator material.

"Mom." Ben appeared at the French doors from the courtyard, probably wondering what I could possibly be talking to his mom about in private. "We're taking family photos now."

"I'm coming," Donna replied. She patted my shoulder before she walked off. "Gorgeous flowers, by the way." The compliment made my heart flutter. Donna paused in front of Ben, giving him a hug. "You're next."

Ben rolled his eyes, but didn't seem too annoyed by it, judging by the small, warm smile he gave his mom before she stepped outside. I thought he would trail behind her, but he lingered at the doorway.

"Can I help you with something?" I asked as my eyes slid toward the wedding cake. Real pink roses were placed on each of its three tiers for a cascading effect, but something wasn't right. It lacked movement. I stole a rose from one of the big arrangements that flanked the stage and added it to the middle tier after cutting off the stem.

"Is that really necessary?" he asked.

Did this man ever stop asking questions?

"Yes, it is." Besides the couple, nothing received more close-up shots than the cake. "I thought you had somewhere else to be."

I adjusted the rose on the second tier, making the rose look like it was spilling over. Then I worked on the big arrangement to fix the gap that the stolen rose left. I worried that I'd gone a little too far with my snippy reply when Ben didn't respond. It wasn't his fault that I had a million things on my mind, wondering what it would take to win this *Wedding Style* contest so I could finally pay myself again. I knew I should get along with him for the sake of the wedding, but there was something about him that made me feel a little off center.

If Ben was offended, he didn't look it. He was still standing at the doorway, head tilted, observing the cake the same way one might stare at a painting in a museum. I stilled, waiting for his assessment.

"Nice."

That was all he said. Nice. And then he was gone, off to rejoin his family.

What was I supposed to do with that? "Nice" was supposed to be positive, complimentary. From Ben, it felt more loaded, but not in the way I wanted. I wanted something more definitive, more glowing than a response that I would say to Beth when she successfully lobbed her empty boba cup into the trash can.

I stopped myself from spiraling before I returned to the cocktail hour. Why did I care so much about Ben's opinion? I wasn't going to see him again after this evening, so why was I letting him ruin this wedding for me? I could take the high road and play nice. Maybe then Ben would learn what the word really meant.

Chapter Five

The reception went swimmingly. Guests were mingling over their steak or salmon dinner. The jazz band onstage performed breezy songs that reminded me of the music I'd hear when I was put on hold by a customer service representative. Pleasant enough to pass the time, yet nothing too rousing. Basically, it was as boring as the boiled chicken breast entrée Jesse requested.

"How could you eat that?" Ethan took great offense at the lack of flavor and the inconvenience Jesse had imposed on the kitchen for her special order.

"I'm trying to bulk up," Jesse said with a full mouth. She followed a strict diet and workout schedule for her next CrossFit competition. She was so dedicated that she decided to forego having a bachelorette party, which was too bad. Jesse knew how to turn up. At least she was able to eat. I thought my dress was too tight standing up, but sitting down was a new level of hell.

"Why aren't you sitting with your parents?" I asked Ben, who'd been eating quietly between Ethan and me. Bob and Donna seemed to be having a lively conversation over at their table up front.

"I'd rather hang out with my friend," Ben explained, referring to Ethan. "Why? Are you asking me to leave?"

"No." How did everything become antagonistic with him? I was trying to make conversation. If my mom were here, she'd want—insist—that I sit next to her so we could be each other's plus one. I tried a more mundane question. "So, how long have you been at Bistro Ynez? I've heard good things about it."

"A few months. Today was my last day."

"What's next for you?" I knew the answer to this, but everything I knew about Ben I heard from other people. I was curious to hear what he had to say.

Ben stopped cutting into his steak for a second before resuming. "I'll be working for my mom's campaign until election day," he said plainly, though this seemed to put him in a bad mood because he remained tight-lipped. He couldn't handle more than a few basic questions when he'd been throwing plenty at me all day. It was getting tiresome.

Onstage, the band leader tapped on his microphone. "And now, I'd like to invite the best man, Steven, and maid of honor, Beth, to the stage to say a few words for the couple."

Steven adjusted his bow tie as he rose from his seat and then searched his phone for his notes. Beth approached the stage empty-handed. She'd memorized her speech because rote memory wasn't only a study strategy for Beth, it was a way of life.

"Come on, Jess," I said, tapping her hand to let go of her fork, "we have to watch and offer moral support."

"Why?" Jesse picked her teeth with her nail. She would deny it, but Jesse was still miffed that Rebecca chose Beth over her for MOH, fearing Jesse would say something crass. "I already know what Beth's going to say, unless she uses the uncensored version with the juicy stories."

Ethan whispered across the table to Jesse, "What kind of juicy stories?"

"Don't you know?" Ben asked. "Beth didn't tell you?"

"Yeah right. Their clique is airtight," Ethan said. "The most exclusive VIP club on the planet. When the four of them are together, it's like us guys don't exist."

"I'm sorry," Jesse said after a beat. "Did you just say something?" Ethan was unamused.

"We don't tell each other's secrets, that's all," I said diplomatically. We couldn't help it if we fell back into our old ways, when it was just the four of us.

"They made me pass the Boyfriend Test," Ethan said.

"He's exaggerating," I said to Ben, not wanting him to get the wrong idea. "It was a stupid thing we used to do whenever a new boyfriend came into the picture."

"It was a checklist, like a real official document," Ethan insisted. "There was a space to get it notarized."

I laughed this off as a silly joke, but it was true. There was a form with a bullet point list of criteria, but no one actually got it notarized. It wasn't that serious. I wasn't sure why Ethan was bringing it up now. He passed, didn't he?

"Hello." Steven paused when feedback squealed from the microphone. "For those who don't know me, I'm Steven Lam, Mark's best man." Scattered cheers arose from their startup friends. He proceeded to tell guests about how he met Mark and the time Mark was there for him after his last app failed to obtain funding. It could have been a heartwarming anecdote but it didn't hit the right emotional notes since Steven was reading from his phone.

"But Beth is your friend. Doesn't she tell you everything?" Nosy Ben was back. Didn't he ever learn not to talk when other people were talking?

"Airtight," I repeated under my breath, hoping Ben would

follow my example in lowering his voice. I scooted my chair, angling it to get a better view of the stage.

"Now, Mark," Steven said, finally looking up from his phone, "this is usually when a best man is supposed to offer the newlywed advice. But you're a smart man—"

"—because you've already chosen Rebecca," I recited to myself.

"I take it that you helped him with his speech," Ben whispered behind me, sending a shiver down my spine. I should have scooted my chair farther away.

"I did."

"You couldn't have made it a little less . . . cheesy?"

I ignored Ben. Rebecca specifically asked me to help Steven with his speech since I was the so-called wedding expert of the group and her request was, and I quote, "Something sentimental, but otherwise forgettable." I understood the assignment. I sensed Ben wanted a response, so I waited until Steven wrapped up. "Sure, Steven could have gone the funny route and shared embarrassing stories. Mark has no shortage of those, but that's not what Rebecca wanted. Ultimately, best man speeches should be about the groom and not the person giving it and Steven accomplished that." In his unmemorable way. I shushed Ben when light applause welcomed Beth for her turn.

Beth accepted the microphone from Steven and cleared her throat. "Hello, everyone. I'm the maid of honor, Beth. I'm here to represent our collective group of college friends, including Jesse and Elise."

I could feel Ben's eyes on me when my name was mentioned. Normally, I would have let this go, but something compelled me to return the glance. Ben stared like he was trying to make two puzzle pieces fit. Fortunately, he gave up shortly after and went back to the speech.

"The four of us are close but I think I know why Rebecca chose me," Beth continued. "Mark and I have something in common. You see, we're both the recipient of Rebecca's heroism. I first met Rebecca at Pepperdine. Rebecca showed up on campus ready to make a difference and the first pet project happened to be a lost freshman"—Beth pointed to herself—"and I'll never forget how she stopped me in the middle of Adamson Plaza, appearing like an angel in her white sorority rush dress, and said, 'Where are you trying to go?' It was like she knew that I was bad at directions. And that's the true beauty behind Rebecca. It's not that she walks with the grace and sparkle of a pageant queen in a sequined dress. It's her big heart. She has a sixth sense for people who could use a little help. That's how she met Mark."

Guests chuckled. Beth had nailed the delivery.

"Did you go to Pepperdine too?" Ben asked, his voice low.

"I did," I replied, keeping my answers short so Ben would get a hint. No such luck.

"I don't remember seeing you at Rebecca's graduation party."

"I'm short. Most people don't see me usually," I said matter-of-factly. I've had a lot of practice being in the background. I grew up eating dinner silently while my parents argued about every little thing, so it was easy to go unnoticed. Considering Ben's side-eye glance, he didn't seem to buy my answer. "I'm not that memorable," I offered instead.

"I doubt that," he said simply.

"I—" I wasn't sure what I expected him to say, but it wasn't that. "I didn't go because I didn't graduate," I finally admitted. College wasn't for me. So instead of wasting money on tuition, I took a break and it freed me to pursue floral design. "And I was working an event that night. It was a movie premiere for some fairy tale musical." I rubbed my fingers at the memory. They were dark from spray-painting roses an ominous gray to replicate the spooky forest set. It was my first red carpet event. I was so excited to see pictures of the premiere splashed in celebrity magazines. Famous actors were mingling in front of my work, but it got old quickly. It didn't have the romance, the drama, or the personal stories that weddings had.

Speaking of personal stories, Beth's speech ended to a round of applause. I'd missed it because of Ben.

"Would you like champagne?" he asked as he raised his glass for the toast.

"No thanks," I replied, holding up my water glass to hide my annoyance. "I don't drink on the job."

Beth returned to the table with a satisfied smile, the same look she had every time she came out of a big exam. I clapped for presumably a job well done. Before taking her seat next to Ethan, she came up to me. "E, one of your lights went out."

My head swung toward the direction Beth was pointing to. It was the nook, which no longer resembled a coral reef. The blue light flickered, which was impossible. I bought the lights brand-new. I excused myself from the table to get to the bottom of it. When I reached the gift table, I found an elderly woman in a black column gown, bent down at the end of the table, yanking on the power cord.

"Excuse me," I said, startling the woman. "Please don't unplug the equipment."

"Oh, thank goodness," the woman said, still pulling the cord like she hadn't heard me. "Would you be a dear and plug in my charger? I'm expecting an important call and my phone is at one percent."

I really wanted to say that her emergency didn't constitute her mishandling my equipment, but she was still a guest and if my estimate was correct, the jeweled necklace she wore was worth more than everything I owned.

"I think there's an outlet in the restroom, which might be quieter than here. Or try the lobby," I gently suggested. I tried to remove the cord from the woman's hands, but this lady was strong. Our quick altercation had me struggling for my breath. Damn you, Spanx!

"No, that won't do," the woman said as she yanked the cord. The blue mood lights shut off, leaving only the faint stream of light coming from the ballroom. She quickly plugged in her charger. Her phone lit up, casting a creepy shadow on her pinched face. "There. That's better."

"E-excuse me." My voice shook from anger, but it sounded intimidated even to my ears. I hated that I couldn't come up with anything else to say because this woman was a guest. Her experience at this wedding mattered too because most of my business came from word-of-mouth referrals from former clients and guests. So, as much as I wanted to say something, I said nothing. What good would it do when she didn't listen to me the first time?

"What's taking so long?"

I turned around at the sound of Ben's voice. He switched on the main lights to the room, making it sterile white. "It's time for—" He stood taller when he saw I wasn't alone. "Oh, Mrs. Reed." His voice became more proper, more polished. "How lovely to see you."

Lovely wasn't the word I'd use.

"Oh, Benjamin! I'd been meaning to say hello, but you know how things are during an election year. Suddenly, everyone cares about me and my money again."

"That's not true," Ben said with a false charm that hadn't presented itself before. Seriously. Who was this guy and where had he been all night?

"I've been around this circus longer than you've been alive. I can spot the song and dance for my money from a mile away." Mrs. Reed scrolled through her phone and talked as if I didn't exist.

Since Ben seemed to know this Mrs. Reed lady, I gathered the courage to try again. "I need to get the lights back on. It's for the bride."

I turned to Ben for some backup, sliding my eyes at Mrs. Reed, giving what I thought was the universal "help me out here" signal. Ben nodded, taking note of this, so I thought we were on the same page.

"Actually, Elise, Rebecca requested the wedding party to join halfway through their first dance." His long arm pointed toward the ballroom like a big flashing arrow. "Mrs. Reed, could you plug the lights back in once you're done? You wouldn't want guests to miss the display that's fundraising for the California Conservation Center."

"Oh, is that what this is for?" Mrs. Reed craned her neck at the arrangement and caught the QR code that led to the donation page. "Oh, that darling Rebecca. I'll be quick, then." She flitted her hand, dismissing me as if we hadn't played tug-of-war a minute ago.

In my state of shock, Ben ushered me back to the reception. "Sorry about . . . pulling you away." Once we were out of earshot, he added, "You shouldn't have done that."

"Me?!" My small outburst caught the attention of nearby guests. I quickly grinned and pretended to laugh it off. "Did you see how that lady mishandled my equipment?" I gritted out through my smile. "Who does she think she is?"

Ben's eyebrows shot up. "You don't know who Veronica Reed is?" he asked in a low voice, pulling me aside near the coffee station. "Veronica Reed as in Reed Medical Group? She's also president of the California Hospital Association. Her husband is Terry Reed, as in Reed Venture Capital. Mark just secured Series B funding from RVC."

Nothing Ben said meant anything to me. I knew nothing about the people who used money and power to influence their neck of the woods. I was merely a simple local florist dumping flowers into a vase. "What does all of this have to do with the wedding?"

Ben clenched his jaw. "I'll tell you this. It's bigger than this wedding or some magazine."

At times like these, I wished I were the kind of person like Rebecca, who could dig in her heels and stare this insufferable man down. Tell him off like Jesse or forget him like Beth. But I couldn't. I just stood there, arms crossed, overcome with a fact I'd been trying to ignore. I'd poured my life savings into my business and if *Wedding Style* didn't work out, I'd have to close my studio, maybe as early as the end of the year. Moisture pricked my eyes and because the universe liked to sprinkle salt in my wounds, there was a ripped seam on the side of my dress right by my ribs.

"Just what I needed," I said, swiping away my tears.

"I'm sorry. I didn't mean that," Ben said quietly. He sounded like he meant it. I shrugged, unsure what to say.

The pianist introduced the next song, "That's All" by Frank Sinatra, and welcomed Mark and Rebecca for their first dance. I didn't feel like dancing anymore since there was a chance I'd flash someone some side boob.

"Do you want my jacket?" Ben said, noticing my predicament.

"No." I collected myself and followed the rest of the wedding party to the dance floor. The Spanx wasn't too far off from the champagne color of the dress. Maybe no one would notice if I danced with my arms glued to my sides. That wasn't weird at all.

"How about this?" Ben seemed like he had second thoughts before he covered the split seam with one hand, his other hand taking mine like we were waltzing. Ben's touch was light but warm. Now that we were face-to-face, I could tell he was trying to help, so I let him take the lead. A temporary truce to fulfill our groomsman and bridesmaid duty.

"I don't like coming to these events," Ben confessed after a few steps, loud enough for only the two of us to hear. "It's so much pressure to say the right thing, knowing people are watching my every move, as if something I did could come back to reflect on my parents' careers, like what happened to Becks."

It took me a second to recall what Ben was referring to. In college, Rebecca had to do a group project for her public policy class where she was supposed to debate her teammates on the topic of raising the minimum wage. Rebecca was assigned to take the opposing stance. Even though she personally disagreed with this, she debated the topic in class, making her arguments with her silver tongue. She wanted to do well because it counted a lot for her grade. This would have all been benign if someone hadn't made a harsh criticism about it on a now defunct app where users posted anonymously.

It snowballed into a story in the student newspaper and then it was picked up by political blogs I hadn't even heard of, connecting Rebecca to Donna Yu, who had been elected for her first term. That was when Rebecca received horrific racist and misogynistic emails from strangers. Rebecca learned that being a woman on the internet and the added association with her public figure parents subjected her to unfair scrutiny. *The personal is political* took on a whole new meaning for her. It took a long time before Rebecca regained the confidence to move on after that.

"We don't talk about that anymore," I said, miming that my lips were zipped. Rebecca wanted that to stay in the past.

Ben nodded in a show of gratitude. "Well, I hope you can understand why I take precautions when I'm in this type of environment, especially with new people. I know it can be . . ." He paused, hoping I would let him off the hook from this apology, but I leaned forward so he knew I wanted to hear it come straight from his mouth. Ben sighed. "I know it can be off-putting. I'm sorry if I offended you today. It wasn't my intention."

"Good intentions don't justify the impact."

Ben dipped his face to hide his guilty smile. "Yes, Becks reminds me of that often."

"That doesn't surprise me," I said. I couldn't help but chuckle at the thought of Ben getting checked by Rebecca.

"Are we good now?" he asked. I wasn't sure when we had begun to dance so close, but I was starting to feel hot all over. Stupid unbreathable satin.

"Yeah." Sure. Why not? The night would end soon. Might as well let bygones be bygones. The corners of his eyes smiled halfway, just like his mouth. I wasn't sure if it was the dancing or the Spanx restricting the flow of oxygen to my brain, but I was feeling light-headed. Luckily the music wound down and I unlatched myself from Ben.

"So can I tell you now how short you are?" With a hand on his back, Ben winced as he straightened himself. I rolled my eyes.

"Don't push it," I said. We clapped for Mark and Rebecca as we walked off the dance floor. "If you want to show me how sorry you are, you can get me a slice of cake."

Chapter Six

The next morning, the wedding party and family members gathered for brunch in a private room at the hotel where guests had stayed. It was a thank-you for everyone involved in the wedding and a send-off to out-of-town guests. Some folks—namely Mark and his coworkers—were worse for wear after drinking post-reception shots of tequila. They nursed their hangovers and regrets over Bloody Marys and omelets. I wasn't faring much better after staying late to break down the event. Guests took the centerpieces home, but the arches and big arrangements went back with me. Fortunately, Steven, Ethan, and Ben helped me or else I would have been stranded at Ellery Estate.

Rebecca and her mom went table to table, chitchatting with guests, while Ben sat between his dad and Emilio. Ben was getting lectured from both sides, but the only attention he gave was to his two sunny-side-up eggs.

"What are you looking at? Or should I say *who* are you looking at?" Beth was by far the smartest one in our group, but sometimes she had things all wrong.

"Nothing," I replied, as I spread cream cheese on my sesame bagel.

"It didn't look like nothing on the dance floor yesterday. Come on. One date."

I glared a hard *no* at her and she knew I meant it, even as she pretended not to see it. No one would admit it, but some alliances were stronger than others in our friendly foursome. It wasn't as dystopian as it sounded. The friendship among the four of us was like a sweater that stretched and shrunk with every wash cycle. We felt it with every life transition—new jobs, new significant others. Or in my case, when I started my studio two years ago right after my parents' divorce. Beth was there for me, listening to me rant in between class about how petty my parents were to each other after arguing through their entire marriage while Rebecca and Jesse were preoccupied with their jobs and wedding planning. Beth knew me better than anyone, so if she was seriously thinking I would date Tom, aka Ben, then I'd have to reconsider her standing as my best, best friend. I was single, but I wasn't desperate.

"Did you tell her?" Ethan asked. I was not going to enjoy this bagel if I was going to have two people conspiring against me.

"Not now," Beth whispered. "I thought—"

"But everyone's here," Ethan reasoned, gesturing around the table. "And Elise should know."

"Know what?" I asked. Beth clenched the napkin on her lap before sighing in defeat.

"Um. I was going to wait until the wedding was officially over, but—" Beth stole another nervous glance at Ethan, who nodded, encouraging her to continue. Instead of finishing her sentence, Beth shot her left arm out from under the table, revealing a sparkling sapphire on her ring finger.

"No shit!" Jesse exclaimed. "You're engaged?!"

"What?!" Rebecca screeched. She excused herself from her

hostess duties and power walked like a lady to our table. "Start from the beginning. I need all the details. How did the proposal go down? And ugh!" Rebecca lifted Beth's ring right up to her eye. "This ring is gorge!"

"Are you pregnant?" Jesse asked too loudly, causing Beth to blush.

"Jess!" I chided.

"What?" Jesse said more quietly this time. "We were all thinking it."

"I'm not pregnant," Beth clarified. "But we've talked about getting married someday, like after my residency, wherever that will be."

"And as you know, both my parents are gone and I don't have much family left." Ethan clutched Beth's hand as he spoke. "And while we were getting ready to come up here, Beth had been talking about how there are policies about how families are contacted if a loved one is in the hospital and the only thing I could think of was that Beth was my family. It just wasn't official yet and I thought, what was the point of waiting? So, I packed my grandma's ring and when we got back to the hotel room last night, before Beth changed, I said, 'Your outfit is missing something.'"

"So I started checking my hair, my earrings, my clutch," Beth said through a laugh, grinning when she caught Ethan's gleaming eyes. "And when I looked up, Ethan was down on one knee and said, 'Beth, if you'll do me the honor of marrying me, I'll hang by your side like a fancy purse and go wherever you go, sugar mama.' And I said yes."

I swooned. It was the best proposal for Beth. Short and simple and so perfectly them. "Oh, Beth. I'm so happy for you." I caught them both for a hug. "I love you two so much."

"You're all going to be my bridesmaids, right?" Beth asked.

"You know it," I said, in agreement with Jesse and Rebecca. As if she had to ask.

"Elise, could you do the flowers?" Beth's voice was tentative. She was like this whenever she felt like she was a bother, even though that was hardly the case.

"Of course," I said emphatically. "Let me know when you have a date."

"Well . . ." Beth fiddled with her ring. "The thing is . . ."

"We were hoping to have the wedding before Beth goes back to school in the fall," Ethan supplied. "The first Saturday in August."

My eyes widened. That was hardly enough time to put together a wedding, but that was their problem. I checked my calendar. "You're in luck. I'm free that day."

Beth beamed, but slowly, her smile fell. "There's something else. Would you be able to help me plan it, E? I am swamped with studying and I don't have time to research all this stuff. I'd be happy to use any vendor you'd recommend that's good and cheap." Beth must have seen me swallow at the ask because she kicked her request into high gear. "It should be easy. It's going to be a small, simple wedding. With my med school loans, we can't afford anything extravagant anyway. Fifty guests max. It could even be at City Hall or . . . something."

"City Hall could be nice," Rebecca said, trying to be supportive. "It's . . ." She struggled to find the right word. ". . . intimate."

I'd been to many lovely weddings at City Hall, but I heard that sad whimper in Beth's voice. I'd also seen her Pinterest account. Her dream wedding was something I'd describe as boho-vintage–rustic farmhouse with a taco truck. If Beth was willing to give me some leeway, I could plan something that I could submit to the

Wedding Style contest. Something that would have the Elise Ngo stamp on it, designed specifically for Beth and Ethan. The more I thought about it, the more excited I was to get started.

"I'll plan it for you Beth," I replied. It was going to be a tight timeline, but I knew some vendors. I could call in a few favors because Beth deserved a nice wedding. If she was going to dedicate her life to caring for others, she should have at least one day to celebrate herself. And Ethan too. "We can discuss your budget and brainstorm what we can do. I'm not going to let you settle on your wedding day. Not when you've settled enough with this guy over here."

"Thanks, Elise," Ethan said, taking my joke in stride. "We know it's fast, but you know us. We'll make do with what we can get. We just want to be able to celebrate with the people we care about the most."

"I'd be honored."

"So honored that you'd be my maid of honor?" Beth asked. Rebecca and Jesse looked expectantly at me because this was a given. This was my destiny.

"Of course," I said. I knew it was too much for me to take on, but I couldn't say no. She was my best friend. I wasn't going to let her down over a few extra events like a bridal shower or a bachelorette party. Besides, Beth wouldn't want anything too flashy, so I could probably manage it.

Beth threw her arms around me for a tight hug. In my ear, she whispered, "You know who's going to be Ethan's best man, right?"

Her singsong voice told me more than I wanted to know. Of course it was going to be Ben.

I STOPPED IN the lobby after brunch to respond to a handful of inquiries from prospective clients, asking for free consultations, when Ben welcomed himself to the leather chair beside me. He looked rather refreshed in a T-shirt and shorts and those cheddar cheese Crocs of his.

"Good morning," he said before doing a quick sweep of our surroundings.

"Wait a sec," I said. I slipped on my sunglasses. "Okay, I'm ready."

Ben blinked. "What are you doing?"

"Just trying to protect my identity in case you're about to spill top-secret information. Don't worry. This meeting never happened." Ben pushed himself up from his seat, muttering indecipherable complaints under his breath. I tugged on his shirt before he walked away. "I'm kidding. Sit down. I'm about to leave, so you can enjoy your solitude in a few minutes."

"Actually, I came to speak with you about something," he said after he sat back down. "I'm here on official campaign business." My ears perked up at the unexpected request. "I have to organize a fundraiser in a couple weeks and I'd like to hire your services for the event. It'll be held at Veronica Reed's house."

My nose crinkled at the thought of spending more time with that woman. "I'm not sure if you know, but this is a popular month for weddings."

"It's on a Thursday, if that helps."

Damn it. "It does," I replied. "But why would you need me? You could dump flowers in a vase and call it a day."

"How long am I going to pay for that comment?" Ben groaned or growled or something in between the two. "If you don't want to, I can tell my mother to go with a vendor she's used before. I only thought of you because I thought you'd want the exposure."

"I—" Now I felt bad. Ben was genuinely trying to help me out. I'd meant my comment as a friendly elbow to the ribs, but Ben didn't seem to be in a joking mood. "I do . . . "

"But?" he said as my voice trailed off.

"Why would you want to help me?" While we'd called a truce, we weren't exactly buds. Maybe he was being nice because I was Rebecca's friend.

"Think of it as being mutually beneficial. This fundraiser is my first task for the campaign. I like what you did for Becks's wedding and I'd rather hire someone I know and trust. The fundraiser should be easier, considering that it's a much smaller commitment than this wedding. If all goes well, I can send more business your way. There are more campaign events in the coming months."

That all sounded good, but I asked the obvious question. "What do you get out of it?"

Ben leaned back in his chair, but his posture was anything but casual. "My mom is running for her last term. This will be the last campaign I'll have to work on. As long as I put in my time and she gets reelected, I'll be free to go back to my own life."

"Living in obscurity?"

"You could say that."

"Okay." Everything Ben said made sense. The fundraiser sounded doable given the timeline and frankly, I needed the money. "Text me the details and we can set up a consultation."

"Sounds good." Ben stood from his chair and extended a hand to help me up. I hesitated for a second before I accepted. Ben didn't have a reaction to my sandpaper touch, not now or when we danced. Either his politeness was far-reaching or he had impeccable control of his facial expressions. "I'm looking forward to it."

At least one of us was.

Chapter Seven

Mornings were my favorite time in the studio. Nothing but me, a warm cup of tea, and Debussy playing on KUSC while I worked on a last-minute order for a longtime client. I grabbed a mason jar vase off the wire shelf and placed it on my butcher board counter. I wandered into my walk-in refrigerator and selected the best blooms I had in stock—buttercream roses and fragrant lavender. I ran my knife along the stem of a silver dollar eucalyptus, watching the spade leaves ricochet off and scatter on the floor. Once the flowers were prepped, I filled the vase, readjusting the placement and length of the stems until it looked right.

I spun the arrangement around to make sure it looked good from all angles when Ben came through the front door.

"Good morn . . . ing," Ben said, immediately struck by the gradient of pastel silk flowers dangling from the floral chandelier above us. "It's like a secret garden in here."

I stayed quiet so he could linger a bit, letting his admiration fill me with pride. The studio was tucked in the corner of an unassuming small shopping plaza on Las Tunas Drive that people rarely frequented. The country cottage vibe of the studio never failed to wow customers. Ben was no different.

"But more homey," I said, "like *Kiki's Delivery Service*." I wiped my hands on my apron before taking it off. "You're here early."

Ben sheepishly rubbed the back of his neck. "I can't sleep in anymore. I spent the better part of the year working breakfast service. The chef would have handed my ass to me if I ever showed up late."

It was hard to think of Ben as a chef, even after meeting him in his chef's jacket. It was a far cry from the ill-fitting button-down and khakis he was wearing today. He looked like he wanted to sell me insurance. I gestured Ben to have a seat at the small desk in the front of my studio where I did all my consultations.

"We're going to meet here?" Ben glanced to his left, then his right. My eyebrows furrowed, wondering what Ben thought was lurking by the wall stacked with shelves of vases or the spools of ribbon on the opposite end of the studio.

"There's no one else here and I don't expect anyone to stop by anytime soon," I reassured him, remembering that the man had trust issues, but Ben continued to stand. He tapped his foot against the leg of the chair.

"Where did you get this? The children's section?" Ben may have said this with a voice as dry as California but I could tell he was secretly laughing at me behind his expressionless face.

"Excuse me. I'm normal height," I said, though I didn't know how true that was. He couldn't blame me for designing my studio to fit me. "You've never considered that maybe you're too tall?"

"Nobody's ever accused me of that before," he said as he lifted his pant legs as he sat down, as if he were about to squat or something. He wasn't tall enough nor were his clothes nice enough to warrant such care.

"Did you bring the pictures?" I asked, moving past Ben's tired "short" jokes. When Ben set up this meeting over text, he'd included a couple pictures of past fundraisers to give me an idea of what to expect but didn't include any from Veronica Reed's house, citing privacy reasons.

Ben presented a mock-up on his iPad. "Here's the setup we had the last time Veronica hosted a fundraiser." I zoomed in on the blueprint and then swiped for the photos. There were two long dinner tables stretched across a marble veranda behind a palatial Italian manor, with views of a luscious green backyard and sparkling swimming pool. I failed to see what was so sensitive that it couldn't have been sent over text or email.

"Veronica has sophisticated taste."

"It has to look nice for what we're charging. We'll be hosting some of our usual donors—the California Hospital Association, the Realtors Association, the Organic Farmers Association— along with some of Veronica's philanthropist connections."

"Is there a theme I need to work around?" I asked.

Ben shrugged. "Whatever's in season?"

Wow. Whoever put Ben in charge of this event had a lot of faith in him.

"Come with me. Maybe it'll help to see a sample," I said as I stood. Ben was only too happy to comply, stretching gratuitously before following me to my workspace. I selected a white linen tablecloth from my cabinet and tossed it to Ben, who helped me drape it over my counter. "I was thinking," I said, moving around Ben as I gathered flowers and materials, "we could match the classic European style of the home. And if you want to do something seasonal . . ."

My voice trailed off as I set a bronze compote vase in the center and inserted a soaked brick of green floral foam. I arranged some pink roses and burgundy dahlias, filling the rest of the space with sprigs of green. "I know it doesn't look very full yet but pretend there is fruit overflowing from the edges. Grapes. Figs. Maybe some artichoke?"

Ben's eyebrows crept higher with each suggestion. Before I got carried away with my vision for an abundance of produce, I asked an important question. "What's my budget again?"

"Not enough for figs or artichokes."

"Thanks." I'd have to think about a cheaper filler that would still look nice so it could stand up to the surroundings. The Reed mansion was so stunning, it could pass for a wedding venue. With the right photos and permission, I could try to submit these centerpieces for the *Wedding Style* contest. "What do you think about cabbage leaves?"

"They're fine for salads." Ben crouched at the workbench, his arms folded as I fiddled with the arrangement some more. It made me self-conscious about things that I didn't think twice about, like the green stains on my fingers. I wasn't used to someone watching me while I worked.

"You lack imagination," I said as I added one last rose.

"I do like it, though."

My attention lifted from the vase to Ben, catching his gaze for a split second before he turned away, gracing me with another glimpse of that Brawny Man jawline. His size-too-big button-down shirt billowed as he straightened to his full height. My eyes were playing tricks on me because suddenly Ben took up so much space in my studio. Even his hands looked ginormous as he palmed the sides of the round vase, picking it up to feel the weight. The same warm hands that held me as we danced a few nights ago.

"I think this will work. So, let's say sixteen centerpieces and a bigger one for the table in the foyer?"

Ben's businesslike manner snapped me back to the present. I

could admit that there was something attractive about Ben but it ended there. Whatever I felt had to be a symptom of being chronically single. I cleared my throat. "I'll write up the invoice."

Ben checked his phone. "I have to get to the office. Send me the invoice ASAP so I can process the deposit as soon as possible. Make sure it's detailed or else it won't clear our campaign account."

Who said bureaucracy wasn't fun? "Don't worry. I'm definitely including everything, plus mileage for making me drive all the way out to Beverly Hills."

"I don't expect anything less. Pleasure doing business with you," Ben said with a two-finger salute. Regret flashed across his face and he shut his eyes for a moment, like he knew it was awkward too, but he left without saying anything else. On his way out, he held the door for a customer coming in, who happened to be my favorite one.

"Hey, Elise," Alex greeted. His face lit up when he saw the mason jar vase behind me. "That one mine?"

"Yeah," I said, shaking the thought of Ben out of my head. I picked up the flower arrangement, enjoying the soft lavender scent as I brought it to the front counter with a blank card.

"You remembered," Alex said with a pen already in his hand.

How could I forget? Alex was the only customer who insisted on writing his own card and he stayed a loyal customer even though he didn't live in the area anymore. I peeked at the note he was writing to his girlfriend, Jas. Lucky girl. "What's the occasion? Anniversary?"

"No, that's not for a couple months. Jas got promoted. She's producing video content for *Angel City Magazine*."

"Oh. I thought she worked at a donut shop. I was going to ask if she could offer a discount. I wanted to order a few dozen for a wedding I'm planning." The idea came to me when I saw a do-nut wall on Beth's Pinterest board. I had some wood stored in the back that I could use to DIY this project.

"She doesn't work there anymore, but I can text you the info to her parents' shop. They take custom orders." Alex signed his card with a small flourish and slipped it in the card holder inside the bouquet. "I'm actually about to go meet her. She's covering the grand opening of a knife-cut noodle shop over in San Gabriel."

"Oh. That sounds like a fun gig." I'd seen videos on my phone that highlighted local businesses. It was a great way to find hidden gems.

Alex withdrew his credit card from his wallet and tapped it on my kiosk to pay. "Yeah, she's been filming food content lately. Supposedly, the algorithms like it. She can explain it better than me."

I wouldn't know. I hadn't had the time to post anything on my Instagram account besides the occasional wedding photo. I'd been banking on the *Wedding Style* profile to happen, even though it wasn't a guarantee. I couldn't put all my hopes in that one basket. I really could use all the press I could get.

"Do you think Jas would be interested in filming here?" I asked.

The question took Alex by surprise, but he took one of my business cards on the counter and stuffed it in his wallet along with his credit card. "I could ask. She's always looking for new ideas."

"And who knows?" I said as I gave him his receipt. "Maybe she'll hire me for your future wedding."

Alex blushed at my harmless teasing. "Maybe in a few years."

With Alex gone, my client work was done for the day. I switched gears to wedding planning mode and conferred in the group chat.

ELISE: Beth, don't forget to put together your registry

BETH: Okay!

I made a note to remind Beth about this in case she forgot. She tended to forget things that weren't on a study guide. Maybe I could get Ethan to handle this.

ELISE: What kind of donuts do you want for your donut wall?

I sent a link to the Sunshine Donuts menu.

BETH: Do you have one???

ELISE: I could make one

BETH: No, I don't want you to go through the trouble

ELISE: It's easy. It'll be fast

Not that I'd ever made one before, but it couldn't be harder than the stupid tree I had to assemble for the launch of an energy drink that tasted like carbonated acid. The brand had a cherry blossom logo and I had to make the cans look like they were growing out of a cherry blossom tree. At the time, I was new to Filigree so I agreed to do it when I had little carpentry skills. My boss, Lorenzo, never explicitly said why I was assigned to this client, but I had a feeling it was because the brand was appropriating Asian culture, which was later confirmed when models arrived in short kimonos to serve drinks. The whole experience left me feeling gross, but I did learn how to build a tree and if I could do that, I could surely build a donut wall.

BETH: I can't decide. A variety? So guests can choose?

JESSE: Don't talk about donuts right now! I miss carbs so much. I had a dream about bread and pasta last night

REBECCA: Good luck on your competition this week!

BETH: Shouldn't you be on your honeymoon?

REBECCA: Chilling at the airport lounge

BETH: When are you coming back again?

REBECCA: In a week. *cry* I wish it were longer, but Mark has to go back to work. I'll be back in time for the fundraiser. E, I'll see you there?

REBECCA: Make sure to dress nice!

Times like these, I wondered if Rebecca thought she was my mother.

ELISE: I'll be gone before it starts

REBECCA: You can't show up to the Reed mansion looking like trash

ELISE: Why? I'll pick up after myself and take myself out

REBECCA: I'm serious

ELISE: No one will see me

REBECCA: Eyes are everywhere

ELISE: Fine. I'll wear something nice

Our group chat ended when Rebecca got called to her flight. With that, I checked one thing off Beth's wedding planning list. Many more to go.

The venue was the most important one. I put out some feelers with some event planners I knew. I wish it were as simple as sending out a few emails, replying to texts, but this was the hardest part to nail down. Good venues were booked a year in advance. I only had two months. A text appeared on my phone and got my hopes up.

BEN: Please send the invoice to Benjamin.Yu@asm.ca.gov at your earliest convenience.

Even his texts felt stiff.

I dug around my laptop to find an invoice template. In the past, my (former) assistant, Sarah, processed the paperwork, but now it was all on me. Fear cast a shadow over me as I thought about my growing to-do list, but I looked at the bright side.

If things went according to plan, I was going to help my best friends get married this summer and save my business in the process. Being busy was a blessing.

Chapter Eight

"Where have you been?" Ben whisper-hissed. Someone needed to give this guy a chill pill. He was pricklier than my legs.

"I texted that I was running late," I said as I set down the big arrangement in the gigantic Reed Mansion foyer. Unlike Ben, I kept my voice quiet to avoid the echo.

"That was hours ago."

"Yeah." I knew hours ago that I would be late because I was caught in traffic. I drove out to the Inland Empire to check out a barn for Beth and Ethan's wedding. As I suspected, most of the good venues were booked in August. I had to expand my search for any kind of farm-like property, which turned up a surprising number of options due to Southern California's agricultural past. However, if they happened to be available, they were too big for what Beth and Ethan were looking for and more than they could afford. "I texted again, saying I was going to be here in twenty minutes."

"Which was forty-five minutes ago."

I really didn't understand why we were arguing about this. Everyone knew that twenty minutes in LA time really meant twenty minutes plus or minus another twenty minutes to account for traffic. I gave proper notice, but Ben was my client so I kept that to myself. "I'm here now," I said, keeping my tone even and professional. "The flowers are ready. I just need to bring them in."

Ben appraised the floral arrangement. It was exactly as we discussed, except I used green grapes—organic of course. "So you decided on a fruit salad."

I took his teasing as a sign that he was pleased. "I didn't think one fruit constituted a whole salad. Is that what they're teaching you in culinary school these days?"

"Ha-ha," he replied dryly. "Do you need me to show you where to go?"

"No, I saw catering go through the side gate." I was planning to do the same.

"Catering's here?" Ben ran off before I could respond. He was more high-strung than normal, which made me wonder if this was his first time running the show.

I didn't want him to worry about me. I made quick work transporting the centerpieces around the sprawling mansion with my trusty cart. I would have been faster if I weren't wearing a black wrap dress and cheap ballet flats that were saunas for my unsupported feet. This was how I knew ballet was not for me. I had weak arches, not to mention a lack of grace and any real coordination.

In the end, the veranda looked like a postcard from Tuscany. The only problem was that it was so hot outside, the flowers had started to wilt. By the time guests sat down for dinner, my vase of abundance was going to look like a bowl of raisins. I went into the kitchen, dodging serving staff, to fill up my spray bottle.

"Damn it!"

I followed the sound of Ben's voice into the adjacent room, which turned out to be a library. I was hoping to run into him to rub it in his face that I still had fifteen minutes to spare, but Ben's face was as wild as his hair.

"Whoa," I said, setting down my spray bottle on an end table. I made my way to the center of the room where Ben stood. "Is everything okay?"

Ben was startled by my sudden appearance, but quickly recovered. "No. My mom is stuck in traffic. Catering is behind schedule. I have to stall."

"That's not so bad," I said. "I saw there were hors d'oeuvres and wine. That should be enough to keep people distracted until your mom arrives. And if she's in traffic, chances are everyone else is too."

Ben shook his head. "You don't understand. This event has to be perfect."

"There's no such thing as perfect," I said. "Shit happens."

"That's not helping." Ben sat down on the brown leather tufted couch and sunk his head into his hands. "We need this fundraiser to go well. People don't fork over money out of the goodness of their hearts. They need to be properly fed and slightly inebriated or else my mom is going to lose to a dumbass like Shawn Tam. If that happens, well fuck. My parents are going to make me go to grad school or some shit."

Shawn Tam. Shawn Tam. Why did that name sound familiar? "Wait," I said as the image of an opinionated young Chinese American man came to mind. "That guy on TikTok?" He liked to make videos of himself saying inspirational monologues that sounded like a bunch of Instagram quotes put together. "He's the guy running against your mom?" His real claim to fame was that he had a law degree, an MBA, and he'd made it rich on investments. He'd instantly become a popular meme among Asian Americans. "You know, my mom sent me a picture of Shawn Tam. The message said, 'Lawyer, MBA, and millionaire by 26.' I wasn't sure if she was comparing me to him or trying to get me to date him."

Ben's face soured. Apparently, nothing I said was helpful. "The guy has been a council member for Alhambra for a few years and suddenly thinks he can jump into the state assembly. The problem is that his stupid meme raised his profile and now we're competing with his popularity."

I sat beside Ben. There was a steely determination in his expression—the deepening crease on his forehead, his tense jaw. It was something. "You really care about this, don't you?"

"Why wouldn't I?" Ben's eyebrows furrowed. I regretted the shock and awe in my voice.

"Didn't you say that this was just something to do before you moved on to your next adventure?"

"It doesn't mean I want to do a bad job."

Rebecca made it seem like Ben was a gallivanting flake, but I wasn't so sure that was true. My phone buzzed from a text. Speak of the devil.

> **REBECCA:** I'm here. I see your bag, but where are you?

I looked at Ben, who was shaking his legs so rapidly that the little antique tchotchkes lying around were rattling.

> **ELISE:** I'm dealing with something right now

I checked the time. There were eleven minutes left until the event officially started. I still needed to put my final touches on the flowers. It would be hours before the sun would set. I didn't want the flowers to wilt under the heat but I couldn't leave Ben when he was a wreck. I thought back to my tool bag. There should be another spray bottle in there she could use.

ELISE: Do me a favor? Look inside my tool bag for a spray bottle. Can you give the flowers a quick spritz?

REBECCA: Got it

"Rebecca's here," I said, but Ben didn't hear me. He was off in his own world of worry. I clamped my hand down on his knee. "Hey! Stop this before you break some priceless artifact. It's going to be okay."

Ben stilled, staring at my hand. Suddenly, I felt like I'd crossed a line. I let go. I remembered that he wasn't very comfortable with touching. I gave him more personal space. "I'm sorry. I was starting to get motion sickness."

"That wouldn't have been good. If you threw up, I would have—" Ben winced as he swallowed. "It wouldn't have been pretty."

"Really? I didn't take you for someone with such a weak stomach."

"Only when it comes to blood and vo—" He pressed his fist against his lips. He couldn't even finish the word. Ben peered at me from the corner of his eye. "How are you so calm at these things? I planned everything, gave everyone crystal clear instructions, and stuff got fucked up. The caterer forgot to include a vegan option. I keep getting texts from people getting lost driving up the hill. I feel like I'm running around with my head up my ass."

I shrugged. "I'm used to it. You gotta focus on the things you can control, not the ones you can't."

"Easier said than done."

"Hey. Look at me."

Ben locked his wary eyes on mine as I motioned for him to take deep breaths as if I were a conductor until his shoulders relaxed.

"The only thing that matters is that everything is done before the first guest arrives. If they don't see how the sausage is made, then it was a success." The corners of Ben's lips curled into a half smile. It was like finding buried treasure. "So, you better get out there. You have"—I checked the time again—"nine minutes."

"Damn it. Do I have to?" Ben grumbled. "I don't know what I'm going to say. It's the thing I hate most about politics. I hate talking to people when they have an agenda."

"But *you* have an agenda!" I laughed. "Why did you agree to take on this job, then?"

Ben shrugged. "My parents and I made a deal after I quit my IT job. They wanted me to go to grad school, but I didn't want to trudge through more school to get another nine-to-five job. So, I enrolled in culinary school for fun."

"How did that go over?"

"Oh, they hated it. But they paid my tuition with the condition that I help with the campaign. It's their way of keeping tabs on me until the election is over." Ben's fingers searched for his cuff links. He seemed to do this when he was nervous. "I can't wait for November to come."

"Am I supposed to feel sorry for you? Because it sounds like you went to culinary school for free and got hooked up with a job."

"Before you accuse me of nepotism, I'm not much better than an intern. Emilio made sure of that. And culinary school was hard."

"At least you could eat your homework," I joked.

"There was that," he said, his voice drifting. His posture straightened as he inhaled sharply, like he'd regained some confidence. I thought this signaled the end of our chat but then he asked, "Do you think you can stay? I could use a friend out there."

My face warmed. Ben thought we were friends? "What about Rebecca?"

Ben paused, letting his apparently tepid feelings seep in. "She's better in a crowd than me."

She was still mad at him, I surmised. The girl could hold a grudge. "I can't," I said, answering his question. "I'm not paying ten grand a plate." If I had that kind of money to throw around, I'd be floating on a yacht somewhere.

"It's not ten grand a plate."

"I can't afford it anyway."

"There's always leftover food at these things," he reasoned. "No one's going to make you leave if you act like you belong here."

"Are you sure about that?" I smirked. "You'd be surprised at the treatment I get at certain establishments. Couple weeks ago, I was at the Ellery Estate—"

"You're never going to let me forget that, are you?" Ben stood and helped me up.

"No, but we can laugh about it now, can't we?"

I decided to test Ben's theory and hung around until someone asked me to leave. Ben had nothing to worry about. Veronica Reed was entertaining her guests as they arrived and Rebecca was in conversation with her own circle of people, enrapturing them with stories of her honeymoon. Classic Rebecca, gifted in her ability to turn heads like sunflowers.

"So what's next?" I asked Ben. He'd loosened up since the event hadn't imploded. "I've never been to a fundraiser before."

"Introductions. A quick quip. Let people eat and drink to loosen them up," Ben said. He picked up a glass of wine off a server's tray, exchanging it with the empty one in Rebecca's hand. She lifted the glass as a greeting, thanking Ben before returning to her audience. "Then down to business. Talking points. You get the idea."

"We have the florist right here," Rebecca said, tapping on my arm. "I stashed your tool bag inside the house," she whispered before roping me into her caucus.

"Thanks for helping me." I scanned the table. From afar, the flowers looked great, glistening in the low sun.

Rebecca waved away the comment like it was nothing. "Elise created these," she said to the man next to her. Phil introduced himself as an organic citrus farmer, representing citrus growers' interests at this event.

"Very nice, though I see you have a grape bias," Phil remarked. The playful comment sparked interest in nearby grape growers. Phil plucked a green grape from the nearest centerpiece. His face soured the second he popped it in his mouth. "See? These don't even taste that good."

"You shouldn't eat them," I said. What kind of person would eat the flower arrangement? "I didn't, er, wash them beforehand."

"Nonsense," Phil said as he chewed. "A little dirt don't hurt."

Despite his critical review, Phil continued to eat another grape and then another. His neighbors farther down the table unfortunately followed his example.

"Not organic," one chastised.

"It has a bitter aftertaste," another grower remarked.

"Don't eat the centerpieces," I pleaded, but nobody seemed to care. "Or at least wait until after dinner?"

"Now you see why I hate these things?" Ben whispered as he picked up a glass of red wine.

I didn't understand why these men would ruin my perfectly crafted arrangements. It felt like a lack of respect for my work, tearing it apart in front of me. Now the flowers were surrounding a carcass of stems.

Rebecca saw the horror on my face and transitioned into her work in water conservation. This easily distracted all the farmers because water, it turned out, was a hot topic. Where it was sourced. How it was divvied up. Where the state government stood in its support of local growers. I tried to follow along, but I was out of my league. I copied Ben and picked off every new appetizer coming out of the kitchen. I didn't take it as far as Ben, who was genuinely savoring the soup spoon of tuna tartare. I was too upset to have intellectual thoughts about bite-sized food.

Donna Yu arrived eventually and not a moment too soon. The crowd was getting tipsy from all the wine being served. After she explained her tardiness, she asked everyone to begin dinner as she made her opening remarks. "I want to thank Veronica for graciously hosting us. I promise you're in for a real treat. I know you all have questions for me and what the future of California holds. I'm running for reelection because my work is not done. California is on the cusp of—"

A chair scraped against the floor, bringing Donna's speech to a halt.

"Excuse me." A woman in a red power suit stood, clutching her stomach. "Where's the restroom?"

"Uh, if you go back inside, pass the dining room and make a left at the hallway," Veronica said, smiling off the interruption. After the woman left, Veronica gestured to Donna to continue.

"As I was saying—"

Phil grumbled, exhaling discomfort. "Was there something in the food?" There was a sheen of sweat on his forehead. "My stomach is not agreeing with something."

Ben and I looked at each other. Dinner hadn't even been served yet and there wasn't anything questionable in the appetizers. If there was, Ben and I would be screwed.

More people started complaining, a few running into the house.

"My mouth is burning!"

"It has to be the grapes," someone asserted. "They didn't taste organic!"

"I promise they were!" I shouted over the commotion.

Rebecca's face paled. "Uh . . . Elise." She waved me over to whisper in my ear. "Um . . . I think I made a teeny mistake."

"What are you talking about?"

Rebecca smiled apologetically. "I, um . . . sprayed the flowers with the Glo-Shine."

Panic churned in my stomach. Rebecca had sprayed my flowers with plant polish and now people—very important people—were running for the bathroom. "Why would you do that? I meant to spray it with water!"

"But it had sparkles!" she said in her defense. "I didn't think people would eat it!"

"Why didn't you say something earlier?" It took every ounce of patience not to shout.

Rebecca's eyes bugged as another person charged past her on their way into the mansion. "I didn't think this would happen!"

Arguing about it wasn't helping. We had a crisis on our hands.

"You should call poison control," I said to Rebecca over my shoulder. I ran into the house to search for my bag. The back of the Glo-Shine bottle probably had some useful information. This would have been a good plan if I knew where my bag was.

A hand gripped my shoulder and spun me around. It was Veronica Reed, gorgeous in her Dior dress, but very pissed at me. "Do you have an explanation as to why I have guests holding their mouths and their asses?" she seethed. "What did you do?"

I personally didn't do anything, but if I had to own up to anything, it was giving unclear directions to a woman whose love of shiny things overrode her common sense. "Mrs. Reed. I am very sorry. If you could give me a sec, I can find out how to treat this."

I desperately searched the room, hoping my bag would turn up when I heard Veronica Reed gasp in horror. When I looked out the window, it was like a scene out of an apocalyptic movie. People were keeling over like dominoes falling one after the other. Some took it upon themselves to throw up over the railing. Donna was frantic, trying to direct people into the house, closer to one of the many restrooms inside.

I ran back out to Rebecca. "What did you find out?"

Rebecca held up a finger while she listened on the phone. "Mild irritation? Sir, it's worse than a *mild* irritation. Everyone is hacking up their insides. I think it's going to take more than a rinse of water."

"Oh, this isn't good, this isn't good," I repeated to myself. Without any better ideas, I handed people glasses of water in case it would help, but I was only one person. "Ben! Could you—" Ben looked like he was possessed. He was dead in the eyes, skin gray. "Ben?"

He violently shook his sweaty head, humming to himself.

"Is that"—I listened closely—"Olivia Rodrigo?"

Ben hummed louder, ignoring me. He got up and moved toward the house, trying to get far away from the chaos. I didn't understand. He didn't eat a grape.

But he has a weak stomach.

Ben was trying to drown out the sound of splattering sickness. When I realized this, it was too late. I watched helplessly as Ben stumbled into his mother, the illustrious Donna Yu, and threw up all over her pressed navy suit.

Rebecca ran off to help her mom. The fundraiser had failed to launch and I was the one left to clean up the mess.

Chapter Nine

Whenever I needed a pick-me-up, I visited Jesse. Her gym was a safe place where I could kick butt.

"What are we working on today?" Jesse asked, pressing buttons on her stationary bike. She liked to start each session with stating our goals.

"To look good for your wedding." I pedaled at a leisurely pace to warm up. I didn't want this workout to turn into a gossip session, even though it was inevitable. Rebecca dished out all the gory details about the fundraiser over our group text, dubbing it "The Hurlicane." I might be able to avoid the topic if I could keep Jesse on her wedding. When I found out it was going to be a traditional affair, memories of the weddings I went to as a kid came rushing back. The door games, the tea ceremony, the eating! We were going to paint the town red, literally, to celebrate this union.

"Tell me you ordered the right size." Jesse didn't have to worry about that. She did all of us bridesmaids a favor by having us wear black jumpsuits that had an adjustable waist. There were no concerns about fit or wardrobe malfunctions, which was good because I fully planned to eat every course at the banquet reception. "Remember, self-love is ordering clothes that fit you."

"Don't worry. I did." I'd learned my lesson from Rebecca's wedding. No more Spanx for me. From now on, I was going to let my flab jiggle freely. "I'm here to be more active," I said, revising my answer.

"Good. Let's go!" Jesse said, pedaling faster. If our bikes weren't stationary, Jesse would have lapped me long ago. "I want to see you push for the next five minutes and then you can tell me why you haven't returned Rebecca's calls."

Busted.

"You saw the group chat." I gripped the handles tighter and pumped my legs as hard as I could until the endorphins kicked in. After Rebecca recapped the fundraiser with green vomit emojis, she apologized to me. Admitting fault in front of the group was supposed to ensure that everyone was aware of any infighting and it usually resolved things. I'd replied, acknowledging it was an accident. "What did Rebecca tell you?"

"You know Rebecca hates it when someone's mad at her."

"I'm not mad," I said through my labored breaths. "I've been busy."

Jesse saw through my lie. "Tell me or else I'll make you do a hundred burpees." She knew my next gig was her wedding, which didn't require much work. A few big arrangements for the tea ceremonies at Steven's house and her parents' house. Tall, skinny centerpieces for the banquet reception at the Chinese seafood restaurant because there was no room on the lazy Susans for anything bigger. After the fundraising fiasco, I wasn't swimming with new, rich clients.

"Permission to be petty?"

"Hell yes." Jesse slowed her pace so the machine would quiet down. "I'm always down for petty shit."

I braked my pedals. "Rebecca doused my arrangements with a

plant polish and somehow I'm the one who got lectured by the organic farmers and conservationists about how I was polluting the environment with chemicals. I thought Rebecca would own up to it, but she didn't because she has to kiss up to Veronica Reed. She thinks she has more at stake, but what about me?"

When I dreamt of owning my own floral studio, it was boundless and in color. I dreamt of thriving, not scraping for every last penny, chasing after some far-fetched contest. I'd entered, but I knew it was a long shot. Last I checked, there were at least two thousand florists listed on the *Wedding Style* website.

"Don't get me wrong. If I were you, I'd be mad too, but I don't want to see this blow up." Jesse wiped her face with the towel hanging on her neck. "I need you two to make up so I don't have bad energy going into my wedding day." Jesse squirted water into her mouth as she changed her bike settings to increase the resistance. "Before I forget, thank your mom for the decorations."

"Will do."

When my mom found out Jesse was having a more traditional wedding, she offered Jesse some free wedding decorations from some uncle she knew who used to sell this stuff. It sounded sketchy, but she procured ceremonial items Jesse had been searching for— banners, a red silk signature cloth, special wedding incense, and a tea set with the double happiness 囍 painted on the sides. These gifts earned my mom a wedding invitation from Jesse's mom, who, if we were being honest, was passing them out like candy.

While it was on my mind, I sent my mom a quick text with Jesse's parents' address to remind her of the tea ceremony. My mom replied right away with a glittery thank-you sticker. She was still getting the hang of texting.

"How are you feeling about the wedding? It's coming up fast."

Jesse grunted as she sped up.

"What's wrong?" Something must have come up with her parents. It couldn't be cold feet. Jesse and Steven had been together the longest of our group. Nine years and counting.

"Nothing. It's fine." Jesse sighed. "It's a lot, you know? When I let my parents plan the wedding, I thought it would be great. All I had to do was show up. But no. My parents and Steven's parents have had tense phone calls about what traditions they want to do at the wedding to make sure everything is auspicious. They argue about everything, like the kind of dresses I should wear and what time Steven comes to the house to marry me. If it weren't for the red envelopes, I don't think I would have agreed to all of this. My cousins told me they received enough to save for a house and that's the only thing keeping me from eloping. Steven's start-up is still in the beginning stages, so we need the help."

"It'll be fun too," I said. "Think of the door games we're going to torture Steven with." Steven had to pass a series of tests before he could marry our Jesse and I didn't plan to make it easy for him.

Jesse was not consoled by this. "Just wait until your own wedding."

I had to wait because I didn't have anyone to marry yet. I used to imagine myself having a traditional, daylong wedding like all the family weddings I'd attended in the past, but hearing Jesse's experience gave me some food for thought. I always thought the best weddings were the ones that honored and celebrated the couple.

"How's Beth's wedding planning going?"

"It's going." If there was any silver lining to having a slow wedding season was that I had time to make calls for Beth's wedding. It gave me an excuse to call up vendors I used to work with. It was nice to know that most of them remembered me, but as I expected, they were booked through the summer. "I haven't been able to find a venue within her budget yet."

"You know Beth will be fine with whatever you can do."

That was true, but "fine" was not good enough. "Fine" was not what dreams were made of and neither was failure.

AFTER THE WORKOUT, I opened my studio and I browsed through Beth's barnyard wedding Pinterest board again. For flowers, she gravitated toward a natural, understated look with wispy white flowers and green foliage. The placement and volume of the arrangements had to be designed around the venue. If I had more time, I could play around with some ideas, but time I didn't have. I was going to have to take one for the team and call Lorenzo, my former boss.

Lorenzo had been in the business long enough to have encyclopedic knowledge of venues and vendors across the region. When I left Filigree, I made sure to leave on amicable terms because I didn't want to burn that bridge. Lorenzo wasn't fond of designers who left, especially if they ended up in direct competition with him. But what kept me on the line when his assistant put me on hold was that Lorenzo was very giving with information, especially if it gave him the chance to name-drop a celebrity client.

"Is that you, Elise?" Lorenzo greeted me like we were two ladies who lunched. "How are you and your quaint little studio?"

He was making me kiss the ring right off the bat. "Lorenzo!" I mirrored his slightly fake friendliness. I could play along if it meant getting some leads. "I'm doing fabulous. Busy getting ready for wedding season, as you can imagine."

"Oh, look at you being modest. I heard that you did a wedding recently at the Ellery Estate. Good for you."

"How did you know that?"

"A little birdie told me," he said cryptically.

If he was keeping that information close to his chest, this was going to be harder than I thought. "Well, I'm calling because I could use some help. Do you know of any barn- or farmhouse-style venues in the area for a small wedding? I have a friend who is trying to get married this summer."

"A 'friend,' you say?" I could sense Lorenzo's air quotes through the phone.

"I would tell you if I was dating someone, Lorenzo."

"You sound awfully invested for a friend," he drawled. "Don't be coy, darling. Who is this for? Does it rhyme with Jennifer Lopez? No, that can't be right because I did her wedding already."

I held in my laugh. This was how Lorenzo disarmed people. Blatant tea spilling was his poetry. "It's not a VIP."

"If you say so," he replied. "But, honey, I hate to break it to you. Barns are so hot right now. I swear everyone in LA wants to wear cowboy boots and pretend they're in Nashville. We did an event out in Calabasas for a Kardashian last week. I can't tell you which one without violating the NDA, but we basically re-created a farm inside a tent in their backyard."

"Oh." If a Kardashian couldn't get their own barn, then I had zero chances here. "I don't think my friend could afford that. It's a much smaller affair than a Kardashian wedding. If you can think of anything, would you let me know? I'm getting pretty desperate."

Lorenzo emitted a long thoughtful *mmm*. "How desperate? I do know someone who bought a parcel of land a while back. It used to be an equestrian center with an old house, but she's been trying to renovate it to rent out. I've lost track how many times this project has been delayed and it's a little out of the way, but it might be worth a look."

"Could you send me the address?" It sounded a heck of a lot better than building a barn from scratch. I wasn't that handy.

"Of course. Anything for 'your friend.'"

There he went with the sly air quotes. After we said our good-byes, I waited for Lorenzo's assistant to text me the venue info. I checked my emails and responded to a few prospective clients seeking quotes for weddings for the following year. I tried to be optimistic about them, but it was common not to hear back when clients were casually shopping around online.

Someone banged on my windows. I shut my laptop and gripped my phone in one hand and my pocketknife in the other. I tiptoed to the front door and quickly relaxed once I saw it was Ben. I opened my door and saw him covering my business hours with a red, white, and blue sign that read "DONNA YU FOR CA ASSEMBLY." No one could argue that it was short and to the point.

"What are you doing?" I asked from the door. Ben and I hadn't spoken since last week's fiasco. I probably should have asked how he was feeling first, but he was looking healthier this afternoon in his campaign T-shirt and cargo shorts. Very, very healthy, indeed.

"Doing you a favor and getting rid of these Shen Yun flyers for you." Little did he know that Shen Yun flyers were like the stray hairs on my chin. I kept plucking them, but they kept coming back. Ben plastered my window with more signs, tearing duct tape from the roll he'd been wearing like a bangle. "Because of last week's mishap, I got demoted to signage and canvassing duties."

"Oh no," I said. I was so focused on my tiff with Rebecca that it didn't cross my mind that Ben would take some heat from the debacle. "I'm so sorry."

Ben shrugged. "It's better than working out of my mom's office replying to racist emails. Do you know how difficult it is to write a diplomatic response to constituents' concerns about the economy and job growth when they also question my mom's citizenship in the same email?" Ben huffed. "If they read her bio, they'd know our family has lived in California for generations. 'Simple fact-checking, dickhead.'"

"You should sign your emails that way and see what they say." Ben pretended to consider the idea. I knew he wouldn't, but it was nice seeing that he had a sense of humor about it, even though the whole situation was fucked up. "How bad was the aftermath?"

"My mom had to personally call each guest to apologize and gave them time to voice their concerns. Worst-case scenario, they split their donations between campaigns, which isn't unheard-of."

"That doesn't sound too bad."

"It's not the lead we were hoping for."

"Oh." It didn't seem like there was much I could do to help with damage control, except to stay out of the way. Stick to my own lane. I checked my phone. I'd received the address from Lorenzo's assistant. When I tapped open the map, the directions pointed to a green patch in the middle of the canyon. "Hey, Ben. How many more signs do you have to post?"

"Not many. I stuck at least twenty by the mall before coming here. Why?"

"Can you clock out of the campaign and clock in for best man duties? There's a venue I want to check out for Beth and Ethan's wedding."

Ben crossed his arms. "Are you asking me to ditch work?"

I didn't think I had to persuade him. Posting signs sounded like the pits. "I'll drive so you can answer emails on the way there," I offered.

"In that thing?" Ben swung his head toward the parking lot. Hesitation grew on his face the longer he stared at my refrigerated truck.

"What's wrong with Jet?" My truck was sturdy, reliable, and temperate. If it were a man, he would be perfect.

Ben quirked his eyebrow at the nickname. His eyes dipped to my phone, tracing the long line that crossed the map on the screen. "I don't think Jet will make it that far." He chewed his lip as he thought. Now I was the one staring. "I'll drive."

Chapter Ten

You can learn a lot about a person by sitting in their car. For example, Ben had In-N-Out Burger for lunch, if not today, then sometime earlier that week. It was hard to tell since he nervously threw the crumpled bag into the backseat before I got in. The drink in his cupholder was a brown sugar milk tea boba. According to the label, it was 25 percent sweet. The math didn't compute with the amount of brown syrup glazing the inside of the cup. It was his version of Diet Coke, trying to be healthy but not really.

Ben apologized for the boxes of voter registration forms behind us, saying that those weren't usually there. They were labeled by language—Spanish, English, Chinese, Vietnamese, Korean, Tagalog. It was kind of funny to see the clutter, like it made Ben a little more human instead of the mysterious version I'd made up in my head.

"Canvassing seems hard," I mused, thinking of the diverse groups that made up the San Gabriel Valley as Ben started the car. "What do you do when you meet someone who doesn't speak English?"

Ben held the back of my headrest and looked over his shoulder as he reversed out of the parking spot. His face was so close, I could smell the combination of his ocean-scented cologne and sweat baked into his skin after a day out in the community. I wasn't sure if it was the hand-eye coordination of steering while looking backward or the way his body stretched taller somehow, but this move was switching on feelings in places I hadn't felt in a long time. What was going on with me right now? I mean, it was possible that after being single for so long, taking care of my own business was not enough to ward off the desire of having a man's body on top of me. But Ben, of all people?

"What do you mean?" Ben replied, not noticing how I was wrestling to clear my baser instincts out of my mental cache. "Registrarse para votar."

Any weird physical attraction for Ben disintegrated at the sound of his flat, mangled Spanish. Good. It was going to take over an hour to get to Granada Ranch, which was located on the outskirts of the San Fernando Valley. I didn't need to spend that much time trying to make sense of wanting something that came with too many red flags. For one, I didn't think he liked me in the romantic sense. Not to mention, he was Rebecca's brother. It was a one-way ticket to Messville. Better to put this time to use and get Ben's input on Beth and Ethan's wedding.

"Ethan said he secured taco trucks for catering. I need to make enough favors for fifty guests." I ran through the list of pending items Beth emailed me to remind me of what was left to do. "Beth is letting us pick our own bridesmaid dresses. What about you? Has Ethan sent you to get fitted for a suit?"

"No. Ethan told us to wear our own suits too."

"This isn't good." I drafted a text to Beth about this. "We're not going to look coordinated at all."

"What's the problem?" Ben grasped the steering wheel at ten and two when a gust of Santa Ana winds pushed the car slightly to the right. "Suits come in so many colors."

I tried not to laugh at Ben hunching over the steering wheel like every auntie I knew. "It's not going to look as nice in pictures."

"Why do you care so much? It's not your wedding."

"Is it a crime to care?" As we headed northwest, the freeway twined around the mountains, yellow from perpetual dry seasons. "Beth has always been there when I needed her. I want her to have a special wedding and I can give her one."

Ben's arms tensed as another gust nudged the car. "It sounds like a lot of extra work for you. Can't they deal with some of these things on their own?"

"I don't mind. You should know more than anyone that Ethan works late and Beth, forget about it. Once she hunkers down to study, she can't be bothered or else she's going to confuse one thing for another. During our first finals week, she asked me if Rome was a city or a country." That was the telltale sign that Beth was in over her head. She mixed things up when she was flustered. "Best not to bother her with this stuff."

Ben pointed in my general direction while keeping his eyes on the road. "What's next on the list?"

"'Confirm wedding playlist,'" I read. To save costs, Beth and Ethan decided to forego a DJ, which meant they had to compile their own collection of songs. "That's going to be hard."

"Can't you google 'Top Love Songs' or something?"

"Benjamin," I said to convey the gravity of this task. His ignorant question was quite telling. "One does not simply google a wedding playlist."

"Why not?"

"First of all, the music selection should be personal and reflect the couple. Secondly, the song selection must match the mood they're going for. Romantic? Celebratory? It's very subjective! And lastly—" I could see Ben's eyes crinkling from his profile. He found this whole lecture amusing, but he had to listen carefully to this next part. This was very important. "And lastly, you cannot rely on any list from the internet. Don't you know that most love songs are sad?"

"That can't be true." Apparently, Ben had never been dumped.

"Here." I connected my phone to his car and played the first love song playlist I could find. "This is why you don't trust the internet."

Ben frowned, confused. "'I Will Always Love You'? What's wrong with this? The title says it all."

"Are we listening to the same song?" I turned up the volume. "They're breaking up!" I played the next song and the next.

Ben narrowed his eyes as he concentrated on the lyrics. "Whoa, these *are* sad. I don't get it. How are these considered the best love songs?"

"Because, Ben. It's about the *yearning*. The angst of not having what you want. The hope of what could have been."

"I'm familiar with the concept. What I don't understand is why so many songs about pain are deemed 'the best.'"

"Because . . . even in love, there are let-downs. Obstacles. Distance." I realized I was spouting anything that came to mind. I didn't think I would be parsing out that love hurts. There was a confused expression on Ben's face that made me wonder if his comment had been rhetorical. "'Best' is subjective too," I said, changing tack. "So, we should get Beth and Ethan's input. I'll ask Beth." Knowing Beth, I'd have to curate a list for her approval or else she'd pick stuff from her usual karaoke rotation. "Summertime Sadness" wasn't the right vibe for celebrating your lifelong love. "You ask Ethan."

"Sounds like a plan."

Ben and I continued to split up tasks, which made Ben realize that his only real job was to keep Ethan on track and to hold on to the rings. I did remind him to write a speech. I offered my services, but he declined because he didn't want it to sound like the one Steven gave at Rebecca and Mark's wedding. Fair enough. I was curious to see what personal message Ben wanted to write for Ethan.

"Are you sure we're going in the right direction?"

Ben's GPS led us into a vast open field of tall, overgrown grass with a single road carved through it. It was the one thing that marked the untouched land. One would never know that there was a city behind us.

Ben rolled down his window and stuck his phone out. "I'm not getting any reception. Are you?"

"Nope." I regretted not getting better directions when I contacted the owner, a woman named Esmeralda. "Let's follow the road. It has to be here somewhere."

"Well, we've already come this far." Ben proceeded down the dirt path, while the grass engulfed us.

"It feels kind of magical, doesn't it?"

"Getting lost doesn't do it for me. If the wedding ends up being here, we should advise Beth to include directions about this part. Look around. There aren't even signs."

That was a good suggestion. I jotted down a note in my phone. "Just keep going. I bet it's right around the corner." As I said this, the car ascended a small hill and at the end of the curving road was a lone Craftsman home. As we drove closer, it appeared that the house had been refreshed with a coat of white paint on the side paneling. The weathered, low wooden fence and lush garden retained a rustic, bucolic charm.

Ben parked the car in the gravel lot. "Nice."

I made a mental note to teach Ben more adjectives. It was better than nice. It was perfect.

I climbed out of the car and hung by the fence. The porch was surrounded by bursts of pink desert peonies and imposing Cape marigolds. What a stunning place for Beth and Ethan's wedding. I wondered if Beth would want a flower crown to complement her vintage lace dress. Something simple so it wouldn't take away from the delicate crochet details and long skirt. Immediately, I thought of eucalyptus leaves, small white English roses. Maybe some thistle as her something blue. Ideas were flooding my brain.

"Elise. You still there?" Ben waved a hand in front of my face until I turned to him. "You disappeared for a second."

"We need to find the owner." I walked up to the front door and rang the doorbell. I tried to sneak a peek at the interior through the plastic-covered windows to no avail.

Ben appeared by my side. "Now that I've spent more time with you, I'd like to rescind my apology. I was fully within reason to find you suspicious."

"Not now." Footsteps approached from the other side of the door. "Can you please act normal for a second?"

"How am I not—"

I cut Ben off with an extra-cheery greeting to the paint-splattered Latina woman who opened the door and had to be Esmeralda. "Hi! I'm Elise and this is Ben. Thank you so much for having us on short notice."

"Welcome." Esmeralda held the door open to let us in. The entire floor was lined with paper and smelled like cut wood. "Pardon the dust. I wasn't planning on showing the house yet but when Lorenzo personally refers a couple, I couldn't say no."

"We're planning this wedding for a friend," I clarified, not wanting her to get the wrong idea.

"Yes, Lorenzo mentioned that," Esmeralda replied. Knowing Lorenzo's penchant for hyperbole, I doubted that Esmeralda believed me.

"How long have you been working on this house?" I asked as I walked around the tarp-covered furniture. It was evident that the house was still in progress, but much of it was refinished. From where I stood, I could see that new cabinets and fixtures were installed in the kitchen. The house still retained some of its character with the original mantel and fireplace.

"Longer than I planned," Esmeralda said wearily. "It was supposed to be done in April so I could get it rented already. When I saw the property, I could see the potential for company retreats, family reunions, and weddings. But then it was one delay after the other. Trying to get the city to come do inspections was a nightmare." Esmeralda guided us through the rest of the first floor. "There's an office, guest bedroom, and a family room beyond the kitchen that's convenient for entertaining. There are four bedrooms upstairs, which I just started working on."

Though unfinished, each room was light and airy, calling nature in. The view out of every window tempted you to go outside. Esmeralda did just that. She led us out the sliding doors and into the backyard, if that's what I could call it. There was a large, dirt-covered oval enclosed with a white fence and stables on the other side.

"This is the riding arena for horses. I'm going to get this soft dirt cleared out so I can replace it with stone pavers. When it's done, I think it would be nice for a large, outdoor wedding."

"We're planning a smaller wedding," Ben said.

I stumbled at how easily Ben referred to us as "we." I mean, yes,

Ben and I were planning a wedding for someone else, but if Esmeralda didn't believe it before, she wasn't going to believe it now.

"Follow me." Esmeralda smiled proudly, like she'd been waiting for this moment. Past the arena, she slid the doors open to an enclosed circular structure. She flipped a switch, turning on a ring of lights in the center of the ceiling, unveiling a big empty . . . what was this? I didn't possess enough farm knowledge to know what this building was for.

"This used to be an indoor pen for horse training," Esmeralda said, reading my thoughts. "I had floors installed so that it could also serve as an event space. Lorenzo mentioned you were interested in the barn, but I haven't been able to get rid of the equipment stored in there yet."

"When do you think you will be ready for reservations?" I started taking pictures with my phone as I got farther inside. The half walls blessed the space with sunlight and a view of the flora around us. The pen offered a blank canvas and inspired so many ideas. Planters around the perimeter. An idyllic white and green color scheme. "I'd like to book a date for August."

Esmeralda blinked in surprise. "Oh, that won't be possible. Conservatively, I'd say the house won't be ready for four months. When Lorenzo called, I assumed you were thinking of a date next year."

"Would you consider letting me book it? The space is amazing. We could work out a discount for referrals—"

"Elise, I think we should talk about this." Ben's voice echoed from the doorway, stopping me from blurting my ideas for cross-promotional opportunities. His silhouette fell away as he drifted back toward the house.

"Excuse me," I said to Esmeralda through an apologetic smile. I ran after Ben, who was taking long strides faster than I could keep up with. His shirt flapped when a sudden gust of wind plowed through the arena. Ben leaned back with his arms crossed against the fence, like a brooding city boy pretending to be a cowboy. "What do you think you're doing?"

"Helping you." Ben was annoyingly aloof again, coming and going as he pleased even when his body was still.

"How are you helping me?" The wind was relentless. It was force-feeding me my own hair.

"Don't you know to walk away if you want a good bargain?" Ben murmured between us with a levity I rarely heard from him. "You were too eager back there."

This was Ben helping? I considered this for a second while I wrangled my hair before it plastered to my face. "We're not haggling for goods here."

"Same principle applies. You're showing your hand too early."

I held on to the fence before I flew away. "I can't leave here without booking it. It's too perfect."

"You call this perfect?" Ben coughed when dust swirled at us. "If it's not ready, then it's not ready. Don't get your hopes up."

Too late. My eyes welled, which was becoming an unfortunate, inconvenient habit. It wasn't Ben's remarks that upset me. He'd said them casually, with good intentions. It made sense to keep my options open, but my heart was set. I didn't care if it was illogical or foolish. I needed to believe I could get the things I wanted. I needed to know that I could do the things I set out to do. Damn it, I needed a win.

"Elise?" Ben watched me carefully with his eyebrows cinched, funneling all his unsaid thoughts down the center of his face. "I can't tell if you're sad or if you want to kill me." He lifted my fist from my side and unrolled my fingers. "Making sure you don't have a weapon."

It felt almost wrong to chuckle with Ben after all the barbs we'd thrown at each other.

"Oh good," he said plainly at my empty hand. "I can't die here. Nobody would know how to find me."

An unexpected, heinous cackle escaped my mouth at Ben's dark humor. I clasped both my hands over my mouth to stop myself, but it only made it worse. My body was shaking and tears of laughter fell down my cheeks. My hair flew in every direction, causing some strands to stick to my damp face. All the while, Ben looked down at me with that comma half smile of his, finding the whole sight funny. He must have taken pity on my mess because his fingers reached for my face, raking my hair back before I became Cousin It.

The crinkles at the corners of his eyes relaxed as he came closer, transforming mirth into something more serious. A heated flash. Suddenly, it felt too intimate to be the sole recipient of Ben's gaze. He must have felt it too because he withdrew his hands and stuffed them in his pockets.

Ben stepped back, swallowing hard. "What was that?"

I tried to tamp down the disappointment. "What was what?"

"You didn't see the sparks?" It sounded like a line, but Ben yanked me behind him as the wind sent a tree branch crashing to the ground and swung the gate open. I tripped on Ben's feet, sending me ass-first into a bale of hay stacked at the arena's entrance. Ben tried to save me, catching one of my flailing arms, but ended up toppling into the wet muddy patch next to me. I groaned, my butt and my ego bruised.

"We better get out of here," I shouted as the wind thundered past us. Ben didn't answer right away. He was preoccupied examining the mud on his clothes.

"Is this . . . is this horseshit?!" he screeched, desperately trying to wipe off clumps of dirt and hay and something else from his hands.

I didn't have the heart to tell him that there was a strong likelihood that he was covered in poop. "Think of it like a clay mask," I offered.

Ben didn't find my comment reassuring. His face matched the storm brewing around us. He opened his mouth, but before a word came out, the light overhead flickered and sparkled like a firework, burning out as quickly as it appeared.

The power was out.

Chapter Eleven

I patted the hay off my clothes before retreating into the house. Esmeralda ducked into her office to call the utilities company to see when the power would come back on. Ben stood over the kitchen sink, scrubbing his arms with dish soap like he was about to go in for surgery.

"We should leave soon," he said, watching the windows vibrate from the raging wind. The summer sunset was extinguishing under the cool-blue sky. We both knew what that meant. I had to concede, at least for the time being.

Defeated, I nodded, handing him a paper towel to dry off.

"I'll go tell Esmeralda," I said. Before I could go searching for her, an alarm blared from my phone. The sound multiplied. Ben's phone was going off too. A message flashed on the screen: POWER OUTAGE ALERT. Power line down at Granada Canyon Rd. Due to high winds, power out until 6 AM.

"Shit." Ben swiped the notification away. "That was the road we took to drive up here."

"So, what? We're stuck here?"

"Looks like it," Esmeralda said, popping out of her office. She palmed her forehead as she processed the news herself. "I wasn't expecting guests so soon," she said with a hollow laugh.

"I'm sorry to put you out like this," I said, wondering where we were going to sleep for the night. I couldn't see if there was a couch to crash on underneath the dusty, plastic tarps in the living room.

"No, don't be. None of us could have predicted this. If I did, I would have installed a backup generator." Esmeralda searched her drawers until she found a flashlight and handed it to us, taking candles for herself. "You two take the master suite. It's ready for use. I'll sleep in the guest room downstairs." I protested, offering to exchange rooms, but Esmeralda insisted. "It's fine. Really. I usually sleep down here when I'm too tired to drive home. I wish I could do more. I wasn't planning to stay here tonight, so there isn't any food in the house."

"Oh, that's fine," I lied while my stomach rumbled.

"The room has fresh towels and sheets. There aren't any toiletries, though. Oh!" Esmeralda exclaimed as she suddenly remembered. "There's a basket of snacks in the room. We had the room staged for photos for the website. You're free to break into that if you'd like."

"Uh, thanks." Ben rubbed the back of his neck. "We'll turn in, then," he said excusing us.

"Let me know if you need anything," Esmeralda said graciously, though I suspected there wasn't much else to offer two stranded guests in this unfinished house.

After thanking Esmeralda, I trailed behind Ben as we climbed the stairs. It was too early to sleep, but without power, there weren't many options.

Ben and I stood at the threshold of the master suite. The worry lines on his forehead reappeared. My guess was that it had something to do with the big heart of rose petals in the center of the king-sized bed.

"Well, this isn't useful." I picked up a petal, which turned out to be fake. I found the picnic basket of snacks that Esmeralda mentioned—a small box of chocolates and a can of "fancy nuts" with a bottle of local white wine. I put them on the nightstand and I swept my arm across the bed, collecting the petals into the basket.

"I'm going to the car," Ben announced, slinking back toward the stairs.

"Why?" If anyone should be uncomfortable in this situation, it should be me. I was the one who thought we had a moment outside and I was too hungry to think clearly about what that meant. Deciding where to sleep for the night when there were no other options available was the least of our problems. "We're both adults. We can both sleep on the bed without tou— bothering each other." I was trying to be mature about this, but Ben already had both feet out the door.

"I, uh . . . I have some extra clothes in my gym bag."

Oh. Of course Ben had extra clothes. He seemed like the kind of person who'd have a contingency plan. I had to go and make things awkward.

I sat down on the corner of the bed. I should let my mom know where I was. My phone had one bar of reception and one bar of battery, so I opted to send her a text even though she wasn't great at texting. To be safe, I texted my friends too.

ELISE: At a venue but road closed. Stuck for the night. Can one of you call my mom? I'm low on battery.

JESSE: I'll tell her. Are you okay tho? Is it safe?

BETH: Oh no!

> **REBECCA:** Where are you? Do you want me to come get you?

> **ELISE:** It's fine

I didn't know why I hesitated before I typed the next message, but it would ease their concerns.

> **ELISE:** I'm here with Ben

There was an explosion of eyeball emojis and exclamation points pushing the group chat up at rapid-fire speed. Never mind. This was precisely why I'd hesitated.

> **REBECCA:** My brother? What are you doing with my brother?

As if I'd forgotten that Ben was her brother. God, they liked to make a big deal out of everything. Rebecca should have known how ludicrous it sounded. Even if I wanted to entertain the idea of dating Ben, there were too many reasons stacked against it. Ben had multiple entry points into my circle of friends. He was Ethan's best friend and, more important, my best friend's brother. I couldn't fathom the gigantic shift dating him would cause.

Rebecca, Jesse, and Beth were my family away from my own tumultuous family. They were the longest-lasting relationship I had, the only one that didn't require me to be a mediator between two screaming adults who couldn't stand to be in the same room together. My friends were the safe haven where I could just be me and I wasn't going to rock the boat over some fleeting feelings. I couldn't let them get any ideas, so I kept my answers simple.

> **ELISE:** He drove

> **REBECCA:** Let us know if there's anything we can do

> **ELISE:** thx

> **BETH:** At least you're not alone

I knew it looked innocent, but I still felt the gratuitous insinuation in Beth's concise reply.

> **ELISE:** My phone's about to die. I'll text when I get home tomorrow

As soon as I sent the message, my phone shut down.

Ben came back with a gym bag over his shoulder and set some clothes on the bed. "I, uh, had an extra campaign volunteer shirt in my car and some sweatpants. I don't know if they'll fit, but they're yours if you want them."

"Thanks." Were those his pants? The thought of sharing clothes had my cheeks hot like fresh steamed baos. So much for being mature. "I texted Rebecca to let her know we were here."

"Oh, that explains the texts she sent me," Ben muttered under his breath. Before I could ask what that was about, Ben took off his shoes. "I'm going to shower. Is it okay if I take the flashlight with me? I don't want to shower in the dark."

"Y-yeah," I stammered. I was absolutely not picturing Ben showering in the dark. What was the point if you couldn't see anything? For him, I meant.

When he shut the door, I got up and changed into the shirt

he left me. I could tell it had never been worn. The stiff material left creases where it was folded. The shirt had an odd fit. It was boxy but not very long. The pants were a whole other story. They were too big and no matter how much I pulled on the drawstrings, they slung low on my hips. Eventually, I gave up and rolled up the waistband.

I cracked open the wine and gave myself a heavy pour to drown out the sound of water. This isn't smart, I thought to myself as bitter notes singed my throat. I had too much to do to let this stupid attraction derail me from my priorities. I still had to come up with a game plan for the *Wedding Style* contest, which I hadn't been able to do when all my free time went into planning Beth and Ethan's wedding. I had to save the studio or else it meant all the sacrifices I'd made from my personal life and my bank account were for nothing.

"Bathroom's free."

Ben stood on the other side of the bed, fully dressed in a white T-shirt and black shorts. He seemed more refreshed, except for the exhaustion in his eyes. His five o'clock shadow had darkened, accentuating his tight jaw. He was probably still mad about being stuck here for the night. I wouldn't blame him.

"Sorry." I swirled my glass. "I started without you." Ben's eyes lowered, lingering at the hem of my shirt. "Thanks for the clothes. They fit. Kind of."

I realized too late that I'd walked into a "short" joke, but instead of taking a cheap shot, Ben said, "I can see that."

When Ben glanced back at my face, I could have sworn his eyes were as dark as his shiny, damp hair. His gaze awakened parts of my body that I hadn't used in a long time. Oh, this wasn't good. I took another sip of wine. I had to say something. Anything. "You look clean. Ya don't smell like shit anymore, that's for sure." I tipped my glass in his direction to congratulate him like I was Leo fucking DiCaprio in *The Great Gatsby*. I knew it wasn't good, but I'd already done it, so I committed to it.

"Uh . . ." Yeah, that was the only appropriate response from Ben. "I'm going to bed."

"Cuz you're pooped?" I no longer had control over my mouth.

Ben groaned at my poor joke. He chose the far side of the bed, sitting up as he scrolled through his phone. I climbed onto the vacant side. I considered lying down, but it felt too early to sleep and Ben was still up with his bright-ass phone. God, what did people do before the internet? I was so bored. "What are you doing?"

"Checking email," he grumbled.

"Why are you mad?" I opened the can of nuts and picked out the cashews. "Did the email hurt your feelings?"

Ben frowned, more at the phone than at me. "It's Shawn Tam. He posted more videos today." He turned the screen so I could watch. It was a supercut montage of him spending time with elderly Asian women in the community. Doing tai chi and pouring tea at dim sum. He was leaning hard into the Asian mom demographic.

"I'm Shawn Tam, running for California State Assembly. I'm running to give back to the community that has given so much to me." While the voiceover was playing, there were captions that listed his credentials with subtitles in Chinese. "What we need is fresh talent who can think outside of the box, not career politicians that don't make good on their promises. That's why I'm leading a grassroots campaign. Join me by donating." A caption flashed to visit the link in his bio. "Vote for me, Shawn Tam. I'm self-made and Asian-mom approved!" The next video of his autoplayed; it was the same as the previous one except entirely in Mandarin.

Besides the fact that Shawn spoke superfast, I was impressed. Ben, on the other hand, was incensed. "*My* Asian mom doesn't like you!"

"Ben. I know it's corny, but is he really the competition?" I squinted at the phone screen. The next video was of Shawn Tam dancing to Blackpink. "He looks harmless."

Ben huffed. "I hate how Shawn Tam panders for likes and popularity. Like his whole 'good Asian' shtick is perpetuating the model-minority myth, as if all we care about is his pedigree."

"Your mom graduated from Yale," I pointed out. "People do care about those things."

"But if you look on his website, there are no specific plans. He can tout his JD and MBA all he wants, but what else does he have to offer? Our constituents are not single-issue voters. What is his stance on health care? How is he going to boost the economy? Improve infrastructure? Combat climate change? How is he going to improve the standard of living with his bad dancing? The nerve of this guy calling my mom a career politician when she's done more with—"

"Shhhhh. You're talking too loud." I sat up and poured a glass of wine for Ben. "You need this more than me." Ben indulged in a sip but he kept ranting about polls and records and other stuff that was killing my buzz. "You shouldn't hatescroll before bed," I said. "It's not good for your sleep."

"Hatescroll?" I heard a tinge of amusement in his voice. I took it as progress.

"You heard me. Take a break. Wind down for the evening." Ben didn't take my advice and kept shooting daggers at his screen. I slid the snacks over to him. Snacks always made me feel better. I looked inside the nightstand, skipping the channel guide for the TV (which was useless at the moment), and took the small note-pad and pen to sketch. I grabbed Ben's wrist, pointing his phone over my lap.

"Excuse me," he said of my brazen move, but he didn't sound too annoyed.

"I need some light." I sketched the layout of the property as close to scale as I could. I flipped to the next page and drew a few ideas for the ceremony. An arch of dark green lemon leaves with Queen Anne's lace for fillers. While I added a few spirals in for white ranunculus, the light on my notepad brightened. Ben had traded his phone for the flashlight.

"What are you doing?" I asked.

"Being nosy," he said, stating the obvious. He picked at the box of chocolates until he found a caramel. "You're a really good artist."

I wasn't sure about that. I wasn't trained or anything. They were nice doodles, maybe. "I'm jotting down ideas before I forget. Let me know if your arm gets tired."

"That looks nice," he said of the bouquet I was messing around with. I was thinking a mix of all white flowers so it would be the same color but different textures would add dimension. "Did you always know you wanted to be a florist?"

"Yeah. Ever since I was a kid." The venue would look great with two long dining tables. I made a note to ask Beth about it along with other ideas. Garlands of leaves instead of centerpieces. Can-dles and . . . and? I lost my train of thought when Ben shifted closer to get a better look at my list. He was so close, I could smell the chocolate he was licking off his fingers.

"I can tell you're passionate about it," he hedged. The round-about way he said this was hiding a question.

"Yeah." I directed my eyes back to my paper, unsure where he was going with this. "I like things a certain way."

"No, I didn't mean it like that. When we were talking earlier, outside," he clarified.

I froze. He was referring to the crying earlier. "It's nothing."

"It didn't seem like nothing. There has to be a reason why you're set on this place. You were about to give Esmeralda the milk and the cow for free to book this half-finished place for a wedding that's not yours. I'm just trying to understand because *someone* recently told me it wasn't healthy to focus on the things we can't control."

I glared at him out of the corner of my eye. How dare he use my words against me.

"That person sounds like a hack." I dropped my pen. Without it, the still of the night and complete boredom left me alone with my thoughts and I didn't like it. So I found myself telling Ben the truth. "I might have to close my studio after Beth's wedding." I sunk into my pillow. Saying it out loud made it feel real. Too real.

"Oh." Ben lowered his arm, shining the light away from me. "But you're so talented."

I smiled weakly. It was nice of him to say, but compliments weren't going to help me at this point. "Thanks, but I'm falling behind on bills. I really picked the wrong time to start my own business."

Ben nodded. He was more familiar with current events than me, so he knew what I was talking about.

In recent years, people had lost jobs or quit if they didn't feel valued. It meant less disposable income for what was essentially a big party. People focused on what was important to them and downsized. Good for other people, but bad for my bottom line. "Anyway, that's why I wanted the feature in *Wedding Style*. If it still goes to shit, then at least I'll go out on a high note, you know?

Rebecca, Jesse, Beth—they mean everything to me. Their weddings should be something to be remembered."

"They don't know, do they?" Ben tilted his head, deducing the answer as he searched my face. "Why not?"

"Their wedding days are about them, not me. Don't tell Rebecca. I'm only telling you because, well . . . you've already seen me cry about it." I placed my sketches on the nightstand. "I swear I don't cry that much. You always catch me at the wrong time."

"You don't have to explain." Ben turned off the flashlight like the interrogation portion of the night was over, showing me some mercy. He lay down and pulled the covers over himself. "I do care when I see tiny florists acting shady and giving attitude."

"Whatever," I said, grateful that the darkness hid my smile. I shuffled under the covers. "Same goes to fake chefs kicking me out of someone else's kitchen."

"I never claimed to be a chef."

"Do you want to be?"

Ben was quiet for a while. I didn't think he'd answer until he said, "I don't know. I only chose culinary school because I thought it would be fun. I grew up watching my grandpa cook. In the kitchen, it didn't matter who you were. Once service started, the only thing that mattered was that you did your job and you did it well. I liked that."

"What are you going to do after the election, then?" I felt greedy, asking another question, but this was the longest Ben had ever spoken. It was as if his thoughts only existed in the shadow of the night. If things had to go back to normal in the morning, then I didn't want to squander the chance to keep this going. Just two voices sharing secrets in the dark.

"I don't know. I haven't thought that far ahead. I'm trying new things, seeing what sticks." The bed dipped as Ben turned and when I heard his voice again, we were face-to-face. "I envy you. It's inspiring to see someone going after their dreams."

"Even if I'm failing at it?" I yawned. The wine was lulling my tired body to sleep.

"Who says you're failing at it? You're doing it, aren't you? Better than me. My family thinks I'm wasting my time being mediocre, dabbling in different things."

"That sounds like something Rebecca would say."

"You guys talk about me?"

Oops. Things were going so well, but there was no way I was going to answer that question, even if it was more curious than accusatory. He probably didn't want to know that my loyalty was to Rebecca. He definitely didn't need to know that I thought about him outside of our interactions together. "Do you always answer questions with a question?"

"Do I? I didn't realize I did that." He sounded surprised, like this was the first time someone had brought this up to him. "Does it bother you?"

"Meh. I've gotten used to it."

"Huh," he said with a small laugh as he shifted to lie on his back. "Be still my mediocre heart."

Chapter Twelve

*B*en Yu *frowns when he sleeps.* It was the first thing to pop into my head when I woke up. While Ben fell asleep easily last night, I had clutched the covers whenever the wind howled outside or sent debris tap, tap, tapping against the window. Somehow, I'd ended up here, sharing the same airspace as Ben, cocooned in the duvet. I knew I really should get out of bed. The view out the window was serene and the roads were likely cleared by now but I couldn't stop looking at the depth of his eyebrows, bookending the bridge of his nose, holding back the waves of concerns. The man had no chill, not even in sleep.

I softly passed my finger between his eyebrows. Instead of smoothing down, Ben's face pinched as he stirred and emitted a low, throaty sound.

Not gonna lie. That sound did things to me.

His eyes were still closed and his frown deepened, which made me inexplicably giddy. "What time is it?"

"I don't know." I was about to roll over to get my phone, but then I remembered it was dead. Ben curled into a fetal position, grumbling about the cold. My blanket-hogging ways had left him exposed to the elements. Oops. I unraveled myself and threw his rightful half of the blanket over him.

Ben moaned as he luxuriated in his newfound warmth, rewarding me with another unintentionally delicious sound. "Forget that I asked. Let's stay in bed all day."

I stopped myself before I read too much into that. Ben probably didn't know what he was saying. He was still half asleep, drugged by this cloud of a mattress. I couldn't stay anyway. I had to get back for Jesse's final dress fitting. "Come on." I shook Ben's arm. "I don't—"

"Ow!" Ben caught my hand and lifted it to his face. He squinted his barely awake eyes at my calloused palm. "Be careful with those."

"You never complained before," I said, trying to free myself from his grip.

"I never had a reason to," he mumbled.

"What?" In between my fingers, I saw Ben's eyes widening like he finally realized how close we were and that I'd heard what he said. I folded my hand to get a better look at him. I thought he would brush off his comment, but the daylight made it hard to hide. Thank goodness, because the morning sun softened his face, including his scraggly scruff. I wanted to bask in his gaze, even if he was regarding me carefully. He was waffling, hot and cold. Call it impatience. Call it lust. I needed to know if what I was feeling was just in my head.

Before I thought better of it, my index finger stretched. I watched him to let him know my intention, to see if he'd pull away. At first contact, he leaned in, our foreheads almost touching as I dragged my finger along his jaw to his chin like I was lighting a match. His thumb pressed the inside of my wrist, on top of my racing pulse.

When his lips parted, I closed my eyes in anticipation. I waited, passing time to the sound of his deep breaths.

"We should get going."

Ben let go of me and slid out of bed. He busied himself with packing his things, back to his normal self. It took a few seconds for the sting of rejection to wear off. My mother used to tell me to find a man who liked me more than I liked him. I never thought it was good advice, but it might have prevented this embarrassing attempt at seduction. It served me right. I always leapt before looking.

After getting dressed, we said our goodbyes to Esmeralda. We thanked her for her hospitality and complimented the five-star bed. She appreciated the feedback, but unfortunately didn't accept my request to reserve the venue.

"I can't afford the liability when the venue isn't ready," she explained. It was a very good and valid reason that frankly sucked balls.

"What are you going to do?" Ben asked during the drive back to the studio. We stuck to wedding talk. It was the only safe topic.

"I don't know." What a day to face everyone. All the bridesmaids, including Rebecca, Beth, and Jesse's cousin Hannah, were supposed to meet to try on our jumpsuits for last-minute alterations. I was hoping to give Beth some good news today, but no such luck. I was back to square one. I should have listened to Ben and not gotten my hopes up. Being an optimist was exhausting. "Worse comes to worst, Beth and Ethan get married but postpone their ceremony if they can't find a venue in time. Maybe get married in someone's backyard. Do you have a backyard?"

"No. I'm subletting Rebecca's old apartment until the lease runs out."

Not too far from me. I shelved the thought. It was neither here nor there.

"Well, there goes that idea." I didn't know anyone else who would be willing to host fifty strangers at their house.

"I think Beth and Ethan will be happy wherever they can get married. I also think you can make a ditch look grand and romantic."

It was nice of Ben to say. It might be my only option. "I better get on it before all the good ditches are taken."

BETH SAT BETWEEN Rebecca and me on the couch at the bridal boutique in Temple City, acting as our buffer to ensure the fitting was drama-free. I told her it was fine. I had mostly forgiven Rebecca after she asked Veronica Reed for photos of the fundraiser, sending me the best pictures of my centerpieces before guests ate the poisoned grapes. They were off-center and not taken at the best angle, but the veranda looked beautiful. And, as much as I hated to admit it, the grapes looked deceivingly juicy in the lighting, so I submitted the photos to the *Wedding Style* contest after all. The first theme was "Exciting Destinations" and Rebecca thought I could make a case for Rome (à la Beverly Hills).

Back in the real world, Rebecca was chatting with the boutique's owner, Janet Wong, while Jesse changed in the dressing room. Janet was a bit of a local legend, having dressed many of the brides in my family for decades. She never seemed to age, which she accredited to her vegetarian diet. My guess would have been the soft lighting in her shop that made us all look like we had filters on our faces.

"There used to be more bridal shops down Las Tunas Drive," Janet lamented as she zipped the dress bag containing Rebecca's jumpsuit. "Couples used to walk up and down the street to book everything in one trip. Photography, flowers, wedding dress, qipao. But now it's out of style. You young people don't want to do big banquet weddings anymore."

"Yeah, I can see that." Rebecca was smart enough not to mention her own nontraditional wedding. "It's a long day. There's the procession to the bride's house, the tea ceremony. Then repeat at the groom's house."

"Don't forget the door games," I said. As the groom, Steven had to bribe his way into Jesse's house and pass a few tests before reaching his bride. Jesse had given us bridesmaids permission to run the groomsmen through the gauntlet. It was an excuse to torture Steven, Ethan, and Mark a little. Hopefully, we wouldn't scare away Jesse's brother Brian or Steven's frat bro Mateo.

"Then there's pictures, the reception at night, outfit changes . . ." Rebecca continued, sighing as if she was exhausted at the thought. "How many dresses are you wearing, Jesse?"

"Three," Jesse replied, shouting from her dressing room. "Cheongsam for the tea ceremony, the white gown for pictures and the beginning of the reception, and ending the night with the áo dài to please Steven's mom." Jesse stepped out in a gorgeous modern cheongsam. There were bursts of gold embroidered flowers in lieu of a dragon and phoenix. The dress was fitted to the waist before it flared into a small train with a thigh-high slit cut in the front of the skirt instead of the side. "Can someone help me? I can't get this fucking thing in."

The "fucking thing" Jesse was referring to was the frog button on the mandarin collar. Hannah went to Jesse's rescue, successfully pushing the silk knot into the corresponding loop.

Rebecca let out a low whistle. "This fits you like a glove, Jess."

"Fuck yeah, it does," Jesse replied. Since her CrossFit competition was over, Jesse had been pumped about life, especially getting off her diet to eat all the things at her wedding. "This was the only dress I was worried about. The white gown and áo dài are more forgiving."

Janet circled around Jesse to check for any adjustments, but she ultimately agreed with our assessment, giving Jesse the okay to change into the next dress. "Are you excited about your big day?"

Jesse snorted. "I want to get this thing over with. Relatives are starting to fly in and coming to my house. It's been hectic."

"What about Steven's family?" Beth asked. "How are they handling everything?"

"They've been okay," Jesse said as she returned to the dressing room. Hannah followed her in to help her change. "They have opinions about certain things, like they wanted a Vietnamese-speaking emcee for the reception and the áo dài, but our parents were able to come up with a compromise. Elise, you're still planning on going to Steven's parents' house to set up the flowers, right?"

"Yeah," I said. The night before Jesse's wedding, I had to decorate both Steven's and Jesse's parents' houses. It was a bit of a logistical nightmare with all the centerpieces and boutonnieres Jesse's mom wanted me to make for all the aunts and uncles in her family. This was the kind of stuff I lived for, I reminded myself. Who needed sleep? "Why?"

"Try not to stay there too long. My family is having a wedding pre-party. There's going to be a ton of food."

"Yes, of course," I said. I wasn't a good cook, but I could help with the eating.

"So, how was the venue?" Beth asked quietly, not wanting to take the focus off Jesse. This was the game we'd been playing for the last few weeks. Nobody wanted to step on anybody's toes or steal anyone's thunder, while they were simultaneously internally focused on their own wedding.

"It didn't work out." I showed her and Rebecca the pictures of Esmeralda's property on my phone, trying to read Beth's expression as I described the feasibility of the space. "The house itself wasn't a hundred percent ready, though, so I couldn't make a reservation."

"Okay," Beth said wistfully, still swiping through my photos. "I need to confirm the venue with my other vendors soon. I don't know how much longer I can hold out."

I fixed on a smile, ignoring the tension in my shoulders. My brain seized, trying to think of a solution. There was so much to do, but not enough hands. I was running out of time and money. Something had to give.

"I was wondering if I should even do a bridal shower or bachelorette party. I don't think I have time after exams for both," Beth added. "What do you think, E?"

Oh shit. I was the worst maid of honor. I'd forgotten I had to plan those events too. There weren't enough weekends to choose from at this point. I didn't know what to do. I rubbed the throbbing pain in my temples.

"Um, Beth." I hated this. I hated disappointing people. "I don't think I have time."

"I can do it!" Rebecca shouted, turning everyone's heads. "Elise already has enough to do. Let me take care of this."

I hesitated. I had a feeling Rebecca was offering out of guilt, but it would be a big help. "Only if you have time—"

Rebecca waved her hand. "It's fine. I'm always down for a girls' trip." Of course she'd made an executive decision on the bachelorette party. "What are you guys thinking? New York? Austin? New Orleans?"

All I heard was the whistling sounds in the ghost town of my wallet. "What about karaoke in Ktown?"

"We can do that anytime," Rebecca said, even though it had been months since our last karaoke night.

"It's expensive and some of us are on a budget," I reminded her.

It was never fun to be the poor one in the group, but it had to be said. Friends didn't let friends go broke.

"How about Vegas?" Rebecca's eyes gleamed. "I know someone who could hook us up with a room. What do you think, Beth?"

Why did I have the sense that I'd been played? Like she started with the highest offer, knowing I would say no, and then suggested something I couldn't refuse? She'd haggled me! It didn't matter because Beth was down for the idea and now Jesse was excited about making up for her own skipped bachelorette party. It was so beyond my control that I had to let it go.

Once that was decided, it was the bridesmaids' turn to change clothes. All of our jumpsuits fitted without suffocating us. Just when I thought I'd escaped any special undergarments, Janet handed us pasties. The thin spaghetti straps that crisscrossed the back of the jumpsuits didn't leave us with many options except stickers for our nips. Mine were flower shaped, naturally.

Once we were done, we split off to our separate ways in the parking lot, promising to check the group chat for bachelorette party planning. Beth followed me to my studio so we could discuss some place-setting ideas before she went back to memorizing the nervous system.

"I'll make this quick," I said, laying out a white dish on top of a larger, gold charger plate. "I found these wooden napkin rings that would look great with these." I held up forest-green napkins for her approval. Beth reached out and instead of taking the napkin like I thought she would, she touched my neck with both hands.

"Hey!" I squirmed and batted her hand away. "That tickles."

"Let me check your lymph nodes. You look gaunt. Did you, ahem, not get any sleep last night?" Only Beth could pull off an angelic look while waggling her eyebrows.

Now I felt ill. Crushes—and getting rejected by them—were not good for my health. There should be a page about it on WebMD. "Don't do that. Nothing's going to happen there." I swore Beth to secrecy before giving the basic rundown of my evening with Ben at Rejection Ranch.

"Give Tom—I mean Ben—a chance." I wasn't going to entertain the idea. I went back to the place setting. "You know, I've gone out with him and Ethan many times," Beth said, not ready to give up. "He's really great once you get to know him."

That was the problem. I had tried to get to know him and look how that turned out. "I don't think he likes me. Not like that. You saw how he treated me at Rebecca's wedding."

"You mean when both of you were so busy talking to each other that you missed my speech?" I shot her a look. She knew that wasn't what I meant. "So he doesn't like crowds. That's not a deal breaker, E. He's a good guy. He wouldn't be Ethan's best man if he wasn't."

That might be true, but I didn't have time to decipher what made Ben hot and cold at the same time. Life was too short for lukewarm feelings. I laid out some wedding favor prototypes I had been working on. One was a vial of lavender potpourri; a tag with their wedding details was tied to the vial with a ribbon. "I could replace this with Ethan's favorite seasoning," I suggested, in case they wanted something more personalized. "Then there's this two-in-one option." I pushed a small potted succulent with a place card stuck in it. "Which one do you like?"

Beth smelled the lavender and sighed dreamily. "This is nice."

I crossed "Choose wedding favors" off the list. Now I only had to assemble fifty of those. "Did you want something different for your bridal shower?"

Beth's face paled as if she saw me kill a spider, even though she hated spiders. "No, forget I mentioned it. I don't know why I brought it up. I don't want one anyway."

"Why not?"

"No one understands my comprehension about this." The word mix-up put me on alert. "The more I think about it, I don't have time to sit around and open presents. I can't. I am way behind on studying and then there's so much to do for the wedding."

"Okay," I said quickly. If it was going to stress her out this much, it was best to forget about it. I had to keep my bride happy, so I changed the subject. "Have you found a bakery for a cake?"

"Ethan asked his pastry chef." Beth recovered now that we were talking about dessert. "He makes great cookies too."

"Who?" I jotted down a list of supplies I needed to order, pretending not to notice the suspicious drop in her voice. "The pastry chef?"

Now Beth gave me the warning look to stop playing dumb. "All right. I'm going to say this once and I promise to never bring it up again."

Oh no. Hard-truth time. Sometimes my friends and I aired our concerns to say our piece with the understanding that the recipient could do what they wanted with it. Like the time Rebecca took one for the team and told Jesse that her shorts gave her major camel toe. Beth hadn't dropped hard truths on me since the time I dropped out of college, when she offered to help me study in an effort to get me to stay. I braced myself, giving Beth my full attention. "What is it?"

"I love you, but you're being picky. You always have been. You quit after the first or second date if things don't click right away."

"It's not being picky. It's called having standards," I countered, fighting the fire that threatened to come out of my ears. I wasn't being naïve in wanting the kind of easy love that they sang about in ballads. I knew what happened when two people who weren't meant to be together were stuck together. I didn't think it was too much to ask for someone to like me as much as I liked them.

My phone buzzed on the counter. The preview of the text revealed a partial photo of a torso in an indigo-blue suit and a stubbled jawline that I now knew intimately. I couldn't pick up my phone before Beth caught a glimpse.

> **BEN:** Would this go with your dress? For Beth and Ethan's wedding

Another example of how crushes were bad for my health. It was making me stupid. Ben and I had discussed what we might wear to Beth and Ethan's wedding, so why was I mooning over this effort to coordinate our look? It was so like him to add the clarification at the end, making sure there was no subtext to this message at all. I scrolled through my camera roll and sent Ben a picture of the lilac wrap maxi dress I wore to Jesse and Steven's engagement party last year. It was the most flattering dress I had that could pass as a bridesmaid dress.

"I think you need to give people time to open up," Beth said, picking up a rose to hide her smirk. "Flowers don't bloom in a day, do they?" I snatched the rose away from her.

I was all for hoping for the best, but the power of positive thinking had its limits. I couldn't manifest anyone to fall in love with me. Even a magic genie couldn't do that.

Chapter Thirteen

The setup at Steven's parents' house was quick. After I delivered the flower arrangements, the only thing Steven's mom asked me to do was help her with the gift trays that Steven's relatives would carry for the procession to Jesse's house. I assembled fruit, teas, and bottles of Hennessy, wrapping them with red cellophane and placing them inside red cake pan–like wedding tins. At Jesse's parents' request, there were also boxes of wedding pastries that I didn't have a taste for except the big almond cookies. Once a tin was filled, I topped it off with its accompanying lid and a red silk cloth embroidered with 囍.

I made the trek up to Jesse's parents' house, which sat on a hilly street in Monterey Park. It was hard to park there on a normal day since it was common for multigenerational homes to own multiple cars. It was exponentially harder to find a spot today since Jesse's relatives were over. I had no other choice but to block the driveway.

I carried a vase of purple cymbidium orchids and curly willow branches to the front door, adding my boots to the mountain of shoes scattered about on the porch. I kicked them to the side so no one would step on them. A middle-aged woman I assumed was Jesse's aunt opened the door and waved me in.

"Hi, Ayi," I greeted to be safe. Everyone was an auntie or uncle except for Jesse's grandma. She was in the corner playing four-color cards and laughing with a group of other octogenarian women. "Where's Jesse?"

The woman shouted over the din of Cantonese aunties chopping on heavy wooden butcher boards while uncles made noodles from scratch. Brian, Jesse's brother, distributed the beer, which kept everyone loose-lipped, judging by the gasps and cackling coming out of the kitchen. The house was already decorated with banners hanging on each side of the front door. A table was set in front of the rosewood altar, where the gifts and an entire roast pig would go. Jesse came out of her room, reaching for the vase when Hannah admonished her.

"Oh, I forgot," Jesse said, flipping her hands to show me her manicure. "Hannah just painted them. Here." Jesse directed me to put the vase down on the end table.

"You shouldn't lift a finger. It's your wedding," I said.

"God, don't say that. I feel so useless," Jesse said, waddling from the foam that kept her painted toes separated.

"It's okay. Beth and Rebecca can help me." I scanned the room, looking for them.

"They're not here. Rebecca is stuck at work on the Westside and Beth didn't even answer her texts. It's down to the wire," Jesse reminded me. Multiple people called for Jesse at the same time, which she answered with a growl. "Look at this madhouse."

"Hey," I said, switching on my soothing voice. "It's fine. How about . . . ?" I angled my head toward the slew of teenage cousins on the couch in their own bubble playing Xbox and Jesse got the message. She changed the Wi-Fi password, taking the Xbox offline, and put all her cousins to work. Once all the flowers were in the house, Jesse went back into her room to let Hannah pluck her eyebrows when another auntie swept me to the kitchen. I wasn't sure if I was going to be put to work until I was plopped down at the dining table and a bowl of chow mein appeared before my eyes.

"Here. Eat." Auntie slid a pair of chopsticks toward me. Now, I didn't presume to know much about anything, but I did know this. When an auntie tells you to eat, you eat. I wouldn't have refused anyway. The chow mein had the thin golden egg noodles that I liked and a rich aroma of dark soy, oyster sauce, and smoky wok hei. Auntie waited until I took my first, satisfying bite before she returned to the counter to finish plating food to feed the rest of the guests.

After I finished my food, I tracked down Jesse's mom and asked her to commit to the number of boutonnieres she needed. Jesse's mom might be shorter than me, but she was a force of nature with the calves of an ox. She didn't mess around, so I didn't press her when she kept giving me the runaround, saying she didn't know exactly how many flowers she needed because their family didn't do RSVPs. They were old-school, hand delivering invitations to all her friends and family. She couldn't get a head count until she called everyone to remind them of the wedding.

"Twenty," she finally said, which was my worst nightmare.

Fuck boutonnieres. Fuck them. It was going to be hell on my hands to make so many on such short notice. After my internal tantrum, I flexed my fingers and went to work. I borrowed a pair of somebody's sandals and gathered supplies from my truck. Then, I went to the backyard to make the boutonnieres at a make-shift station. Jesse's mom told me all the tables and chairs set up for tomorrow's festivities were off-limits and directed me to a spot by her kumquat tree where she apparently kept the rest of the help. There I found a row of small blue plastic children's stools, where

Ethan and Ben were seated and peeling carrots over newspaper pages lining the ground.

"Fancy meeting you here," Ben greeted as I set down my bucket of orchids. Over the course of the last two weeks, Ben and I had texted about wedding stuff but nothing else. I had hoped that enough time had passed to get over him, but seeing Ben, squatting impossibly low on this flimsy chair, knee-deep in root vegetables, still managed to keep me off balance. We were in the presence of other people—a whole village of people—so I fixed on my smile and put my feelings aside.

"I should be saying that to you." I lowered myself into my designated baby chair, careful not to let my thighs eat up my cutoff shorts. "Why are you here?"

"Jesse called and said they needed more cooks," Ethan explained, gliding a paring knife down a daikon the size of my arm. "And then her mom put us on prep." He laughed, genuinely amused that his restaurant experience in high-end kitchens had no bearing in Jesse's house. He was nowhere near Asian auntie status. Ethan elbowed Ben. "Just like the good old days, am I right?"

Ben's face broke into an embarrassed smile as he fished out another carrot from the big plastic colander and I didn't think I'd ever recover from it.

"What's so funny?" I asked, nimbly wiring each orchid to create a stem.

Ethan smirked. "When Tom"—Ethan shook his head as he corrected himself—"when Ben finally moved up from washing dishes, his first task was to peel potatoes. This fool got so much shit from the chef for throwing the skins away because it was one of those farm-to-table, use-every-scrap kind of places."

Ben kicked off a peel that landed on his orange Crocs. They appeared radioactive under the old fluorescent floodlights. "If only he could see me now, littering on top of yesterday's *World Journal*."

"A disgrace," Ethan joked. "What would you do if I didn't come save you?" He hauled the heavy colander of peeled vegetables and propped it on his shoulder. It was an obvious excuse to flex.

"I hate it when you tell that story." Ben laughed easily as Ethan returned to the kitchen through the sliding doors. This little bromance of theirs was adorable.

"How have you been?" I asked, picking off the best-looking flowers. I kept my voice neutral, even though my stomach flipped when I thought about the last time we saw each other.

"Busy," he said. "I'm back in the campaign office. They have me on the phones now. 'Hi, this is Ben calling to remind you to reelect Donna Yu. Will we have your support this November? A vote for Yu is a vote for you!' I'm having a blast." I couldn't help laughing at Ben's sarcasm. "What about you?"

"Same," I said. "So . . . Tom, huh?"

"Short for Thomas."

Benjamin Thomas Yu. It suited him. "Do you ever miss your double life?"

He shrugged. "It was easier. Less chance of anyone googling me and finding out about my family."

"You act like they're so bad." I tied a ribbon around the boutonniere. One down. Nineteen to go.

"They're not, but I learned at a young age that people determined my worth based on who my parents were. If they could come speak at our school. If they could donate money. Friends who wanted internships. It wasn't really fun, being a stepping-stone. I shouldn't complain. It's not like I didn't benefit from it. I only got my first job because my boss at the time played tennis with my dad. But, I wanted to know how people would treat me if I was Tom. Plain old Tom."

Ben was painfully earnest. It was a shame that he was only like this in the evening while we were shrouded by darkness, like he didn't trust anyone to see this side of him any other time. While I didn't really understand what it must have been like to worry about people's hidden agendas, I did know what it was like wishing to be seen and loved as I was.

"Give yourself some credit. You're hardly old."

"Ha-ha," he said, sounding a bit sad.

"How old are you again?" I knew he was younger, but I wasn't sure how much younger.

"Twenty-seven." We were only a year apart. Ben handed me another wire as I was about to reach for one. "My mom had Rebecca and me almost back to back. In her mind, it was more efficient that way."

"It doesn't sound like it would be," I said. "But what do I know? I'm an only child."

"Did you ever want siblings?"

"Sometimes, when I felt lonely," I confessed. "But then, I had friends."

I was concentrating so hard on handling the delicate flowers that it took a while before I realized a silence had fallen between us. When I looked over at Ben, he was peeling, lost in thought.

"What's wrong?" I asked. "Reminiscing about your former life in Hell's Kitchen?"

A half smile appeared on Ben's face, followed by a silent laugh. "No. Being Tom was fun for a while"—Ben peeled the next carrot in a spiral—"but he was a chump too."

"Why do you say that?"

Ben checked our surroundings, glancing into the kitchen, where Ethan was roped into wrapping egg rolls. When he seemed certain that we were alone, he said, "Because he got caught up in the kitchen hierarchy, wanting to prove something to himself. So much so that when Ethan suggested a double date with his girlfriend's best friend, he said no. And now he lives with regret."

I froze. This didn't make sense. I saw him run out of bed with my own two eyes. "But . . . the other day . . ." My whole body flushed, remembering our small touch. All of my senses went haywire, except for my ears, which tuned into the frequency of Ben's low voice.

"You caught me off guard. You've caught me off guard from the first day we met."

I laughed nervously, trying to wrap my mind around that statement. The day we met? Where he grilled me until I was a well-done steak? I was going to need him to explain that to me, but then he said, "But life is complicated right now with the campaign. Half the battle is getting the word out and keeping up appearances. It consumes my time and it's only going to get worse the closer we get to November. I don't want you to get swept up into it."

"My life is complicated too," I retorted. My hands flew as I finished a boutonniere, fueled by Ben's excuses. It wasn't like I'd placed an order for a distraction in the form of Ben's handsome face and companionship. *You've caught me off guard from the first day we met.* Damn it. Now he had me tracing back to every interaction. I didn't need this either. "You're right. It's not a good idea. God, what would Rebecca think?"

"Elise." Ben grabbed ahold of my wrist, breaking the rhythm I had with my little assembly line. He was lucky that I didn't accidentally pierce him with the pearled pin. I was about to tell him this when he placed a flower in my palm—a rose made entirely out of a carrot ribbon.

"What is this for?" As much as I hated to admit it, I loved the carrot rose. I didn't know what to do with it, though. It was too cute to eat and too perishable to keep.

"A gift from Tom." Ben cleared his throat, but his voice still came out hoarse. "He would have tried to impress you with this before he knew about your knife skills. He would have found you intimidating because of how honest and pretty you are, but he would have been more confident. He would have asked you what your tattoos mean and where's your favorite place to go and if you wanted to catch a Wednesday matinee because our weekends were booked." He sighed. "And it's also an apology from me and my sorry ass for leaving you . . . in bed. I can't begin to tell you how sorry I am."

Ben's breathing was audible, uneven, like that morning at the ranch. But this time I could see him. His face was as open as I'd ever seen it. His pleading eyes hung on my face, gradually lowering to my mouth. My heart raced, thinking about how he wanted me then and how he wanted me now, but my self-preservation kicked in. Crushes were no good for a person like me, who could take a glimmer of hope for requited love and amplify it to the light of a thousand suns, forgetting how badly it burned. It was nice that Ben had cleared the air, but it wasn't enough. The pursuit of love couldn't be half-assed. It was whole-ass or nothing.

"Elise!" Jesse's mom shouted from the kitchen, startling me. "Brian needs your ladder!"

Saved by the Los. "I better go."

I used every inch of my quads to jump off the plastic stool and head inside the house. Ben called after me, but I didn't look back. This was for the best. We'd addressed the elephant in the room and we could go back to planning Beth and Ethan's wedding through texts with clear consciences.

In the living room, I found Brian, red-faced from a combination of beer and struggling to open my ladder. He apparently didn't see the lock on the side. Over his shoulder was the red curtain that was going to drape against the wall to make a nice backdrop for the tea ceremony. I was going to do that later and frame the top with red roses.

"Hey, Brian," I said, injecting a dose of cheer I usually reserved for first graders. "I can hang the curtain. Give me back the ladder."

"I got it, I got it," he slurred. Brian kept trying to pry the ladder open. The more I reached for it, the more Brian swung it away, almost tripping over himself. His grandma looked up from her card game to yell at him, which started a disorienting chorus of Cantonese aunties shouting things I didn't understand.

What happened next felt like a series of snapshots. Brian climbing my half-open, tilting ladder. Ben's hand on my waist, grabbing my shirt as I ran. Me, catching Brian to break his fall. Kind of. He was bigger than me and if I'd paid more attention in physics class, I could have explained how we ended up on the floor, side by side. The details were kind of fuzzy after that. The last thing I remembered at Jesse's house was Ben's wide-eyed face, calling my name.

"You're lucky you don't have a concussion like your friend over there, Miss Ngo," the nurse said as she wrapped my throbbing wrist. She said it was a mild sprain, but I begged to differ, no matter what the X-rays said.

"What?" That couldn't be right. I tried to touch the bump on my head with my good hand, but Ben was holding it. Nothing was making sense. Jesse yelling at Brian, who was in the bed next to us, wasn't helping either.

"You idiot! You think I wanted to be at the hospital the night before my wedding? You almost killed my friend!" Jesse was still holding her fingers apart. Someone needed to tell her that her manicure had probably set by now.

"I'm fine," I said, but Jesse didn't hear me.

"Miss, you have to keep your voice down," the ER doctor said as she continued examining Brian.

"Apply ice and rest your arm for at least forty-eight hours. A mild sprain should take a few weeks to recover. Try to elevate it as much as possible," the nurse said as she finished wrapping my hand. She typed a note into her computer. After she gave me a brochure on how to treat a sprain, she closed the curtain behind her like she hadn't dropped bad news in my lap.

"I need to hang the flowers for the ceremony," I said. "Who's going to set up the reception?"

"Are you really worried about that right now?" Ben asked. "You just took a hard fall."

"Didn't you hear the nurse? Concussion-free, baby." I winced, not sure why I added the "baby" at the end. Ben misinterpreted this, thinking I was in pain, and began to call the nurse back. I reached for the call button before Ben could punch it. "I'm fine."

"You're not fine. Did you really think you could catch Brian? It was like watching an ant get stepped on."

"I have to deliver the flowers."

"How are you going to do that with one hand?" Why was Ben asking questions I didn't want to hear? After seeing my long face, Ben sighed. "Are the flowers hard to do? Would you be able to tell me?" I was touched that he'd offer. I nodded, but stopped when I felt woozy. Ben looked like he was about to reach for my face, but Jesse pulled back the curtain in a single motion. Ben shot to his feet, letting go of me like I was chopped liver. "How's Brian?"

"So, change of plans for tomorrow," Jesse said at normal people's volume, which was terrifying because it was not normal for her. She closed her eyes as she took a deep breath. "Brian needs to rest, per doctor's orders."

"Oh no," I said. "I'm sorry."

"Why are you apologizing?" Jesse asked. "Because of you, Brian missed the coffee table. This could have turned out much worse."

See? This ant was a hero. I tried to give Ben a smug smile, but he was not having any of it.

"Are you going to be okay for tomorrow?" Jesse asked. After I nodded, Jesse sighed. "Well, take your pick, E. We've got a groomsman buffet. Who will it be? Mark, Ethan, or Mateo?"

"What about me?"

Jesse and I stared at Ben. Did he just volunteer as tribute?

"What about you?" I asked.

"You need someone to help you tomorrow, Elise. You can't drive your truck or handle the flowers." To Jesse, Ben asked, "What color is the suit?"

"Black."

"I have a black suit."

"I think you can fit Brian's tux."

I lay back as the painkillers kicked in and let them hash things out. If this was how the universe wanted to mess with me and put Ben in front of me when I wanted space, then fine. Jesse's wedding crisis was averted. That was the most important thing.

Ben wanted to be a groomsman? Let him. He was going to find out real soon what exactly he'd signed up for.

Chapter Fourteen

Mr. and Mrs. Vinh Lam & Mr. and Mrs. Edward Lo
Request your presence at the wedding of their children
Steven Lam and Jessica Lo
On July 8th
Tea ceremony at nine o'clock in the morning (family only)
Church ceremony at noon
Reception at six o'clock in the evening
888 Seafood Restaurant

*J*esse and twenty of her closest single female friends and relatives were stuffed inside her childhood bedroom, passing the time as we waited for Steven and his family to arrive. I took the time to relay last night's turn of events to Rebecca and Beth since I didn't get a chance to tell them after the hospital. It was too much to text with one hand.

"You shouldn't put any weight on it," Beth reiterated, checking the wrap on my arm.

"What about the flowers?" Rebecca asked. "Do you need us to do anything for you?"

"Um, so Ben's going to help me. He's filling in for Brian."

Beth fluffed her wavy hair, grinning like a sly fox. "Oh really? How nice of him."

Rebecca's face was like that meme, trying to decide whether this was a good idea or not. She considered it for a second but ultimately disapproved. "He didn't need to come. We would have helped you."

"He volunteered." It wasn't the time or place to hash out the confusing feelings between Ben and me or whatever drama that was going on between Rebecca and Ben. There had to be a connection between the two, but the wedding was about to start. Excitement rippled from the front yard and into the house. "They're here!"

All the women in the room got into their places while Rebecca, Beth, Hannah, and I peeked out the door. Steven beamed as he crossed the threshold into the living room, holding Jesse's bouquet of coral-pink peonies. Then came Mark, Ethan, and Mateo, hoisting a whole roast pig, inching slowly but surely toward the altar. It would be a solid minute before I saw Ben, stuck in between a pig and a line of guests behind him. There was a look of slight terror on his face from being perceived by a room full of strangers. He looked lost as he made his way into the house, clueless as to what he should do next.

Brian's tuxedo didn't fit perfectly on Ben. The sleeves were too short and his pants were kind of tight (objectively speaking) but somehow it was very Ben, uncomfortable again in a suit. As if he knew I was staring at him, Ben's gaze steered toward Jesse's room. My stomach flipped, even though he probably couldn't tell my one eyeball apart from Beth's or Rebecca's through the sliver in the doorway. Just as it was implausible that his fingers, the one clutching my bridesmaid bouquet, fanned out to wave at me right before Rebecca shut the door, sending a zing to my heart.

Once the palpitations settled, I had to get my game face on. I couldn't get bowled over by Ben's presence. He said it himself. His life was complicated and so was mine. If I could get through Jesse's wedding day unscathed and with my heart intact, I would consider it a win.

"They're coming." Rebecca took it upon herself to get everyone in their places like she was getting a battalion ready to defend Jesse's honor.

Steven knocked on the door. "Ladies," he called out like a valiant knight. "I'm here for my bride."

"Show us the money," Rebecca demanded. A red envelope slipped underneath the closed door. She picked it up and looked inside, silently counting the cash. "We're going to need more than that."

"This is all I got," Steven said, as another envelope appeared under the door.

Rebecca opened the door, just an inch. "I'm sorry to tell you, but this is not enough to see our precious Jesse. Pony up the big bucks!"

"I didn't want to do this, but—" Steven and the groomsmen rushed to the door. We thought they would wait before forcing their way in, but a couple of Jesse's gym buddies barricaded the door, shutting the guys out in two seconds flat. They were pure muscle in tea-length dresses.

"Steven, you're not going to see Jesse that way." Rebecca laughed off the exhilaration, tucking a tendril behind her ear. "Let's talk calmly, like adults. If you can pass a few simple tests, you can see Jesse. You can get help from the guys."

Hesitant murmurs came from the other side. "All right. We'll play," Steven said. "What do you got?"

Rebecca opened the door wide enough so that only we

bridesmaids were visible to the guys and wedding guests. A flash from someone's cell phone blinded me temporarily. It was a dizzying reminder that the wedding was going to be recorded for posterity, so I had to put on my most winning smile. I made a conscious effort to give every groomsman equal eye contact, though Ben did no such thing. His gaze darted between my arm and my face and not much else. Why was he making this harder for me?

Beth stepped out with a covered tray. When she revealed a big bowl of bitter melon soup, there were mixed reactions from the guys. Mark pinched his nose. Ethan seemed intrigued, leaning over Steven's shoulder to get a closer look. Ben looked like he wanted to gag. Steven swallowed hard, bracing himself.

"This is all you got?" Steven poked the hunk of stuffed bitter melon with his soup spoon. He was all talk until he slurped some of that algae-green broth. "Why is this cold?"

"Sorry. It's been sitting out for a while," Beth said.

Steven groaned. "Is this really necessary?" He reached inside his jacket pocket for another red envelope, but Jesse shouted words of encouragement from where she sat on her bed.

"Eat it for me, honey!" She tried to say it with a double entendre but couldn't make it through without snorting.

"You heard her," I said. "The bride gets what the bride wants."

Steven closed his eyes and took another spoonful. The crowd of guests behind him egged him on to eat more. Figuring quickly that the only way out of this public suffering was to take a healthy bite, Steven picked up the bitter melon with his fingers and stuffed it into his mouth, to much fanfare.

"May I enter the room now, ladies?" Steven said, fist-pumping the air.

"No," Rebecca said. "The next test is for all the groomsmen."

The guys protested at the suggestion, even more so once they saw me fanning myself with wax strips. "Show us your legs!"

"No way." Ethan backed away and hid behind Ben. "Don't come near me with those things."

"It's not going to hurt," I lied. I handed each of them a strip and showed them the proper technique to get every hair out down to its follicle.

Mark was down. He rolled up his pants in no time. "Come on, men! Let's do this!"

"You're only saying that because you don't have any leg hair," Steven said as he adhered the strip to the side of his calf.

"What's wrong with a little maintenance?" Mark asked, showing off his baby-smooth shin.

Ben got spooked when a random uncle massaged his shoulders for encouragement. He shot me a look like this was an act of betrayal, making him wax his fine leg hair in front of a ton of people. I would have felt bad, but it was all in the name of love and carrying on tradition and maybe a little payback. I slapped the clear strip onto his leg and gave it a quick rub to make sure it was nice and stuck.

On Rebecca's count, Steven and his groomsmen ripped off their wax strips with a piercing howl. They writhed in pain. A small part of me felt bad but I was soothed by the uproarious laughter from Jesse's family.

"Evil." Ethan whimpered at the bare pink rectangle where a field of leg hair once grew. "You're all evil."

"I wish I could see!" Jesse shouted.

"Don't worry," Beth said. Cell phones darted out to capture their suffering. "There's plenty of video."

"Jesse!" Steven hobbled to the door. "I'm coming for you!"

"Not so fast," Rebecca said. "We have one last test and this was by Jesse's request. She would like to see you do twenty push-ups with a groomsman of your choice lying underneath you." The crowd tittered while Ethan and Mateo groaned in disapproval.

Mark tried to rally the guys. "What's wrong? Afraid of a little full-frontal push-up action?"

Steven took off his jacket and rolled up his sleeves. "Let me talk amongst the men." The groomsmen huddled around Steven with some quiet chatter. After some finger-pointing and nodding, Steven emerged. "Okay, I made a decision." He took a deep breath, holding everyone in suspense about his choice like he was about to use a lifeline on a game show.

When he opened his mouth again, he stunned everyone with a battle cry.

Steven charged forward, leading the groomsmen in a surprise attack. All the ladies moved to reinforce the door, but it was too late. Steven pushed his way through, barreling past Rebecca, Beth, and me.

"Yes!" Steven huffed and puffed as he raised his arms in victory. Like a knight in shining armor, he knelt down in front of Jesse, presenting her with her bouquet. "Am I worthy, Jess, without the twenty push-ups? Will you marry me and let me love you for the rest of our lives?"

It was sentimental coming from Steven and he said it so freely in this crowded room of women and in front of Jesse's extended family, who were all waiting beyond the crooked, unhinged bedroom door.

"Hell yes," Jesse said, accepting her flowers.

Guests cheered and made way for Steven and Jesse to walk out to the living room for the ceremony. Hannah and Mateo followed behind them. Then Mark and Rebecca. Ethan whined to Beth about his waxed leg as they waited for space to clear.

Ben handed me my bridesmaid bouquet. I resisted the urge to smell the flowers I'd arranged myself. After taking a quick assessment of our surroundings, he whispered, "Are you okay? You weren't standing behind the door, were you?"

I shielded my blushing face with my bouquet. "I'm fine. Thanks for asking."

"You're having a good time," Ben said like he wanted confirmation of his observation. A question in the form of a sentence.

"I am."

"Good." Ben let out a deep breath and offered his arm, which I accepted. This was becoming second nature for us. "Tell me that's the worst of it."

Even though he'd gone through enough, I couldn't resist watching him squirm a little more. "Haven't you heard of the ancient dance that is supposed to bring the bride and groom good luck?" A sheen of sweat appeared on Ben's concerned forehead. "Oh yeah. It's been passed down through five thousand years of Chinese culture. I'm surprised you haven't heard of it. It's where the groomsmen perform an elaborate choreographed lip sync to the Backstreet Boys' 'I Want It That Way.'"

"Oh really?" he replied dryly, but I heard the amusement in his voice.

"It's one of my favorites."

"I think I missed that part in Shen Yun." It was hard to stay mad at him if he kept this up. "So what's next?" he asked as we were about to thrust ourselves back into the chaos.

"We're just getting started."

THE WEDDING CEREMONY was over in three bows. The tea ceremony was a longer ordeal. Jesse, being one of the youngest in her family, had a slew of elders to offer tea to out of respect and to receive her wedding gifts. An hour into it, Steven's pockets were overflowing with red envelopes and Jesse had donned more gold chains than a rapper, but the line of elders waiting for their turn was going strong.

Rebecca, Beth, and I decided to take turns since pouring tea for Jesse wasn't a three-person job. My feet were sore and my smile had wavered. Jesse would have to look back on her tea ceremony pictures with me beside her, looking constipated while tipping the teapot with my one good hand. When Beth turned the corner to relieve me, I passed the porcelain tea set into her arms and ran off like it was a relay race.

I followed the smell of food into the backyard. It was like being in a busy mall food court except with more plastic, pastel-colored stools. On one side, there was a buffet table with a row of foil party trays with favorites like chow mein, shrimp fried rice, and Peking duck. On the opposite end, Jesse's aunt—the same one who had pulled me aside to eat—helmed the outdoor stove, frying a fresh batch of egg rolls in a wok. There was another aunt butchering the whole roast pig like a boss, handing shards of crunchy pork skin to little kids like candy.

I fixed myself a plate and took a seat next to Rebecca, across from Mark and Ethan. They were in mid-conversation about Beth and Ethan's bachelorette and bachelor parties.

"What do you think, Elise? It's a bad idea to have a joint party," Rebecca said, wanting me to back her up. "Isn't the point to have one last wild night before getting tied down?"

"I thought you liked getting tied down," Mark chimed in.

I grimaced at Mark's TMI comment. "I don't have a preference either way. You should ask Beth."

Rebecca pouted since that wasn't the answer she was hoping for. "Don't you want to have a girls' night out?"

It had been a while since our last girls' night out. I couldn't explain why, but when the four of us were together, we were extra loud, extra rowdy. It was probably because we were drunk. I was still foggy about how we got ourselves banned from The Wiltern. One second we were dancing to Ellie Goulding and then next thing I knew, I was eating intestines at Ahgassi Gopchang.

"Where's Ben?" I asked casually, as one would when they couldn't find their designated partner whom they almost kissed.

"Why?" Rebecca asked, annoyed at the change of subject. She quartered a flaky wife cake and nibbled on a piece once she saw the lotus seed filling. "When did you two become so buddy-buddy?"

"Well, you know we've been collaborating on events and we're helping with Beth and Ethan's wedding," I hedged. "I need to go over the plan for today. Why do you ask?"

"I didn't think you'd get along so well."

Okay. Something had to be going on. "Are you two fighting?"

"Why would you say that?" Classic Yu move to avoid answering the question. "If you're looking for Ben, he's over there. Jesse's aunt asked him to serve food."

I followed her line of sight. Ben was going table to table, passing out plates of the chopped pork. At least he was doing something useful, unlike Mark and Ethan, who were day drinking until they'd become ripened tomatoes. But I should have been the proactive one because Ben served his last plate to none other than my own mother. Between work and the accident last night, it completely slipped my mind that she would be here. She tapped on his wrist to bend down and whispered something into his ear. I couldn't see Ben's reaction. He kept his head down, nodding as he listened and responded. When she was done, they both happened to look up, catching me snooping. Ben's eyes smiled, and call it a hunch, but I knew they were talking about me.

"Excuse me." I took off from the table. I was planning to catch up to my mom eventually but it had become an urgent matter. "Hi, Ma." I greeted the other aunties and uncles sitting around the table. "I see you've met Ben."

"Do you know this boy?" she asked in Teochew so we could talk secretly but openly in front of everyone.

"Yes. Why?"

"He asked me who I was voting for." I snorted. I didn't think Ben would try to court the elderly vote at Jesse's wedding. "Then I said I don't know. My daughter helps me vote."

Help? My refugee mother wouldn't vote at all if I didn't take her to a polling place myself. She didn't see the point when governments never did much for her. She did like getting a sticker, though. Never underestimate the power of a sticker.

"Are you having a good time?"

My mom nodded. It was nice to see her socializing and enjoying herself. It had been a while. The sun kissed her face, bringing it a nice glow that probably, ironically, came from layers of sunscreen. She was wearing a cute blue sheath dress that she'd worn once to a different wedding years ago. It still held up.

My mom gave Ben another once-over and waved him closer. "Ben. I have a question," she said, switching back to English. "You know, Elise has been single for a *looooong* time. Do you have any single friends who might want to date her?"

I muttered obscenities under my breath. What was up with my mom's sudden interest in my love life? Was Beth right that matchmaking was in our genes? Because here was my mother, angling closer to Ben like a wolf. It was as if the wedding had activated an instinct in her passed down from our ancestors to pair single people together to ensure our survival, only to see her daughter die of embarrassment.

"Mom. I'm right here." Now I was the tomato.

"Oh?" Ben ignored my comment, making it no secret that he was enjoying my discomfort. "I guess I do," he said, trying to be helpful. Helpful to whom? The jury was still out.

"Do you know someone who will treat her good? Someone nice? Anyone like that?" All the elderly guests at the table smiled at me in an encouraging albeit nosy way. Fabulous. I always wanted an audience while I died inside. "Bonus if he's rich and handsome too."

"Ma," I interjected in Teochew. "What happened to not relying on a man?"

"It's true. You can't rely on a poor man, but a rich one—"

I threw my hands up. I didn't know who this woman was.

"I'll let you know if I think of someone," Ben said, having way too much fun with this.

I kicked his shoe to get him away. "Ben and I have to leave soon for Steven's house, so you'll have to excuse us." I leaned down and gave her a one-armed hug. I was working my way up to giving her a full hug since my mom was never big on PDA. My therapist told me to start with baby steps. My mom reciprocated with a quick pat on my back. "I'll see you tonight. Do you need a ride?" The restaurant wasn't far from our house, but parking was going to be horrendous.

"Miang, miang," she repeated in Teochew, emphasizing that there was no need. "I'll go with my friend," my mom said, pointing at the auntie next to her, who smiled genially. I had no idea who that lady was, but she seemed harmless in her cute yellow pantsuit and thick platform sandals, which never went out of style with aunties of a certain age.

"Okay." I nodded my goodbyes and then dragged Ben by the arm to the side of the house since there was no privacy anywhere else at Jesse's.

"Why are we here?" Ben asked, trying not to touch anything in the alley. We were in between the black trash bin and the green recycle bin.

"I'm taking you away before you set up a voter registration table in the backyard. Have you no shame?"

"You know who doesn't have shame? Shawn Tam doing tai chi with old ladies in the park." I was starting to think Shawn Tam was Ben's white whale. Talk about obsessed. Honestly, I was wondering if the guy really existed. "You'd think old people would be bad at technology, but I saw them watching Shawn Tam videos on their phones. He is everywhere."

"I highly doubt they're on TikTok."

"Who said anything about TikTok? Videos feed into every social media platform. It's hard to tell which is which anymore."

All right, I hadn't brought Ben here away from the party to stop and smell the garbage. "What else did you say to my mom?" Their conversation had seemed chummier than an overview of November's ballot.

"Someone's being paranoid," he said, smirking at the hypocrisy of his statement. "Nothing. She saw me talking to Becks and asked me if we were friends. I said I was her brother and your mom mentioned how much she always liked Rebecca. How she met my parents once."

"That's good." I wasn't sure why I cared so much. It wasn't like I expected my mom to say anything terrible. She cared too much about saving face. Then it struck me that I wanted my mom to like Ben. I didn't want her to write him off the way she wrote off all men after my dad let her down. Ben wasn't like that. Sure, he had his quirks and he infuriated me at times, but he'd become someone I could count on.

"But just so I'm prepared, can you tell me which one is your dad?"

"Oh." I didn't know what to make of Ben anticipating meeting my dad. "None of them. My dad's in Vietnam. My parents split up a couple years ago." I didn't know why it was still weird for me to say it. While the divorce had been tense at times, they'd tried not to complain too much about each other to me. Now that two years had passed, Mom and Dad seemed to have moved on. I guessed I should too.

"I'm sorry." Ben paused for a moment and I was afraid I'd made things awkward. But then he said, "A couple years ago? When you started your studio?"

I was surprised he remembered that. "Yeah. Just in time for me to lose my parents' health insurance." I swung my bad arm to emphasize my joke, but it didn't land. Ben didn't laugh, but he did give me a thoughtful frown (my favorite of his frowns, if I had to choose).

"A big leap of faith," Ben mused.

"Right into the fire." I shrugged. "What can I say? I like to live dangerously."

Ben glanced at my arm. "Not too dangerously if you don't have health care."

"That's what Beth's for. She's my health care." She was also the lucky recipient of the occasional "Is this normal?" text with a TMI picture of a skin rash. "Before you send me links to health insurance websites, I do have health insurance." It was crap, but I did have it.

"Good to know. I can sleep soundly now."

I poked a finger in his chest. "You sleep just fine."

As I said it, I noticed how close we were standing. We were inches apart, closer than we had lain together in bed. His chest rolled, steady like ocean waves as he breathed. His tux was a little short, but he'd cleaned up nice. His hair was neatly parted, except for the pieces that fell over his forehead as his face dipped lower. Ben's eyes were a warm amber brown like tea, steeping with contemplation.

"Elise." Ben said my name like it was written in cursive, round and smooth. An invitation, but for what? He was the one who'd said it was complicated. We'd both agreed we shouldn't start something we couldn't finish.

"What?" It was a challenge. If he wanted something, he was going to have to tell me. I wasn't going to make the leap unless I knew there was a safe landing. He had to meet me halfway. "What do you want?"

"You." The expression on his face was at once vulnerable and full of resolve. It was as if this man who kept his feelings under lock and key had given away his secret with this one word.

Me. He wanted me.

I angled my head up for a kiss. His mouth was soft, lulling me to sink into him. Wherever he moved, I followed, testing the waters to see how far we'd go. When Ben's beard scraped against my lips, I involuntarily moaned. The sound unleashed something in him because the next thing I knew, my back was pressed against a wall. His hands cupped my face as he kissed me fully. It made me greedy for more. I held on to his lapel, trying to bring our bodies flush together.

Then there was a loud rattle. Ben and I jumped apart in time to see Boss Auntie toss a bag of empty Tsingtao bottles into the recycle bin. She pushed her way in between Ben and me to throw out the big greasy cardboard tray that had carried the whole roast pig, sending a plume of garbage stench into the alley, and slammed down the trash can lid on her way back to the party. She did not give a fuck about anyone or anything, least of all a bridesmaid and a groomsman making out.

"We should stop," I said as I caught my breath. Because yes, a big-ass wedding was still going on while we were hiding (kissing!) in the alley. I brought my good hand to cover my swollen lips as Ben used his to protect his nose from the unique tang of hot trash.

"I better go finish my food," I said. Unlike Ben's, my stomach wasn't sensitive to pungent smells. Now that there was some distance between us, I was thinking clearly. The backyard had become more crowded in the last few minutes. The tea ceremony should be ending soon. "We should go before they come looking for us."

"They" meaning our friends, who would freak out if they knew what we were doing.

Ben's mouth twisted as he surveyed the herd of guests from where he stood. He straightened himself, pulling on his jacket sleeves, which barely reached his wrists. "Can we talk later? Alone?"

The question would have been easier to answer if he didn't add that last part. The only body I'd be joining at the hip today was Jesse's, helping her change into her other dresses and touching up her makeup as best as I could with one hand. It was going to be difficult to find a moment alone, but I agreed anyway. That sliver of hope was beaming bright like a full moon.

Chapter Fifteen

"How long do we have to stand here?" Rebecca complained at the end of the receiving line, not loving her Louboutins today. In all fairness, the day had been ruthless on our feet. After Jesse's house, Steven brought his bride back to his parents' house for another tea ceremony, which Ben and I ditched early to set up the church. After all was said and done, we still had to stand for the long Catholic ceremony, where I tried to look natural while staring at the back of Jesse's head and not at Ben's face in the background.

Since our encounter in the alley, we did have some brief moments alone when he helped me transport flowers. We didn't exactly talk, though, unless I counted giving Ben directions as he steered my truck. Then I had to teach him how to drape tulle along the pews. Ben complained a little when he took off his jacket and rolled back his sleeves, saying that this was too much work for one person. Didn't he see that I was suffering too, watching him lift and carry vases into the church?

There wasn't a good time to have the kind of conversation we needed to have, so we agreed to act normal until we figured things out. We were put to the test when we took pictures at the Pasadena City Hall to pass the time in between the ceremony and the reception. The photographer kept posing me so that I'd hide my janky arm behind Ben, which had me pressed against him all afternoon.

The marathon continued after we arrived at the restaurant. The rest of the wedding party joined in to distribute the centerpieces and I had the chance to rest for a bit while the bridesmaids touched up our makeup. One hour had passed since the doors opened for the reception, but only a third of the guests had arrived so far. At this rate, the reception wouldn't start until nine.

"Why did we have to wear heels when Jesse is wearing sneakers?" Beth asked.

"She's the bride. She can do what she wants," I said through my tired smile. Every inch of my body hurt, including my eyes. "Can you go take pictures of the guests?" I asked Preston, Jesse's photographer. We'd run into each other several times in the last year and I'd made his wife's bouquet when he got married. He was nice enough to take a few extra pictures of the flowers for me to submit to *Wedding Style,* but he needed to cool it on the flash. I'd seen enough stars to fill the sky.

"Uh, okay," Preston replied in his monotone voice, "but the lighting isn't great in here."

I didn't know how that was possible when the entire ceiling was chandeliers.

"You guys can go," Jesse said. She massaged her cheeks since she was in between pictures. "My aunt's family is coming and they're going to want a big family picture."

"Do as the bride says!" Rebecca ran off like she'd seen a sample sale.

Beth and I joined Rebecca, taking our seats next to our respective partners at the table reserved for the wedding party. It was the only table in the restaurant with a red tablecloth, red napkins, and red-faced groomsmen.

"You're drunk," Rebecca chastised Mark, assessing the half-empty glass of Hennessy.

"What?" Mark asked innocently while he filled more glasses with ice. "There was nothing for us to do."

"You were supposed to usher guests to their tables."

"Fuck, I don't know what Steven was thinking giving us that job," Mark slurred. "None of us speak Cantonese or Viet. Everyone sat wherever they wanted like a free-for-all so what was the point?" He spun the lazy Susan around, presenting Rebecca, Beth, and me with our own tall glasses of Coke and Henny. "Who cares? We're at the reception. It's time to party."

"I'm disappointed in you," I said to Ben. His eyes blinked a few times like he was trying extra hard to focus. When he realized I was talking to him, Ben replied with a hiccup and then another. I thought he'd be embarrassed, but then he giggled uncontrollably. Oh my god. I didn't take Ben to be a happy drunk. "How much did you pour for him?" I asked Mark, who was too busy laughing at Ben to answer.

Ben took my glass off the lazy Susan. "Elise doesn't drink on the job."

Rebecca shook her head in disapproval. "We'll get our turn at your bachelorette party," she said to Beth. "You ace that test so we can have some fun."

"Duuuuuuuuuude!" Mark bellowed. He stashed the two-liter bottles of soda under the table to clear the lazy Susan for dinner. "*We* should go to Vegas."

"How much fun are we talking about here?" Ethan asked, putting on a concerned fiancé act but then pounded his chest for a burp.

"Oh, you know. A little shopping and some pool time," Rebecca said innocently, though everyone knew that you didn't go to Vegas for such leisurely pastimes. My wallet was facing a slow death.

"So . . ." I never liked discussing money stuff with my friends. It was a bummer to be the poor one. The hardest part was finding creative ways to opt out or suggest something more budget-friendly. "We're driving, right? I can drive. It's been a while since we did a road trip."

Rebecca's nose wrinkled. "Um, no. I am not going to sit in a car for four hours when we can fly there in one." I wondered if I could win Rebecca over by suggesting that we stop by the Alien Fresh Jerky place in Baker. She might have a refined palate, but she loved herself some of that sweet and spicy "alien" meat. "Don't worry about planning this," Rebecca said to me, misreading my concern. "I told you. Mark and I have a friend who can hook us up in Vegas. I think I can get a suite at the Cosmopolitan comped. I'm still working on table service." Upon hearing this, Beth's eyes gleamed with excitement. "Leave this up to me." Since I didn't appear relieved by this news, Rebecca thought she'd upset me. "I'm not trying to step on your toes if you want to plan the party. I ran it by Jesse and she was down, but we can do something else if you have other ideas."

"No, not at all. I really appreciate it. You plan the best girls' night out anyway," I said, trying my best to sound cheery. I fixed on my smile and let it go. If everyone else was on board with the plan, then I had to make it work somehow.

"How many more courses are there?" Ben asked as he had every time the waiter took one plate away to make room for the next. He stared at the remnants on his plate for clues. "Cold cuts, Peking duck and . . . and . . ." Guests tapped their chopsticks on their glasses and plates to request a kiss from Jesse and Steven. The newlyweds stood and obliged with a solid smooch. The interruption caused Ben to lose count, so he gave up. The liquor had rendered his brain useless for the night, but at least he was having a good time, clapping offbeat as the reception entered the karaoke portion of the program.

One of Jesse's uncles kicked things off with the Teresa Teng classic "Yue Liang Dai Biao Wo De Xin." This song had a stronghold on all the family weddings in my life that John Mayer's "Daughters" could never. I looked over my shoulder and spotted my mom three tables away. She instantly met my eye like her mother's intuition told her I was searching for her. Her eyes twinkled as she waved at me from afar while mouthing the lyrics, just as she had over the years. It filled me with nostalgia of a simpler time.

"This song is a banger," Ben said with a drunk man's conviction. He closed his eyes like he was moved while he incorrectly sang the title lyrics. I laughed at his blasphemy.

"You can't get the title wrong, Ben. It's like you're mocking the pure innocence and sincerity of Teresa Teng's declaration of the moon representing her undying love."

"You feel very strongly about this."

"I do!" I couldn't let him desecrate the song that was embedded in my childhood memories.

Ben watched me, smiling. He was saying something, but I couldn't hear over the singing.

"What did you say?" I dipped my head toward Ben's shoulder, training my eyes to look straight ahead so we didn't look like two people who had sucked face a few hours ago.

"You're purrrrdy," he whispered into my ear. I coughed into my hand and nodded, pretending he'd said something mundane, but I struggled to keep a straight face. He was so drunk and cute. Damn it. He was going to blow our cover. I was about to go back to eating when he added, "Glad you're having fun. You did all of this. Flowers." I assumed he meant that to be a complete sentence.

"You too," I reminded him. I wouldn't have been able to do it without him.

"Here." Ben stopped the lazy Susan and sloppily scooped the last two honey walnut shrimp onto my plate. "Before Ethan eats it all."

"I'm sharing with Beth!" Ethan claimed of the mound of shrimp on his plate.

"You keep saying that to yourself," Ben joked. He turned his attention back to me and nodded toward my plate, encouraging me to eat. The gesture couldn't have lasted more than a second, but it made my face warm. I nudged the steamed bun on his plate with my chopsticks, reminding him to eat so he could sober up.

"Heads up," Jesse said, stuffing her face before she had to kiss Steven on command again. She was eating so fast, I was afraid she was going to choke. "After Steven and I make our rounds to each table, we're going to cut the cake and then," Jesse pointed at me, "you're up."

"Me?" I racked my brain. I'd finished the flowers. Wedding games at the reception were reserved for the bride and groom and there was no way I was going to help Jesse with getting an egg up one of Steven's pant legs and out the other. "What do *I* have to do?"

"Your favorite part," Jesse said. "Bouquet toss."

Oh hell no.

The bouquet toss was the amalgam of everything I hated. First, there was the public callout for single ladies undoubtedly paired with Beyoncé's "Single Ladies." Then, there was the destruction of the bouquet I'd crafted. To prevent this, I'd made a special, smaller bouquet for Jesse to launch overhead so she didn't have to ruin hers. And yet, an hour later, after Jesse and Steven finished visiting every table in the restaurant, there I was on the dance floor, battling other women with only one good arm.

Jesse launched the bouquet into the air to much fanfare. As I watched it fly close to the chandelier and fall toward me, I felt that pull deep in my chest. I secretly wanted to catch that bouquet because, patriarchal rituals be damned, I did hope that one day I would get married. I wanted this silly bundle of flowers to grant me that wish, but I couldn't get myself to reach for it. It meant admitting in front of my friends and my mom that I, a single lady, far removed from marriage, wanted it so badly that I considered shoving Steven's teenage cousin into the fish tank.

So, I kept my hands at my sides as the bouquet fell splat at my feet. Nobody tried to catch it or pick it up. The emcee, a short Asian man who'd switched among Cantonese, Vietnamese, and English throughout the night with an energy as loud as his orange shirt, handed the flowers to me to keep the show going. I was now the de facto winner of this bouquet.

"Do I need to check your reflexes?" Beth asked as I returned to my seat. "Jesse aimed right at you."

I removed a broken peony from the bouquet. "Did Jesse tell her family to let me catch it?" There was no way it wasn't rigged. There were plenty of disappointed aunties questioning their single daughters in the crowd.

"Probably," Rebecca chimed in, followed by a piercing *woo!*

On the dance floor, Steven successfully removed Jesse's garter with his teeth and spun it around his finger to entice a tepid group of bachelors. There were a couple bros I recognized as trainers from Jesse's gym and a handful of kids spinning around, unaware of what was happening. Ben was on the edge of the group with his hands stuffed in his pockets, visibly uncomfortable as he stood next to rowdy uncles. I'd seen him look happier reading emails.

"Gentlemen!" the emcee shouted into the microphone, trying to hype up the men. "May I remind you that the person who catches the garter will get to take a picture with the gorgeous lady who caught the bouquet, Bridesmaid Elise!"

"'Caught' is a stretch," I muttered as a blinding spotlight found me. The DJ changed the music, riling up the group of bachelors. Some of the men threw their arms up, anticipating the garter toss. Ben stayed put, but his hands were now out.

Beth sidled up to me and whispered, "Are you hoping a specific person will catch it?"

"No," I lied.

"Elise," Beth prodded, teasing me, knowing I was full of shit.

I didn't answer. I couldn't because I watched with bated breath as Steven flicked the garter behind him, straight to the floor, where a little boy fumbled it like it was full of cooties. Guests laughed, but soon erupted into gasps as men tripped with arms stretched to catch the ring of lace. A victor emerged and the emcee ran over to raise up his arm.

"Look at this strong man!" The emcee asked the guy his name. "Give it up for Kyle!" The emcee flexed as he shouted into the microphone like he was calling a wrestling match.

Kyle, it seemed, never skipped arm day or leg day or any-part-of-his-body day. The guy was *fit*. He could pass as Lewis Tan's stunt double.

"You didn't answer my question," Beth said, finishing her second glass of Coke and Hennessy. Drinking apparently made her more astute and I wished she would apply this toward her studies and not to me.

I pretended not to hear her and put on a good-natured smile as the emcee called out my name and requested my presence on the dance floor. Ben passed me on the way there, grumbling to himself.

"Ladies and gentlemen. Our future bride and groom. Who

knows?" he teased, joining Kyle's and my hands together. "Maybe one day to each other."

"Oh no." I shook my head and tried to laugh it off, but Kyle lifted my hand to his dry lips, playing to the crowd.

"You're a cute little thing, aren't you?" Kyle said.

There were too many wrong parts with that statement, so I dropped the act and tried to slip my hand away. Kyle, unfortunately, had a strong grip, which he leveraged to pull me in and throw me over his shoulder like a caveman.

"Put me down!" I screamed, but Kyle didn't hear me because the entire restaurant was howling with laughter. This wasn't fair. The emcee was supposed to play tricks on the bride and groom during the reception, not me. Thank goodness I was wearing a jumpsuit because my butt was on display for the Lo-Lam extended family to preserve on their cell phones.

"Let go of me!" I pleaded with Kyle again when I heard more voices join the chorus of laughter.

"Kyle teaches boot camp on Tuesdays and Thursdays," Jesse announced into the microphone. "You can sign up on my website!"

"How much do you lift, brah?" Mark asked, snickering like a fucking idiot.

"Let her go!" Beth squeaked. "She doesn't have health insurance!"

"I do!" I shouted. "It's very expensive!" Seriously, what the fuck? Everything was too loud. The music. The laughter. I knew it was all fun and games, but I'd had enough.

"Put her down."

Ben's voice was firm and calm as he said those three words. It was all he had to say to get Kyle to stop. When my feet touched the ground, Kyle raised his hand for a fist bump.

"It's all good, yeah?"

We'd see if it was all good if I punched Kyle in the face the way Jesse taught me in her kickboxing class. I curled my fingers into a fist, but before I could wind up, an arm hooked onto my waist.

"Come on. Let's go, Rocky," Ben said, pulling me off the dance floor.

"I still have some words for Kyle," I said to Ben as he walked me back to our empty table. "Where is everyone?"

Ben released me and pulled out my chair. "Jesse's mom asked Hannah to help count red envelopes. Rebecca and Beth left to help Jesse change. Mark and Ethan are scouring the restaurant for unopened bottles of Hennessy."

"Good luck with that," I said as I sat down. I double-checked my outfit to make sure all the goods were covered. A waiter dropped off a tray of orh nee and strawberry wedding cake for dessert while an auntie sang another Teresa Teng hit, "Tian Mi Mi." It was hard to be in a bad mood when this song was on, and the night was coming to an end. Elderly guests headed toward the exit before the dancing portion of the evening started. I sighed into my bowl of steamed taro paste, feeling the exhaustion in my bones.

Ben held my hand and it took me a second to realize that we were alone. There was a touch of pink on his face, but Ben appeared mostly back to his usual self. "Do you want me to take you home?" I was about to remind him that we had to stay after the wedding ended to break it down, but then he added, "So we can talk?"

My house, where I lived with my mother? No thanks. "How about your place instead?"

Chapter Sixteen

I'd been to Ben's apartment before when it was Rebecca's. He'd traded Rebecca's sleek, modern furniture for something I'd call thrift store chic. There was a well-loved leather chair next to a bookcase filled with trinkets that didn't exist before. Campaign signs where a coffee table should be. On the other side of the living room was an old, vintage telephone desk with a real rotary phone that appeared to be for decoration rather than function.

"I like what you did to the place," I said, kicking off my heels.

Ben threw his jacket on the back of the couch. "Thanks. Most of the stuff I inherited from my parents. Some of it belonged to my grandparents."

"Like that map with all the state quarters?" I teased. It took up an entire shelf on his bookcase. It was hard to miss.

"That was my dad's. My mom stuck it in one of the boxes when I moved in. She hated it." Ben laughed. He threw a thumb over his shoulder. "You want something to drink?"

"Yeah." I followed him into the small galley kitchen, noting the shiny new knife set and more appliances on the counter than I knew what to do with. I only knew how to use a Zojirushi water boiler for my tea and instant ramen. Ben opened his fridge, gesturing to the door, which had more drinks than one person should have at a time. I pointed at the Brita pitcher. "Water for me."

I observed Ben as he moved around the kitchen. I added "reaching things" as another thing Ben was good at. Besides that, there was something noticeably different about him. He was calmer here in his own home without anyone to answer to. What a difference it made, seeing his relaxed though tired face.

"So . . ." Ben handed me the glass of water.

"So," I repeated after taking a sip. If he thought I was going to extricate all his concerns from a loaded "so," he had another think coming. I set down my glass and leaned my hip on the counter. "You wanted to talk. Out with it."

Ben also leaned against the counter as he ran his hand through his hair, undoing his perfect part. "I don't know where to start."

"How about the beginning?"

Ben glared at me but there was nothing behind it. "Do you remember when I said my dad helped me set up my first job?" I nodded. "It was at a construction firm, doing basic IT tasks. Most days, I was telling people to try restarting their computer. That kind of stuff. I didn't mind it. I knew I had to start at the bottom, but I began to move up. I didn't think anything of it until I was promoted over someone who'd been there a long time. That was when I found out that the company had existing contracts in Monterey Park, when my dad was still a council member. People found out and it made it hard to stay when everyone hates you. So I quit. Took some time to figure out what kind of person I wanted to be. Who I could be without my family. I turned my back on them for a while."

That explained why Rebecca had rarely spoken of Ben in the last few years.

Ben loosened his tie. "I didn't want to join the campaign but firing a hundred orders of eggs benedict didn't pay the rent in LA. I had to come crawling back and my mom needed someone she could trust on the campaign staff. She wanted to lead a clean campaign, but the polls are closer than we anticipated. It's neck and neck."

"What does that have to do with me?"

Ben's expression grew serious. "When I hired you, you became a contractor."

"Is there a rule that you can't date me?"

"It would be frowned upon."

"That doesn't tell me anything. You frown about everything."

Ben frowned, almost on command. I pointed this out by tracing the downturn of his mouth. He didn't find it amusing, at least I didn't think so until he caught my finger in between his teeth.

"Ow," I said, when in reality, the playful bite sent a zing through my body.

"I'm sorry," he said, not sounding sorry at all. He kissed my finger, then trailed his hand up my arm as he studied the sleeve of black and white peonies.

"My favorite flowers," I said since he'd been wondering about my tattoos. It wasn't the deep answer that most people seemed to expect.

"And what about this one?" Ben stepped closer as he turned my arm around, his thumb pressing on the small dandelion close to my elbow.

That one was different. "Um . . ." I wasn't sure why I was getting nervous. It had been on there so long that I'd almost forgotten it. No one had ever asked me about it. "I know dandelions are technically weeds and no one likes them on their lawn but . . ." I shrugged. "It represents to me persistence. The ability to grow anywhere. And they end with a wish." I groaned as I heard my own words. "Was that corny? I never said that out loud."

"It's the most romantic way to think about a weed." He chuckled. "I like it." Ben tucked a loose curl behind my ear. His fingers grazed my cheek as his eyes lingered on my face with the push and pull of uncertainty. It should have been illegal for him to look at me like that and not kiss me.

"What is it? Am I that scary?"

Ben teased me, widening his eyes like he didn't want to say the quiet part out loud. I wanted to punch his arm, but then he dropped his hand and gave me his real answer. "The campaign is going to get more intense and, well . . . I'm going to get more, you know, *stressed*." He said this like a euphemism for his panic spiral into every worst-case scenario. "I don't know if I want you to see me like that again. Rebecca says I'm incorrigible when I'm stressed." I laughed because it was kind of true, but then his mouth twisted. "Speaking of Rebecca . . ."

I bit the inside of my cheek. I knew it was inevitable, but I was hoping to get through our conversation without really talking about Rebecca. What could I say? It was the optimist in me. Ben and I found ourselves in a staring match, neither of us wanting to dive into it, but then I blinked first. Damn fake eyelashes. "I don't think Rebecca's going to like this."

"I don't either, but I want to know why you think so."

I let out an exasperated sigh. Ben was too smart to play dumb. "You're her brother. I'm her best friend. She's going to think it's weird."

Maybe he *was* dumb because his face looked like he was trying to add two and two, but he kept getting five. "Is that all?"

"What do you mean, is that all?" I was so appalled by his reaction. *Is that all?* It was everything!

"She'll get over it." He shrugged. "I don't really care what she thinks."

"This is why she likes me more than you!" I gave him a hard poke in his (firm) chest.

"You *are* more likable than me." Ben slid his hands on the counter on either side of me. It was annoying how good he smelled after the long day we'd had. "We agree."

"Ben! What if we . . . you know . . ." We weren't really anything yet, so it was awkward to bring up the possibility of breaking up. So I tried to put it more simply. "What if this ends up being a mistake?"

He leaned down until I was met with his rich, autumn-brown eyes. "I worry about a lot of things." There was a soft rumble in his voice, like it had come a long way. "I'm not saying this wouldn't be hard. We might have to keep this between us for a while, but I've never once thought that you'd be a mistake."

My tired body was overcome with a rush of renewed energy. Every hair on my head down to my toes felt electric. Ben had laid out all the risks, but if he was willing to take the leap to see where this took us, he didn't need to tell me twice. I was born to fly.

Ben choked on his surprise when I crashed my mouth into his. Once he gathered his bearings, his arms engulfed me, bringing us together. He kissed me like he was savoring it, his beard scraping the edges of my lips, letting me taste the vanilla cake and strawberries on his tongue. I gasped when he lifted me up and carried me toward his bedroom.

"I'm going to get spoiled if I keep getting carried like this," I said, clenching my thighs around him. I moaned when I felt him harden.

"Fucking Kyle," Ben gritted out. "Had his grabby hands all over you."

"You waited long enough to save me," I teased.

"Dude was built like Captain America!"

I laughed at his defense and began to unbutton his shirt until he paused just short of his bed with a strained expression on his face.

"What's wrong?" I blinked. "We can stop if you—"

"No, it's not that," he said in between ragged breaths.

Then why did we stop? I racked my brain. Was he worried about something? Was there something we hadn't covered? "It's been a while," I confessed in a hushed voice, "but I tested the last time I was with someone. We're good to go in that department."

Apparently, I guessed wrong because Ben stuttered as he tried to respond. "U-Uh . . . that's good to know, and, uh, same but, um . . . I wanted to make sure . . ." He reconsidered his words. "I know this isn't the most ideal situation. I don't want you to regret it."

Oh, Ben. So thoughtful and overly cautious at the same time. Did he miss the part where I said it had been a while for me and when he shifted to get a better grip on my ass, I nearly passed out from his length rubbing against all the right places? How could I explain this in a way he'd understand?

"Ben. Can I ask you a favor?" His hooded eyes followed my tongue as I licked my swollen lips. "You see this jumpsuit? I need you to take it off for me."

Ben got the hint and put me down in search of the hidden zipper. In the heat of the moment, I forgot that the jumpsuit was an all-or-nothing situation because once it was off and the cool air hit my skin, there I was, nearly naked with my bits covered. The flower pasties were unfortunate. It made for an anticlimactic reveal. Ben seemed to think so too.

"Are you trying to torture me?" Ben was speaking directly to my breasts.

"You're the one who still has clothes on." I tried not to curse when I peeled the pasties off. They looked like Band-Aids and hurt like them too. "It's not like you haven't seen them before."

"Not like this."

I glanced up at the sound of Ben's husky voice. He'd taken off his shirt and was unbuckling his pants, but his eyes stayed on me. "You tell me if there's anything you don't like." His pants fell along with his boxers. My mouth dried. Ben's ill-fitting clothes hadn't done his body justice. He was strong and tall. A striking mix of sharp and smooth edges. Ben palmed his erection and I lost all sense of time and space. "Okay?"

I mumbled some agreeable noncoherent nonsense as he led me to his bed, climbing over me. Ben dropped kisses on my temple, my lips as he lowered onto me. "Your skin is so soft," he said into the hollow of my neck.

I bucked when he laved his tongue on my aching nipples. It felt good but I needed more.

"Ben." I dragged my nails along his jaw as I lifted his head up. "You don't need to be so gentle." I impatiently rocked myself against him. Ben clamped a hand on my hip to stop me.

"I do or this is going to end too fast for both of us." Ben sat back and I regretted rushing him. I missed the weight of his body. "You don't know how long I've wanted to touch you like this." Ben frowned at the faint pink mark his hand had left.

"I didn't think you liked me." I squirmed when he dropped a kiss on my hip. "You always kept your distance." We were a far cry from bickering at Rebecca's wedding in our fanciest clothes.

"I knew if I touched you, it would feel too good." Ben and I groaned when his fingers reached in between my legs, proving his point. "You're so wet." His fingers went in slow circles, testing me, applying more pressure with each pass. Ben watched me unravel, like it was his plan all along. I felt my pleasure climbing, but then Ben stopped. I whimpered my complaint until he slipped off my panties and threw my legs over his broad shoulders.

"You don't have to," I said automatically. The guys I dated before skipped this part.

"You don't like it?" If I wasn't mistaken, Ben looked almost disappointed.

"I-I don't really know," I admitted. My skin was too hot from embarrassment and the sight of Ben staring at the most sensitive parts of my body.

"Guess there's only one way to find out."

If I was being honest, it took some getting used to. It felt almost too intimate, but soon I found myself feeling lost. Ben was methodical in his approach, starting with flicks, then languid circles. Every move was intentional. His eyes never left mine, like he needed to see me every time I called his name. When he ramped up the pressure, it didn't take long for my orgasm to crash through me like a wave, sweeping me off my feet and setting me adrift. It wiped everything from my mind, except Ben. My body craved being closer to him, to feel his warmth on top of me again. I snuggled against his chest, my hands reaching for him.

"Elise?"

My eyes snapped wide-open at the sound of Ben's strangled voice. Where did this sheet come from? I gasped in horror. Did I . . . fall asleep?

"Oh my god, I'm so sorry," I blurted.

Ben lay beside me, kneading my thigh. "It's fine."

"How long was I out?"

"Not long. Half an hour maybe?" If he was bothered that I'd fallen asleep, he didn't show it. I, on the other hand, was mortified. Half an hour was too long. "You had a long day," Ben reasoned, trying to help me feel better. He brushed my hair back and dropped a reassuring kiss on my forehead. A good night kiss.

"No," I repeated, more adamant this time. "Unacceptable."

Ben was taken aback. "Are you . . . mad at me?" He couldn't finish the question without laughing.

I rephrased. "This wasn't how the night was supposed to end."

"How was it supposed to end?" Ben propped himself up on his elbow, waiting for me to say it.

My skin flushed. It was becoming a habit around Ben. If he wanted me to enlighten him, then I would. I reached down in the space between us and wrapped my fingers around his impressively hard erection. Ben shuddered and rolled on top of me for a downright filthy kiss, swirling his tongue, making sure I tasted me on him. He took both of my hands, laying them over my head. "Keep them here."

Oh. Anticipation rippled in my veins.

Ben produced a condom from his nightstand and rolled it on his length. He kissed my collarbone, working his way up to my mouth when he pushed himself inside me. He groaned on my lips and I wanted to eat it up. It was easily becoming my favorite sound.

He experimented with a few slow pumps. When he hit the right angle, he picked up the pace. My fingers itched to touch him, but when I reached for him, he gently pushed my hands back down. Sweat beaded on his forehead as he gripped my hips and thrusted harder, muttering. I felt myself climbing higher and higher when his mouth found the sensitive spot behind my ear, and told me how beautiful I was. How I drove him crazy.

"Ben." I could barely get his name out. Tears formed in my eyes as I shattered. Ben crashed into me when he came soon after.

When I reached for him this time, he let me. I guided his face to mine for a soft kiss.

"Was that okay?" Ben thumbed away the tear at the corner of my eye. "Was that what you had in mind?"

I nodded with a stupid grin on my face. It was the best I could do since words weren't exactly forming in my head.

Ben beamed, blinding me with joy. "Good."

"Good" was right. No matter what the future held for us, this much was true. Everything about Ben felt good. So, so good.

Chapter Seventeen

"What are you doing today?"

I didn't think my morning could get much better. Ben woke me up with a good morning kiss, which led to good morning sex. We were in the kitchen now. Ben was making me waffles and I helped myself to a cup of tea. The whole scene felt very domesticated, except I was a hot mess with my smudged makeup and wrinkled bridesmaid jumpsuit.

I scrolled through my phone, fawning over Jesse and Steven's wedding photos. Preston had released a preview of the same day edits on his Instagram account last night during the reception and he sent me the photos I requested to my email. The pictures came out better than I remembered the scenes in real life. It was amazing what you could do with a little bit of editing and Photoshop. Ben set a stack of waffles in front of me.

"I have to clean the studio. I still need to find a venue for Beth and Ethan." The wedding was in a month. If I didn't find a place by the end of the week, City Hall was going to be the only option left. "And then I need to work on my *Wedding Style* submission. Why?"

"I have the day off," he replied, taking the seat across from me. "I thought we could go somewhere."

"Benjamin Yu," I said slyly as I cut into the waffles. It had the most satisfying crunch. "Are you asking me out on a date?"

"Maybe." Maybe I still had sex brain, but Ben made eating look hot. I couldn't stop staring at how his mouth moved or how he licked off the maple syrup from his lips. It was probably because I knew where his mouth had been and all the things he could do with it.

Yup. Still had sex brain.

"Um." I wanted to take the day off, but I didn't know how to not work. The studio wasn't going to organize itself. I was already stressing out about taking the weekend off for Beth's bachelorette party in a couple weeks. I palmed my forehead. "I can't."

"Can I ask you a question?" Nothing ever stopped him before. I wasn't sure why he was asking for permission now. "When do you make time for you?"

"What do you mean?"

"When do you take a break? You just had a big event last night."

"Yeah, I did," I said lasciviously, leaning into the double entendre. This was what happened when I spent a whole day with Jesse.

Ben remained composed and pressed on. "What do you like to do when you're not helping other people get married?"

"I—" The question made me itchy. It had been so long since I'd had time to think about anything besides running the studio. "Does bingeing K-dramas count?"

Ben angled his head, considering me. "You deserve a break."

No shit, but it didn't mean that I could take one. There was a reason why it was called "drowning" in debt. When you dive into the water, it looks clear and harmless. You always think you can swim back and make it to shore. You never think that the water will pull you down, making it harder to kick your way up. At some point, I realized swimming back to land was a pipe dream. All I could do was stay afloat.

I sipped my tea and glanced at Ben over my mug. I knew he meant well, but it was easy for him to talk about taking a break. He had options. His family supported him. I only had my two hands and one was currently out of commission.

"I don't have time." My words came out sharper than I intended, so I added, "I have to call venues and pray for a cancellation." I scrolled through my camera roll and sighed longingly at the photos from Granada Ranch. "What are the chances Esmeralda will change her mind?"

"Are you still hanging on to the ranch? Beth and Ethan can't be choosy at this point."

Ben was right. I was wasting my time, but the perfection of the location, even in its unfinished state, haunted me. "I keep wondering if I had approached it differently, maybe Esmeralda would have said yes. Like, maybe if I was more charming like Rebecca, I could have persuaded Esmeralda somehow."

Ben gulped his coffee like he needed to rinse the bad taste out of his mouth. "What do you think she can do that you can't?"

"I don't know. But she makes things happen. When she asks for something, people say yes." Ben didn't seem to know what I was getting at so I tried to show him. I hunched over a little to push my boobs together and slid my hand over Ben's, stopping him from taking his next bite. "Ben," I asked, imitating Rebecca's cool affect. "Can you pass the syrup?"

Horrified, Ben pointed his butter knife at me. "Don't. Ever. Do. That. Again." He grimaced as he shuddered. "I don't care if Rebecca does that, but you don't need to do that."

"Fine." I dropped the act, even though it was fun teasing him. "I wish I could have a do-over." Who knew if that would have made a difference. I wondered if I was dreaming too big. What good was it doing me, chasing something unattainable? "Oh well."

"Finish up," Ben said, guzzling down his coffee. "Let's go."

"Go where?"

Ben was already halfway out of his seat. "Granada Ranch. I love the smell of horseshit in the morning."

I didn't know how to take him seriously with that facetious comment. "W-why what?" My brain hurt with too many questions swirling around. They were coming out jumbled. "We can't just drop by!"

Ben swiped his car keys from the end table by the door. "Let's go cruising."

In this economy? "What's gotten into you?" I washed down my breakfast with the last bit of tea as Ben slipped on his shoes. This was really happening. "Why would you want to spend your day driving to the middle of nowhere?"

Ben held on to my shoulders, his fingers tightening with conviction. "Because you can't give up."

"Why not? People do it all the time." It was healthy to accept defeat. Sometimes the only thing to do was to cut our losses and move on. "Why not me?"

Ben shook his head, looking almost annoyed at me. "Because you are the most driven and stubborn woman I have ever met and I don't believe for one second that you are incapable of getting what you want."

History had proved him wrong, but I'd have been lying if I said it wasn't nice to hear. "Do you really mean that?"

"I do," Ben answered without hesitation. "I hate to see you get down over this. If you want a second chance, go get it."

"What if this ends up being a big waste of time?"

Ben half frowned as he shrugged. "Then at least you know you did your best."

"You don't have to."

"I want to. Besides, I'm the best man." Ben played the part and offered the crook of his arm. "I have to make myself useful some-how."

Who was this man standing before me? I wanted to keep him. "Let's go for a drive, then."

We made a pit stop at my place so I could change into a tank top and shorts. It wasn't what I would usually wear to meet a vendor, but I already had boob sweat before nine A.M. (thanks, climate change!). I called Esmeralda and luckily, she was on-site and wel-comed us for another visit. We swung by the studio so I could make a small arrangement for Esmeralda with leftover roses from Jesse's wedding.

Sunday traffic was light so we made it to Granada Ranch in good time, which, under normal circumstances, would have been cause for celebration. But it gave me less time to think about what I wanted to say. Ben tried to hype me up like this was Friday night football.

"Remember," he said, parking the car in the gravel lot. "Go out there and be confident."

"Wasn't that what I did last time?" I got out of the car and looked up at the house. It was as picturesque as I remembered it, perched in the middle of fields of tall, golden grass that was ma-jestic like a lion's mane.

Ben carried the vase as we trekked up to the porch. "You were about to offer your firstborn child for this reservation." I shot him a glare. I didn't think I came across that desperate. "Okay, fine," he backpedaled, apologizing with a kiss on my temple. "It wasn't that extreme, but I don't think you need to resort to favors and discounts when you have so much to offer. I don't want you going in there thinking you're the underdog."

"Aren't I? Esmeralda already said no before."

Ben stopped me from ringing the doorbell. "We're here. It's too late to have second thoughts. Don't waste this chance going in with that mentality."

He hadn't seen my dismal ranking for my first *Wedding Style* entry. "You're right," I said to appease him. I appreciated the encouragement, but after years of trying, only to fall short of my goals, it was hard to muster the faith in myself. I might be an optimist, but reality had a way of rearing its ugly head like an uninvited guest.

"I mean it. You're too talented to think you're coming in last." Ben held up the vase like he was presenting evidence. "No one can drop flowers into a vase like you."

This guy. I rolled my eyes at him, but I couldn't help but smile too.

The door suddenly opened. "I thought I heard voices," Esmeralda said, welcoming us in.

"I brought this for you," I said. Ben handed over the vase to Esmeralda. "A late thank-you gift for lodging us."

"Oh, you didn't have to," Esmeralda said as she smelled the roses. "They're lovely. Come on in."

"Wow." The house was further along. The dust and tarps were gone. The room we stood in wasn't fully furnished yet, but there was enough to visualize guests mingling by the fireplace or sneaking out drinks from the kitchen. "It looks great."

Esmeralda placed the flowers on an end table and gestured toward the stairs. "Let's go upstairs. I completed two more bedrooms." We toured the finished rooms, listening to Esmeralda as she recounted visiting multiple stores to find fixtures that resembled the original ones. It was apparent how much pride she'd put into the work. "Let me show you the outside."

Ben shot me a wary look as we followed Esmeralda to the deck. No doubt he had poop on his mind, but I held his hand in case he needed help steering clear of horseshit. Esmeralda directed us to sit at a patio table that faced out to the riding area, which looked untouched since we last visited.

"Thanks for having us again." I tried to find shade underneath the umbrella. "It's great to see the house coming along." I cleared my throat. There was no easy transition, so I just came out with it. "I was wondering if you would reconsider letting me reserve the space."

"You know, I was about to call you to see if you were still interested, but you beat me to it." Esmeralda chuckled lightly.

"You were?" I reined in the shock in my voice. Esmeralda had seemed so adamant about delaying. "What changed your mind?"

"I think it would be good to see how this event goes, as a test run. And honestly, my investors are getting antsy. It always comes down to the money." Don't I know it. "Speaking of which," Esmeralda continued, "I seem to recall you mentioning that it would be a small wedding. The starting basic package is four thousand dollars."

I swallowed the knot in my throat. I knew it was going a little too well. That was the top of Beth and Ethan's budget. "That was more than what I was expecting."

"That's the going rate at venues this size," Esmeralda explained.

I wasn't sure how to proceed. I could ask Beth and Ethan to see if they could increase the budget. Ben reached for my hand underneath the table and gave me the kind of look like he was trying to send me a secret message. I loved that he thought I could read his mind, but we weren't there yet. It was enough to have him next to me, encouraging me. The best I could do was spout out more details.

"The guest list is fifty people. They'd only use the house and the indoor pen. Maybe some pictures by the garden." I tried to keep my voice even and businesslike, even though I wasn't sure if this was going to do any good. "No one would be loitering beyond these spaces, except for the food truck they want to bring in for dinner. I was thinking it would pull up to the side of the house." Then, inspiration struck. "I know that is your most basic rate, but that's assuming the entire property is fully furnished and completed. Couldn't you give us a small discount?"

Esmeralda didn't look too convinced. We were at a standstill. She was trying to get her money while I was trying to save as much as possible. The urge to beg was filling my chest, but I held strong. I'd said what I needed to say and I could walk out of here with my head held high. "If not, then I'll look at other venues. Given the short timeline, I do have to move on to other options, but thank you—"

"Wait." Esmeralda stopped me from leaving. "The best I can do is offer a ten percent discount and I would need a deposit upfront." The tips of my ears burned. It was a modest discount, but every little bit helped. Beth and Ethan might go for it.

"Let me call them." I excused myself from the table and walked around the side of the house until I reached the garden. Maybe seeing the pretty location would take away the sticker shock.

"Hi." Beth picked up the video call after the third ring. She was in study mode, armed with a ginormous cup of coffee, a tight ponytail, her glasses, and flash cards in every color scattered around her desk.

"Sorry to bother you." I was surprised she'd taken my call. Her exam was in a week.

"It's fine." Beth stretched her arms back. "I was taking a break anyway. Wait." She brought her phone closer to her face. "Where are you?"

I gave her the rundown on the cost as I walked over to the indoor pen, describing all the flowers and setup for the ceremony. I didn't want her to think I was trying to sell her on the place. It was still her wedding. I tempered her expectations and was transparent about how the renovations were still not fully completed, and the driving distance too. Beth was quiet as she listened to me go on and on, so I wasn't sure if I'd lost her. "What are you thinking?"

Beth flicked her pencil nervously. "That sounds like a lot, E."

I was afraid she'd say that. "Hey. I understand. I can send you some ideas I had. Maybe you and Ethan can see if there are any times available at City Hall—"

Beth cut me off. "I meant for you."

"Me?" Where was this coming from all of a sudden?

"It sounds great, but I don't want you to overdo it. You were running ragged yesterday."

"All in a day's work," I said, dismissing her concern.

"But you're also a part of the wedding," Beth said. "I've asked so much of you. I didn't think you'd go back to the ranch."

"Of course I would," I said. "I'd do anything for you."

"Stop it." Beth rubbed her eyes underneath her glasses. "I won't be able to study if you make me feel mushy."

"Why don't you come over, then? Take a look at it yourself?"

I didn't think Beth would go for it, but then she threw her pencil down and said, "Okay. I was too hungover to study anyway."

An hour later, Beth showed up with Ethan and they fell in love with the ranch immediately. While Esmeralda went into her office to put together an invoice, the four of us waited at the dining table. Ben and Ethan got wrapped up in hush-hush chat about

Ethan's bachelor party. I was riding a high like no other, thrilled that things were falling into place.

Beth poked my arm. When I turned to face her, I found her leaning forward with her arms crossed. She started a staring contest with an arched eyebrow.

I wasn't going to play this game. I blinked. *What?* I silently asked her.

Beth pursed her lips. *You know what.*

Her eyes darted to Ben. I shook my head, but she was not having it. She pointed one finger at me, another at Ben. Then she brought her hands together to form a heart.

I shut my eyes and let out a long-suffering sigh. *Nothing's going on.*

"You're a bad liar," Beth whispered.

"I didn't say anything," I countered quietly.

"Something's going on," she insisted. "I see the way he looks at you."

"Like how?"

We both looked across the table. Ben, confused by the sudden shift of attention, gave me a full-on Neanderthal frown before slinking back to his conversation with Ethan.

"Pass me my smelling salts," I said facetiously as I fanned myself dramatically. "I'm going to faint."

"Fine. Deny it all you want." Beth kept her eyes on me as she pushed her glasses back up her face. "The truth will prevail."

"Okay, Your Honor." Beth should consider switching careers. Luckily, Esmeralda came out with the paperwork, taking the heat off me. It was a wake-up call that Ben and I hadn't thought this through. If we wanted to keep our relationship under wraps, we had to be much more careful.

Chapter Eighteen

JESSE: How did the test go?

BETH: I survived!

ELISE: I'm sure you did great

REBECCA: Congrats!

BETH: I'm going to sleep for the rest of the week

REBECCA: Wait! Don't forget to send me your guest list for your bachelorette party!

REBECCA: . . . Beth?

ELISE: I think she's hibernating

JESSE: What do you guys think about wigs?

I set up my laptop on my work counter and logged into my bank account. Because of the last few weddings, I had enough to cover this month's bills. My studio would live to see another day, but I wasn't out of the woods yet.

I opened a new tab and logged into my *Wedding Style* account. It had been weeks since I last submitted an entry. My rankings had dipped to 1,747. I considered myself a good designer but could I prove that I was better than 1,746 other designers to win? I needed to try something else. Something that could get me quicker results.

I decided to send an email that had been sitting in my drafts for a while.

SUBJECT: Story Feature/Elise Ngo Floral Design

Hi, Jas,

I'm Elise. I'm an acquaintance of Alex. I saw him last month and he mentioned your promotion (congrats by the way!). I don't know how stories get chosen to be featured at Angel City Magazine, but if you're interested in stopping by my floral studio, I'd love to show you around. I'll include the links to my website and socials if you want to see my work.

Thanks,
Elise

I tried to practice some patience and see if Jas would ever reach out to me, but sometimes you have to create your own luck. I still went ahead and submitted the photos from Jesse's wedding. There was a picture from the tea ceremony that stood out. The practice of serving tea to elders with the red and gold backdrop was steeped in tradition, but the red roses that Ben helped me arrange throughout made it feel more current. The photo fit the "Modern Tradition" theme perfectly, so I didn't want it to go to waste. At this point, what did I have to lose?

I wrote a quick caption about Jesse and Steven, bowing to Jesse's parents to show their respect, and some notes about my design. I clicked *submit* and looked up from my laptop to find Ben walking through the door.

"What are you doing here?"

Ben and I were supposed to meet up later tonight at his place to assemble wedding favors. We figured wedding planning activities were a good cover in case our friends were suspicious. I wasn't expecting him to show up at noon with a plastic bag of bánh mì and pennywort drinks. "I brought you lunch from Bánh Mì Mỹ Tho."

"What kind?" I stuck my nose into the bag and inhaled the smell of fresh bread and pâté. No, I couldn't be distracted. "What are you doing?"

He slipped into the back of my studio, admonishing me as he scanned the storage area. "How did you move the arch? You're supposed to rest your arm."

"You'd be amazed with what I could do with one hand," I said. The arch was nothing, but because of this stupid sprain, I couldn't tie a bow for shit. I stole a sip of my refreshing green drink and picked out the sandwich with the different cold cuts.

Ben pressed a kiss on my temple. "I can't wait for you to show me."

My face prickled with pink. I wasn't used to flirting with Ben. My comment was purely innocent, but now my mind was in the gutter. I couldn't stay there too long because Ben was spinning around like he was searching for something.

"Do you have a pop-up canopy?" he asked.

I removed the jalapeños from my bánh mì. It was already too hot in here. "It's in the back corner. Why?"

"Could we borrow it? My mom is back from Sacramento. She's hosting a coffee chat at the Alhambra Farmers Market on Sunday and ours broke."

"Sure." I wasn't going to use it. My Saturday plans were to escape the summer heat by staying in my studio and hand-letter table cards if my wrist cooperated.

"Did you want to come? I think there's space for you."

"Um." There was no delicate way to say this. "I don't have anything to ask your mom."

"Not that. Have you ever considered setting up a table at the farmers market? I've seen other local businesses there. It could be a way to get your name out with residents in the area."

"Look at you," I teased. "You pretend that you don't care for public service, but I see the Yu in you."

"Har har. Just because I'm not in politics doesn't mean I can't contribute to the community in my own ways," he replied. "Come on. It'll be fun."

I wasn't so sure about that. I'd done bridal shows before and never got much traction. I wasn't sure if spending a morning next to organic vegetables would do much good for me. "It's not like I have anything to sell." My table would look lackluster compared to an actual flower grower's.

"You don't have to sell anything. Didn't you say you wanted exposure?" I did, but this wasn't what I had in mind. "What about this?" Ben pointed at my flower chandeliers and the wall of pink and white roses that I rented out for photo booth backdrops. "This would look nice behind your table. People can take pictures and you'd get your name out there."

"I don't know."

"Some things are better seen in person," he said, circling his arms around me like he was lassoing me in. "Please come. The same five people come out to these coffee chats and if I have to spend my day out, I'd rather spend it with you."

When he put it that way . . .

"All right," I said. If it brought me a few new clients, then it would be worth it. It gave me a better chance at salvaging the studio than if I stayed in and practiced my calligraphy. "I'll do it."

On Sunday, I set up my booth near Alhambra High School. I was in between a lady who made fresh jiānbǐng and a farmer who had cauliflower in every color. It was so beautiful, I almost forgot that I hated cauliflower. Cauliflower wanted to be rice, but it could never be rice.

After the first hour of baking in the heat with a few onlookers but no takers, I promised myself to never get lured by good bánh mì. Donna Yu's table was set up at the end of the block, so I didn't see Ben except when he briefly stood in the middle of foot traffic to hand out coffee. He quickly retreated back under their canopy, probably realizing it was a bad idea to stand under the sun in his suit while holding hot coffee. He probably hated every second of it.

I snickered. It was bad of me to laugh, but the thought of his grumpy face made me smile. That had been happening a lot, the out-of-the-blue smiling. It was because this thing with Ben and me was new. It had to be because there was still so much to know about each other and things to figure out. Even though we brought up how we might break the news to our friends—Rebecca, namely—neither of us broached the topic again. I knew I couldn't keep it a secret forever, but I wasn't ready to face their questions. I couldn't imagine how Ben would fare under my friends' judgment whenever a new boyfriend was introduced.

My friends and I met Steven first since he had been with Jesse forever. He bribed us with boba, which was very effective bait for us poor college students. Beth met Ethan through Tinder, which made us suspicious. This was when Rebecca created the Boyfriend Test, which evaluated new boyfriends on a twenty-point scale in areas like kindness, spontaneity, creepiness, humor, and so on. It was supposed to be a secret, but Ethan knew something was up when we stared at him when we first met him at karaoke. He eventually won us over when he sang a compelling rendition of "Ring of Fire." Mark scored the lowest on the Boyfriend Test because he had more swag than he deserved, but we gave him a pass because he was good to Rebecca. Once, he planned a surprise barbecue for Rebecca's birthday and grilled in an outlandish cowboy costume. The test must have counted for something since every couple was still together.

I was getting ahead of myself. Ben and I needed more time before subjecting ourselves to that much scrutiny. Ben didn't like being the center of attention anyway.

"Excuse me. Can I take a selfie here?"

I couldn't believe my eyes. It was Shawn Tam in the flesh. I wasn't starstruck per se since Shawn looked like some rando I might bump into at the supermarket, but I was momentarily stunned. I was so used to seeing him on my phone screen that I didn't think he was a real person.

"Uh, yeah." I welcomed him inside the booth. "I can take the picture for you if you'd like."

"I got it," he said, proceeding to take pictures from his preferred angles. He was trying too hard to look cooler than one could in business casual clothes. "I'm Shawn, by the way. I don't think I've seen you before at the farmers market."

"It's my first time here," I explained. "I'm Elise. My studio is based in Arcadia."

Shawn's face lit up. "I'm not sure if you're aware, but I'm running for state assembly for the Forty-ninth District, which includes Arcadia." Before I could answer, Shawn jumped into a rehearsed speech about his qualifications that I could have repeated to him verbatim from all the videos I'd seen of him. His marketing was unoriginal but effective. "I hope I get your vote this November."

The in-person version of Shawn Tam was less interesting than his digital alter ego. He had a dad outfit—a purple gingham dress shirt and khaki pants—but was without the dad dance moves from his TikToks. "I'm still undecided," I lied.

"Perhaps you can share your plan to increase housing." Ben appeared at my side, butting in to our conversation. He was out of breath, like he'd rushed over here. "That might help sway the vote."

"Ben," Shawn said as if they were good friends. He extended his hand, which Ben reluctantly shook. "It's good to see you when you're not replacing my signs with Donna's."

Ben didn't bother with niceties. "I did no such thing. I was very careful to put our signs around your ugly ones."

Shawn laughed this off. "There's no need to resort to name-calling. I thought your mom was against smear campaigns."

The way Shawn emphasized "your mom" ruffled Ben's feathers. "I'm not smearing anything. They're ugly so I'm calling them ugly."

I brushed my hand on Ben's arm to remind him I was still standing there. "I don't mean to interrupt," I said, "but you're both in the middle of my booth. Can you take this elsewhere?" Anywhere. Somewhere far away from here.

Shawn projected his professional veneer again. "Of course. We shouldn't stand in the way of your breathtaking flowers. Thank you for your time, Elise." He gave Ben a curt nod and left to find his next victim.

"You should've left things alone," I chided Ben when Shawn was out of earshot. "He was being polite."

Ben was affronted. "You were fraternizing with the enemy."

"*Your* enemy," I corrected.

"Why didn't you tell him you were voting for Donna Yu? I would have loved to see the expression on his face."

"He's so bland. I don't know why you're worried about him." I smiled at a young family that strolled by. The toddler pointed at the flower wall, but they didn't stop. "What's the worst thing that could happen if your mom loses the election?"

"She might pick up gardening." I wasn't sure if Ben was joking until he added, "She'll call Rebecca five times a day, asking about grandchildren." Ben shifted his tone. "I don't know. Before Shawn Tam, it wasn't a question of whether or not we'd win. The Yus are winners. Present company excluded."

Ben's self-deprecation was colored with sadness, no matter how he tried to play it off like a throwaway comment. I wanted him to explain what he meant by it but Ben managed to flag down a middle-aged woman to stop at the table. "Would you like to take a picture?"

The curious woman's eyes bounced around the tent until they landed on me, twinkling with recognition. "Ah! I know you." I pointed at myself to make sure she had the right person. She confirmed with a nod. "Yes, Jesse's wedding. I'm her aunt."

That didn't narrow things down. There were hundreds of aunts at the wedding, but I played along. "It's good to see you again. You have a good memory."

"Hard to forget when that man with the big muscles picked you up." The auntie glanced at Ben, but didn't give him a second thought when she realized he wasn't the man she was thinking of. "I didn't know you own a flower shop."

"It's a studio," I corrected her. She tilted her head in confusion, so I said, "Yes. I made all the flowers for Jesse's wedding too."

The auntie's mouth popped open with excitement and she retrieved her phone from her purse. "Can I get your information?" she asked as she snapped a photo of my business card. It seemed redundant to answer since she already took it. "My niece is getting married next year at NBC Seafood. I'll have her call you. I'll send it to my friends too. Some of their kids should be getting married soon."

"Thank you!" I said, but the auntie was already off on her merry way, stopping at the organic honey stand two tables over. I never knew of an auntie who dawdled, but I knew plenty who gossiped. Why didn't I think of tapping into the auntie grapevine to get referrals before? "That was promising." I knew it wasn't a guarantee, but it got me imagining myself in my studio next year. "You're really good at this," I said to Ben. "You're like my good luck charm."

"It was nothing." Ben shied away from the compliment, trying so hard to look unaffected, but a splotch of pink appeared on his neck. "It was all you. All of this"—he gestured at the flowers surrounding us—"is you."

I didn't know how much I needed to hear that until he said it. Each petal, each stem carried my dreams, crafted by my own hands. It hadn't always been easy, but the studio was brought to fruition because of me. I palmed the back of his neck and pulled him down for a kiss. I kissed him until I felt it in the tips of my toes.

Ben stared at me for a second after we broke apart like he was debating if he should kiss me more, which I would have been on board with, but then he scanned our surroundings. I realized too late that I probably shouldn't have done that, but it didn't seem like anyone had noticed. Patrons continued to walk by, browsing fresh produce and foodstuff. The jiānbǐng lady next door glanced curiously at us as she cracked an egg, but it could have been a case of accidental eye contact.

"I should get back to the coffee chat," Ben said. "I might have gone over my fifteen-minute break." I was bummed to see him go, but then he said, "Can we meet up later? My place for, er . . . 'wedding planning'?"

I barked out a laugh, blowing any intentions to keep a low profile. Ben was not smooth at all. "How good are you at tying ribbons?"

The left side of his face scrunched in confusion. "Is that code for something?" he whispered.

I couldn't seem to stop laughing. Ben was too much and I couldn't get enough.

Chapter Nineteen

*N*ow that her exam was behind her, Beth emerged from hibernation in full bridal mode. It was like she was an evolving Pokémon and leveled-up her powers. She dedicated her same intense ability to cram toward her wedding. It was a welcome transformation with two weeks left until the big day. Beth organized the schedule, sent digital invitations, and had programs printed. It was great because it relieved me of so many decisions that never felt like mine to make, even when she gave me free rein over her wedding for a while. Now the wedding was starting to feel more like hers.

"I scheduled the officiant," Beth said, running down her checklist while Rebecca, Jesse, and I camped out in her apartment in Alhambra to finalize details.

"What do you think?" Rebecca held up T-shirts that had "Beth's Besties" scrawled on the front.

"Cute, but check these out." Jesse proudly presented a white tank top with "Lo's Hoes" printed in big bold letters.

"Nice, Jess," I said. "Real subtle."

"Don't you hoes forget it." Jesse turned up "Rack City" on her phone and gave us a preview, shaking her ass in my face. I pushed her butt out of the way and measured Beth's head for her flower crown. All the bridesmaids were getting one, but Beth's was going to be the trickiest to make. I had to attach her veil to it and I had to figure out the best way to style it together.

Rebecca and Jesse busied themselves, compiling goody bags for the bachelorette party. Our group doubled to eight people after Beth invited her med school posse. They all seemed nice on the massive email Rebecca sent out with the itinerary.

Beth rattled off the next item on her list. "Do you have enough jars?"

"Yes." I twisted floral wire together to form a hoop and added some fake flowers to create a prototype.

"Those lantern candleholder things?"

"Yes," I said. Beth scrolled through the list on her phone at least three times. Now, I'd seen brides get nervous before the big day, but this was different. "Is something going on?"

"Well . . . I was thinking . . ."

I didn't like the sound of that. Every time a bride called me up with "I was thinking," it meant I was in for a budget-busting request.

Beth bit her thumbnail and mumbled something I couldn't make out. When I asked her again, she repeated herself a hair louder than a whisper. "Can the flowers not be white?"

I clutched my heart and nearly dropped dead. For weeks, every discussion about flowers had only included the color white. When we discussed linens, she picked swatches with names like "lamb" and "winter's breath." They might as well have been called "copy machine paper white."

I needed to lie down. If this was any other client, I would've said no. The flowers were already ordered. It was too late to make a big change to the design. But it was Beth, so I asked, "Why do you want to change it?"

"I don't," Beth said. "But I finally showed my parents the

inspiration photos for the wedding and they flipped out at the white flowers because white flowers are for funerals. They aren't very traditional, so I didn't think they would care, but they're afraid of what my other family members would say."

I ran my hands through my hair. I had to think. What was a feasible solution that wasn't going to cost me too much money? "Can I add some touches of color or do I have to replace all the white flowers?"

Beth thought about this for a while, slowly nodding when she came to a conclusion. "I think my parents would be okay if there was some color mixed in. What were you thinking?"

I googled some images to give her an idea. "If you want cooler tones, we can add a watermelon pink or peach. On the warmer side, we can add this blush-pink shade with a burnt orange. We can keep it on the lighter side if you don't want it to look like autumn."

"Oh, I like that." Beth exhaled. At least one of us was happy. Now I had a last-minute order for roses and carnations to put in.

"It's going to cost extra," I said gently.

"I know. It's okay," Beth said, though it didn't sound entirely okay. Who liked eleventh hour changes? "I'd rather have this dealt with so I don't have a room full of offended relatives."

"Is there anything else?" Since we were making changes, she might as well tell me everything now or forever hold her peace. I didn't want any more surprises.

"There is one more thing," Beth said. I braced myself. "Do you think we could add string lights where the taco trucks are? It didn't look like there was a lot of lighting there and it would be hard for people to get food in the dark."

Beth was right. From what I remembered, the only lighting was a floodlight off the side of the house. It didn't add much to the ambience. "Let me ask Esmeralda."

"I already did. She said it would be okay to bring our own lighting."

"Damn, you gotta do your own lighting too?" Rebecca chimed in. "They're not ripping you off, are they?"

"Everything about weddings is a rip-off," Jesse declared. "Not you, though, Elise. You're worth every penny."

"Thanks," I said. "I don't have any string lights, Beth." Rebecca was right. Venues typically had that set up already. This was going to be another expense. "I don't have anyone who could install them either." I was handy, but it was a job for more than one person.

"You don't think you can hire your old assistant back for a day? Or your cousins?"

I couldn't afford Sarah and I would never inflict my cousins on Beth's wedding. "Maybe we can get one of the guys to help."

Beth nudged my shoulder. "Do you mean one guy specifically?"

I coughed. Damn. It was very Beth of her to be thorough about her facts. I glanced at Rebecca and Jesse. Luckily, they were too absorbed with the stuff they'd bought for the weekend to notice. "What kind of lights did you want? I kind of like globe lights," I said because this conversation was not about me. I was here for the bride!

Beth threw me an impatient look. I wanted to tell her but I wasn't ready. This group of women was my rock. When other parts of my life were falling apart, they were my constant. If they knew I was dating Ben, it would be the biggest bombshell to our group since the day I told them I was dropping out of college. I'd missed out on so much since I wasn't in Malibu with them during the academic year. It was hard to feel as close as they were with each other, even though we'd all gone through seasons apart after college. And now that they were all getting married, we were bound for another shift. To what extent, I wasn't sure, but it was coming.

Beth opened her mouth, about to weasel any information out of me that she could, when her front door opened. It was Ethan, carrying grocery bags, and behind him, a specific guy.

"What are you doing here?" I asked. Ben was just as surprised to see me.

"I live here?" Ethan said, knowing full well that the question was not intended for him. "Ben went with me to run some errands." Ben seemed overwhelmed when he saw the group of us taking over Beth's living room. After a pregnant pause, he managed to greet everyone.

"Hey." That was all Ben said. He avoided my attempts at eye contact and was all kinds of awkward, dillydallying in between the kitchen and the living room, not knowing where to go. He was not helping me play this cool.

"Ben. Are you scared of us or something? Come sit down," Rebecca said, scooting over to make room for him on the floor in between her and Beth and directly across from me. "I thought you'd outgrow being shy."

Ben whipped his head toward Rebecca, taken aback by the sudden criticism. "I'm not shy. I just don't like people."

"Excuse my brother." Rebecca turned her body away from Ben as if he wouldn't hear if she wasn't looking at him. "He's always been this way. Remember your tantrums whenever we had to take family photos?"

"They were used in campaign mailers," Ben explained in his defense.

"Which then meant we stopped taking family photos altogether," Rebecca countered.

Part of me wanted to break this argument up and another part of me wanted to grab some popcorn. It was rare to get a glimpse of the Yu sibling dynamic.

Ben's eyes lowered, as if he was seemingly humbled by this. "Fine," he conceded. "Honest question. Why is it so important that Mom had to portray herself as a mother? What did that have to do with her professional work? How does that get her more voters?"

Rebecca's iciness melted a bit, but she wasn't ready to give up. "But that was an innocuous ask. I know there's shady people in the world, but there's plenty of good people too, like . . ." Rebecca swept her arm around the room. "Like everyone here. You like us, don't you?"

"I suppose," he said as he glanced around our little circle. His eyes lingered on me a second longer, but then something in the goody bag snagged his attention away. "Is that a penis in the shot glass?"

Rebecca scooped the bags away from him. "This doesn't concern you."

Ben was nothing but concerned. "Why is it so veiny? And why are you celebrating marriage with dicks?"

"Do you really want to know?" Jesse replied. "We do have some vagina cookies to be inclusive. Some of Beth's other friends aren't fans of the peen."

"I don't know why there's such a focus on genitalia either, Ben," Beth offered, "but when in Vegas."

Ethan chose a fine time to enter the conversation. The angel that he was, he set down a tray of potato chips and dip. "We're going to Vegas too."

"Excuse me?" Jesse said. "This isn't a combined party, is it?" To Jesse, there was nothing more sacred than our girls' night out. It happened so rarely these days.

I snuck a glance at Ben. Neither he nor Ethan struck me as the party type so it must have been Mark's doing.

Rebecca seemed to have drawn the same conclusion. "Where are you guys staying?"

Reluctantly, Ben answered, "The Cosmopolitan."

Rebecca's eyes fluttered in annoyance. "Beth, it's your call. Do you want to," Rebecca emitted a deep, disgruntled sound, "do a joint bachelor/bachelorette party?"

"Well, I don't think it was Mark's plan to have a joint party," Ethan interjected. "I think he used the same Vegas contact as you, that's all."

That didn't seem to make Rebecca feel better. Her nose flared as she breathed flames. "I'm going to have a word with Mark." She excused herself to take her phone call outside in the hall.

Beth scooped a generous glob of dip on her chip. "How did Mark take over your bachelor party? I thought you'd planned it, Ben."

"Mark wasn't as enthusiastic about a vineyard tour in wine country," Ethan said. "And some of my buddies wanted to go to Vegas."

"And you wanted to go too," Beth surmised.

Ethan smiled innocently like the cardigan-wearing Danny Zuko. "I mean, it's been a while since I've gone there."

"You don't need to explain," Beth said. She gave him a peck on the cheek. "I trust you."

"But do you trust Mark?" Rebecca asked as she reentered the apartment. "He was being very secretive when I asked him about the bachelor party." She alleviated her annoyance by helping herself to snacks, but seemed to have taken this relatively well.

"You're not mad?" I asked.

"Well, he told me he'd give me their itinerary if I shared ours so we agreed to mind our own business. Beth is ours for the weekend," Rebecca said to Ethan, clutching on to Beth's arm.

"I trust you too," Ethan said to Beth. "The rest of you, not so much."

Ben slightly narrowed his eyes at me, reminding me of the first day we met. He was trying to suss me out. I schooled my face into a neutral expression, giving nothing away because girls' night out was a need-to-know situation and Ben didn't need to know. That didn't stop him from reminding Rebecca not to post anything on social media or to do anything illegal.

I snickered. It was funny watching someone else be the recipient of Ben's nagging. I finished my sample crown with some fake roses from Dollar Tree and tied on a scrap of white tulle I had laying around the studio. Beth tried it on and checked her reflection on her phone.

Beth squealed and then I squealed because her joy was infectious. This wedding was finally coming together, and this moment? Worth it.

Chapter Twenty

W hat's the plural of 'penis'?" Rebecca asked as she strung a glittery banner of pink and purple penis cutouts across our hotel room. She'd booked two adjacent hotel rooms to accommodate our group, but ours was the party room. She decked it out with penis balloons, pink streamers, and a tub filled with ice and every imaginable kind of liquor. I guess none of us were going to shower during this trip.

"Uh . . ." I bit into my penis cupcake, which I should have known would have cream filling inside. I wiped the corner of my mouth. "'Penises'?"

"'Penes,'" Beth answered clinically.

"'Peenies'?" Jesse giggled after taking a loud staticky sip of her drink through her penis straw. "Not 'peen-eye'?"

I mouthed the word but it didn't seem right. "How do you spell that?"

"P-E-N-I," Jesse replied as she refilled her red Solo cup with the concoction that Rebecca had made from a mix of vodka, rum, and . . . something. After a few cups, my memory had faded. All I knew was that it looked like pink lemonade and tasted like bad decisions. "I'm gonna go with 'peni.'"

I laughed. It was inane conversations like this that made me miss my friends when we weren't together. We used to hang out every week, which turned into once a month. If it weren't for their weddings, we wouldn't have spent this much time together this summer. Sometimes, it made me wistful that girls' trips like this would be harder to come by. I'd seen the writing on the wall as I watched each of their relationships and careers take off. Their lives were becoming fuller and I felt the squeeze. Our close circle of friendship was changing shape.

Damn it. It was too early in the night to get emo. I turned up the dance hits from my phone and finished my drink.

Beth's med school friends knocked on our door and came in with a couple bottles of white wine and a cute box of cookies that didn't look like an appendage. It was hard not to imagine them as the smarter, alternate universe version of our group. Megan was like their Rebecca, but in a Meredith Grey kind of way. Zoha was tough as shit, like I could see her running an ER. She was their Jesse. Sofía and Tina were more chill and go-with-the-flow like Beth and me. That had to be the reason why we all became fast friends when we'd met earlier at lunch.

Rebecca handed each of us our goody bag and instructed us to all hold out our penis shot glass and sloppily poured vodka for everyone. "Now that we're all here, let's toast to Beth." We cheered to Beth with a chorus of *woo*s but we were less thrilled after the vodka burned our throats.

"What's our plan for the night?" Megan asked, picking the red penis gummy candies out of the bowl. Rebecca and Megan exchanged details while the rest of us got dressed. We had two hours until dinner and that wasn't enough time to get ready for a night out. It took time to look hot, especially when some of us (me) spent most of the time grazing the snack table. I had to ask Tina where she got the cookies because they were good.

I put on my black cocktail dress and as soon as I zipped it up, Rebecca appeared behind me, shaking her head through the mirror.

"No," she said. I didn't even know what she was saying no to until she descended on me with a needle and thread.

"What are you doing?" I asked. I think I asked. I could have sworn my mouth moved. I peered down and Rebecca was sewing across the hem of my dress, shortening it by two inches.

"You came to Vegas with a church dress?" Rebecca asked, working quickly like some magical elf seamstress. She legit looked sparkly and pretty like she could be Legolas's Asian cousin.

"In your email, it said 'black dress' for Friday."

"A *sexy* black dress was implied," Rebecca said. "I need party-era Elise."

My partying days were behind me. I didn't think my dress was that bad. When Rebecca was done with me, I was wearing a long silver wig and there was a black lace garter on my thigh. I scanned the room. If I had to put a theme to all of our outfits, it would be "video game vixen." Each of us had a different candy-colored wig and garters like some kind of crime-fighting squad going to a rave. Beth, in a skintight white dress and a tiara, was the most demure.

"This is kind of too short," I said, making sure my dress covered my butt.

"No one's going to notice," Jesse said, twirling in her own black dress, which had more cutouts than fabric. "It's Vegas. You can walk down the street naked and no one will care."

After a group picture and one last drink, we were about to head out. Zoha grabbed the box of cookies, but stopped to check the weight in her hands. She opened the box and seemed dismayed as she counted. "Uh, who ate the cookies? We were saving them."

I raised my hand and looked around the group. I guessed I was the only one. "I'm sorry. I didn't know. They were really good!" I added quickly, as if that was any kind of consolation. Sofía's and Tina's eyes bulged out.

"How many did you eat?" Megan asked, suddenly appearing next to me with her arms crossed. Why were all the doctors freaking out?

"One?" I held up my fingers to my face to count. "Two?"

"Elise. They're edibles," Zoha explained to me like I was five. "Are you okay?"

Edibles? They didn't taste any different from regular chocolate chip cookies. Well, they did have an earthy flavor.

"I'm fine." I was a little tipsy from the drinks but everything seemed normal except . . . where did the clouds in our room come from?

"We should keep an eye on her," Zoha said.

"I think she's fine." Rebecca grabbed my shoulders and looked directly into my eyes. "You good?" I nodded until Rebecca's hands clasped my head to get me to stop. "Um, yeah. Jesse, you buddy up with Elise."

"Fine. I'll be her babysitter. One last thing before we go." Jesse handed everyone a sheet of paper. My vision was a little blurry, so I couldn't make out the list except for two words in all caps: SCAVENGER HUNT.

JESSE WAS RIGHT. Nobody blinked an eye at our skimpy outfits when there were people strolling down the Strip with their asses hanging out. We did catch stares for other things.

I hightailed it past the designer shops in Caesar's Palace, where the clouds on the ceiling looked very real. Jesse might be the athlete, but I was faster in heels. "I better get two points for this!" I was out of breath when I reached the replica statue of David. With everyone hot on my tail, I quickly took a selfie with that tower of naked glory.

"Damn it." Jesse panted when she caught up to me. "Let's see the picture." It took her half a second to give it a score. "One point only."

"What?" I took the scavenger hunt list from my clutch and unfolded it. "It says here, 'Take a picture with a statue. Extra point if it's sexy.'"

"Your picture isn't sexy."

"What's not sexy about it?" I'd given it my best kissy face. I shouldn't have thrown up a peace sign, but it was a force of habit. "He's naked."

"You have to do something more like this." Rebecca went around the statue and mimicked David's pose with an exaggerated booty pop. It was like Asian Ariel wanting to show off her legs in her new burlesque show.

"Two points for Rebecca!" Jesse totaled the points on her list. "You need to catch up, Elise."

"I should get a point," I said. The scavenger hunt had tiers of challenges with different points assigned. Rebecca and Jesse were hellbent on winning. Rebecca easily found a random guy who shared the same name as Ethan and got his number. Jesse was the first person to get a free drink and was far in the lead after she faked a loud orgasm in the men's bathroom.

"I can't do some of these," Beth said as she reviewed what challenges were left.

I glanced at the list over Beth's shoulder. I couldn't see her doing any of these things.

Ask a guy to take off his shirt.
Ask a guy to give you a lap dance.
Kiss a bartender.

"You could still dance on a table or take a body shot off one of us." Beth's eyes slid to me, silently asking me if I was volunteering.

"Yes," I said resolutely. "I got you, girl."

Beth looked at me like I was her hero. "I love you, Eliiiiiisse!" She opened her arms, urging me in for a hug. Lovey-dovey drunk Beth was the bestest. I leaned in when she squealed right into my ear, blowing out my eardrum, and pushed me out of the way.

I toppled over into Rebecca, who was still taking more pictures. The wig lowered her inhibitions. When I recovered, I saw the cause for all the commotion. Beth had found another bachelorette party and took a selfie with them, earning herself five whole points. I was dead last in this competition. From now on, it was every girl for herself.

"Where is everyone? We're going to be late," I said. Nobody was listening. I walked Beth back and situated her next to Rebecca, who couldn't decide between filters for her Instagram story. Where was Jesse? And where were the doctor friends? I was too tipsy to be corralling drunk friends. That was like the something leading the something or however the saying went. I shouted Jesse's name, earning stares from passersby, like I was being obnoxious. But they didn't understand! I couldn't find our group and there were five different hallways connected to this statue. They could be anywhere!

Beth straightened her pink, plastic tiara. "E. My other friends decided to play slots after dinner. Don't you remember?"

Honestly . . . no. I couldn't recall where we ate, but I did remember being mesmerized by the Bellagio fountain show playing to Andrea Bocelli. It was fucking beautiful.

"Yo!" Jesse sauntered back, waving her scavenger hunt list in the air. "I took a picture with a cop. Look. He's right there."

Rebecca, Beth, and I swung our heads to the man Jesse was pointing at.

"Jess, that's a dude in a cop costume," Rebecca said.

Jesse propped her hands on her hips, affronted. "How do you know?"

"Cops don't wear their uniform with their shirt unbuttoned," I said. "And he's walking with an Elvis and a Ninja Turtle."

"I think it still counts!"

Jesse argued her case for her ten points the entire way to the club, our final destination of the evening. We met up with the doctors at the entrance and skipped the long line, courtesy of Rebecca's mysterious Vegas contact, and walked right in. There was a swarm of people around the bar, which created a bottleneck to the next room.

"Damn, it's crowded in here," Jesse shouted over the thumping music. She danced in place, looking for a way to infiltrate the dance floor. It was hard to see in the dark.

"Where are you going?" Beth yelled as I climbed up the short set of stairs that divided the VIP section from the dance floor. Clubs weren't really my scene and I honestly didn't know what I was doing. What I did know was that the music was too loud and I was tired. I just wanted to sit down or drink until my feet didn't hurt anymore. There was a good solution to my problems and it was number twenty on the scavenger hunt list: "Steal a bottle from a VIP table."

I found the perfect target. There were a couple of white guys who were really feeling the music and dancing with their eyes closed.

"Getting points!" I shouted. Beth shouted something back, but I couldn't hear her over Tiësto.

Right as I went for it, the bass dropped and the place went wild.

Smoke was blasted into the club from all directions and I couldn't see for shit. I danced my way around, trying to blend in with a group of partygoers at the closest table. Through the fog, I could make out a bottle of vodka in a bucket of ice, but I wasn't close enough to grab it without getting noticed.

Rebecca and Jesse caught on to my plan and did me a solid by barging in and dancing with the kind of booty-shaking abandon that would make anyone blush.

"You!" Rebecca drunkenly shouted at the first man she came across. "Will you give my friend a lap dance? She's getting married!"

Jesse pushed Rebecca aside and took advantage of her booming voice. "No, take off your shirt!"

Megan and Zoha jumped into the action, cheering, creating the perfect diversion. I swiped the bottle and looked for Beth.

"What are you doing?" a man asked from somewhere behind me.

I froze, clutching the cold bottle. Fuck. How do I get myself out of this?

"Will you take off your shirt?" I couldn't think of anything so I started repeating everything Jesse was saying. "Will you give me a lap dance?"

I sensed the man moving closer and saying something, but I couldn't hear between the music and the fear of getting caught. For some reason, his voice reminded me of Ben's.

It was absurd feeling wistful while a mob of people were jumping up and down to throbbing beats. Ben would be disappointed in my petty theft and remind me that an upstanding citizen wouldn't steal. Then he'd laugh at the predicament I'd put myself in because I was a terrible burglar.

Which I was because the man grabbed my arm, breaking me out of my sentimental haze. He ran his thumb over my tattoo like he was brandishing a weapon. Shit! Not only was I caught, but I was easily identifiable in a lineup.

"I'm sorry!" I shouted as I wriggled myself out of his hold. "I'll put this back! I'll never steal again! Please don't call the police or take off your shirt!" I returned the bottle to its rightful place and slid away toward Rebecca and Jesse before we got kicked out. Before I reached them, Rebecca shrieked. A second later, Jesse let out a jarring scream, stopping me in my tracks. Out of the corner of my eye, I spotted Beth on the other side of the velvet rope, wide-eyed, covering her mouth with both hands. Panic ran cold through my veins. I couldn't move.

Someone latched on to my arm and then it was my turn to scream. "I don't want to go to jail!"

I just wanted to have a fun night with my friends before it was too late to do stupid shit because they were becoming wives and responsible adults, kicking ass and saving lives. What if this was the last time we could do something like this? I fought back a sob. Oh no. The emo was coming back. I blinked away a tear, which dissolved the cheap glue on my false eyelashes. Damn it! I'd spent so much time putting those on.

Lights flashed behind my shut eyes in rapid succession, the syncopated beats overriding my heart. I waited and waited in anticipation for the drop, fearing the consequences of my drunken, stoned stupor. I still had so much life to live! As the music reached its climax, my body sagged under the condemning silence. The verdict?

A burst of laughter.

I didn't understand. I was near tears—tears! Why were people laughing?

My eyes blinked open, but my vision was impaired by my flopping falsies so I pulled them off. By now, the smoke had cleared.

Next to the white guys were Mark, Steven, and Ethan, who heckled their very confused significant others. I glanced at the hand that gripped my wrist and there was Ben. It was disorienting, seeing him when I was just thinking about him, as if I'd summoned his presence. Never mind the disparate dress codes in this club that allowed Ben to enter looking like he'd just come from the post office. I wouldn't be surprised if he had voter guides in his jeans pockets.

"Ben?" I asked. He nodded, confirming his presence. "Who are those guys?" I pointed at the two dumbfounded strangers in the group.

"Those are Ethan's buddies at the restaurant," Ben yelled his explanation. "I didn't mean to scare you." In a more discreet sign of reassurance, his thumb brushed circles inside my wrist, dialing down the noise that surrounded us with every turn. Everything else fell away and all I saw was Ben, tall and handsome. He leaned in closer, removing the need to shout. "Don't worry, sticky fingers. I'm not going to call the police."

"Oh my god," I muttered as I hid my face in his chest. I couldn't believe I'd said that. Was there a magician in this town that could make me disappear? "What are you doing here?"

"I was about to ask you the same thing. First you try to steal our booze and now my lines." Ben tsked in feigned disapproval. "See? I knew there was something about you."

"Some instincts you have." I wrapped my arms around Ben, nestling in his steadiness and fresh scent. God, I wanted to stay here forever.

"What. The. Fuck. Is happening?"

Rebecca's voice was a rude awakening. Somehow, in the darkness and dance music, I'd forgotten we were in the presence of our friends. I detached myself from Ben and found dropped jaws all around, waiting for an explanation.

I looked at Ben and mouthed, *Follow my lead*. I started with the obvious. "I'm drunk."

Ben quickly added, "She had trouble standing—"

I pointed at the floor. "I almost fell on that . . . that—"

"That ledge," Ben said, finishing my sentence. It would have been convincing if he hadn't pointed down at the level floor. Our friends' eyes volleyed between Ben and me as we lobbed more excuses.

"My feet hurt."

"Her feet hurt," Ben repeated.

"It was hard to hear," I shouted, enunciating every word. "That's why we were standing so close."

Ben cupped his ear and inched closer to me. "What did you say?!"

"This is like a bad improv class," Jesse said, before helping herself to another drink. "It's so obvious you're fucking."

"What?!" Ben and I said at the same time, which didn't help our case.

"Stop lying," Jesse continued as she helped herself to a cocktail. "My aunt saw you kissing at my wedding."

"You knew?" I asked.

"Drop the act," Beth said, hugging me. "Ethan and I predicted this would happen. Long and behold, it did!"

"'Lo and behold,'" Ben corrected her. Whoa, he was fluent in Beth-speak too.

"That's what I said," Beth insisted. "Long and beyond."

Rebecca's mouth pressed into a thin line. It was hard to tell if she was mad or disappointed. All she said was, "We're going to talk about this later." At first, she directed that comment to Ben but then her eyes slid to me, sending a chill down my spine.

I might not be going to jail, but I was in deep, deep trouble.

Chapter Twenty-One

Ben and I sat in our designated seats on opposite ends of the leather couch. It was like we were being grounded, which would have been a better punishment. If we would so much as look at each other, Rebecca would sigh forcefully, dampening the party like a wet blanket. It was enough to keep Jesse and Beth from inquiring more about Ben and me. I could tell questions were on the tips of their tongues, but one glance from Rebecca would keep them locked away.

If I wanted to see the silver lining, Rebecca's frostiness about the whole thing saved me from having to explain what Ben and I were doing. I wouldn't know what to say except that we liked spending time together. I assumed Ben would say the same, but I didn't really know. *Casual* was not in his vocabulary. His choices resulted from careful deliberation, asking himself a gamut of what-if scenarios. Even now, I sensed the weight of his concern as we sat apart, separated by six friends standing between us. I wondered if he was starting to regret this whole thing.

"How the hell did you crash our party?" Jesse asked Ethan as she bobbed along to the music with a drink in her hand. "Was this your plan all along? To spy on us?"

"Mark took us barhopping and we ended up here," Ethan explained, sipping his old-fashioned.

"What are you talking about?" Mark asked. "You ladies crashed *our* party. We were minding our own business when you tried to bait and switch us. And why would we spy? Rebecca said she had a nice weekend of 'pampering and shopping' planned." He ran his fingers through Rebecca's wig until he got stuck in a tangle. "Because people come from all over the world to get R & R in Vegas," he said, imitating Rebecca, much to her displeasure.

"It's not like you guys were having a quiet evening," Rebecca said, turning the tables on Mark.

"Do you see us taking our shirts off and giving lap dances to anybody who asks?" Rebecca chafed at Mark's sarcasm. "Come on. The night is still young. Let's go dance." Rebecca pursed her lips, casting a watchful eye on Ben and me. Mark tugged on Rebecca's hand. "The kids will be fine."

To prove it, Ben took out his phone. "Go," he told Rebecca. "I have to work on my best man speech anyway." He said this like it was a chore, another task on his long list of things to do, but this was Ben's idea of making lemonade out of lemons.

Rebecca relented and left with Mark to the dance floor. The rest of the group followed them, not before Jesse and Beth left their purses with me to babysit. I kept a watchful eye on my friends' colorful wigs as they bobbed and weaved into the darkness like they were ghosts in a Pac-Man game. I waited until they bumped and grinded their way into the crowd before I talked to Ben.

"What do we do now?" I asked. Ben didn't reply right away, too engrossed in the email he was typing. He probably couldn't hear me over the noise and I wasn't in the mood to shout.

My phone vibrated in my clutch. When I retrieved it, there was a message from Ben.

BEN: Wanna get out of here?

The idea was tempting. I was starting to get the munchies but leaving wasn't as easy as it sounded. I couldn't ditch my friends in the middle of Beth's bachelorette party.

ELISE: What about Rebecca?

BEN: Becks will get over it

BEN: I promise she's more mad at me than you

I doubted that. Rebecca had reacted with a simmering anger that I'd only seen when someone backstabbed her, like when a colleague took credit for her idea at work. This time, Rebecca had directed her glare at me and it was hot enough to incinerate me from the inside out.

ELISE: What are we going to tell her?

Ben replied quickly.

BEN: The truth

I shot Ben an annoyed look from across the couch. His response told me nothing. He tried again.

BEN: Let's not talk about that here

That was fair. I shouldn't press him on our relationship when we were surrounded by half-naked people grinding against each other. My skin was getting sticky from the heat in the club so I started dabbing the side of my neck with the back of my hand. From the corner of my eye, I saw Ben watching me. His eyes touched my body where his hands couldn't. Sometimes, he didn't need to say much to get his point across.

> **ELISE:** Is it the silver hair? Is it doing it for you?

> **BEN:** I don't need extras

I was teasing him, but if he was going to take my question seriously, then I'd love to hear more.

> **ELISE:** What do you need then?

> **BEN:** You. But you know that already

> **ELISE:** I do? In what way?

Ben shook his head as he typed.

> **BEN:** Rather not say

> **BEN:** Not over text

> **BEN:** But I can show you

I loved watching Ben as he typed these messages. On-screen, he sounded so smooth. Had we been apart, I wouldn't have known how Ben bit his lip as he nervously typed these mildly flirtatious texts. It was cute.

"All right, kids," Mark unceremoniously announced, bursting Ben's and my little bubble. I cursed him for his horrible timing. "Detention's over."

The rest of the group trickled in and gathered their things. "Where are we going?" I asked.

"Strip club." Mark's eyebrows waggled as he thrust into Steven. Ben shot down the idea with a succinct and stern no. Mark wasn't having any of it. "You got better ideas, best man?"

Ben gave up on Mark and appealed to Rebecca. "You're going to let Mark go to a strip club?"

"What's wrong with that?" Rebecca asked. "Last I checked, stripping wasn't against the law."

"So, our groups are going their separate ways?" This was the best option, I told myself. This was never meant to be a joint party. As much as I wanted to stay with Ben, we should go back to our original plans.

"Or we could go to the strip club too," Jesse suggested rather suggestively.

"I am not going to a strip club, especially not with my sister." Ben looked like he was ready to gag, which gave me the best/ stupidest idea.

I picked up an empty glass. "Jesse, pour me a shot."

"YES! I like where your head's at, E!" Jesse eagerly poured out the rest of the tequila across a row of shot glasses. "Drink up, bitches!"

"Woo!" I shouted, riling Jesse up even more. I knocked back a shot of tequila and chased it with a lime. I winced as it burned its way down my throat, giving it a minute for the liquid courage to kick in because things were about to get messy. I clasped Jesse's hand. "Jess, I think I'm gonna throw up."

"NOOOOOOOO!!" Just as I hoped, Jesse's voice ripped through

the club, catching the attention of clubgoers around us. "You can't yack here. Can you make it to the restroom?"

I shook my head as I folded over, clutching my stomach. Beth sat beside me and handed me a bottle of water. "Here. Drink this."

"What's going on?" Ben rushed over, ignoring Rebecca's death stares. "Elise?"

I couldn't get myself to look at Ben. He'd know I was lying and I needed his weak stomach for my harebrained scheme to work. I slapped my hand across my mouth and pretended to heave. The sequence of events after that was a little hazy.

Ben violently doubled over, trying not to vomit on anyone. Jesse panicked and couldn't stop repeating, "Fuck!" At one point, Beth called for Ethan to help me up. Rebecca paced around in panic, muttering, "This is like the fundraiser all over again. So help me, Ben. You better not throw up on my Jimmy Choos!" Mark was fed up with our drunken shenanigans and shouted, "You're going to get us kicked out!"

Suited-up security guards shined their flashlights at our table and shoved their way into the melee. "You're outta here," one burly guard said, like he was umping home plate.

Steven held his hands up, trying to de-escalate the situation, but the guard latched on to my arm and easily pulled me to my feet. This didn't sit well with Ben, who reached for me but was thwarted by the other guard.

"Elise, are you okay?" Beth was the only person who'd asked about my well-being. This was why she was a real one. "Text me where you're at."

I looked over my shoulder and showed her a secret smile as Ben and I were dragged to a hidden side door to let her know I was perfectly fine. It was me, Elise. I thrived in chaos.

Chapter Twenty-Two

If you asked me, the plan worked like a charm. The security guards led Ben and me through a secret maze behind the club and into a staff-only elevator. The only time they spoke was into their earpieces, giving status updates on disposing the trouble. In no time, Ben and I were pushed out the side of the building, where people lined up for taxis.

Ben leaned one hand against the wall while the other clutched his stomach. "So you really thought, 'I'm going to get us out of here by getting Ben to spill his guts'? You didn't have any better ideas?"

"I got you out of going to the strip club too." That had to count for something, right? Ben needed to look at the bright side for his small sacrifice. I took a deep breath and stretched my arms. "You know what that is? That's the taste of freedom."

"So patriotic of you." Ben's face soured as he inhaled the thick Vegas air. "It smells like ass."

I didn't know what he was talking about. Well, okay, it did smell like wet dog farts, but was he going to let that stop us from having the time of our lives? "Let's go. The night is calling!"

I grabbed Ben's hand and walked down the Strip, marveling at the bright lights. Where else in the world could we find the Eiffel Tower, bikini-clad women with massive LED Carnival wings, and the magical stylings of Criss Angel within the same block?

"Thank you!" I said, accepting a card from a man handing out flyers on the street. It turned out to be a picture of a nude woman. "No, thank you!" I tossed it in a nearby trash can.

"Where are you taking me?" Ben asked, reeling me closer to him so I wouldn't bump into the herd of tourists walking in the opposite direction.

"'Where are you taking me?'" I mimicked, right down to Ben's scrunchy face. "How can you be so grumpy? We're in Vegas! Anything is possible! The world is full of color! You can't let life pass you by when adventure is out there waiting for you!"

"Why are you talking like an inspirational poster?" Ben stopped me and held my face while he stared into my eyes. "Are you high?"

I burst into a fit of giggles. "You're so cute, Benjamin Thomas Yu. I could eat you up." Speaking of which, my stomach growled like a monster awakening after a thousand-year-old curse. I pushed Ben's hands off me and searched for my next feast. I pointed across the street. "Over there yonder!"

Ben grabbed my arm before I was run over by an eager taxi driver. "I don't think you should be leading the way."

"We're already here."

Ben turned to the storefront and then back to me. "Walgreens?"

"Where you'll find the most interesting people in the world," I said, stumbling through the doors. I zigzagged through the store, throwing anything that tickled my fancy into my basket. A box of Corn Pops. A jar of nacho cheese. Two Klondike bars. A pack of Hawaiian bread. Oooh! This pink feather boa was so soft! I took it off the rack and threw it around my neck.

"Okay," Ben said, taking the basket away from me. I was

bummed when he put away the box of marble-cake mix, but that made sense. How were we going to make the cake swirl in the hotel room? "That's enough."

"But what are *you* going to eat?"

Ben had the face of someone questioning his life choices, pinching the bridge of his nose, but a smile appeared. "Let's get you back."

I went to pay, but I couldn't find my clutch. There was nothing in my hands. I checked inside my dress. I had nothing on me. That wasn't good.

"Beth texted. She has your stuff," Ben said as he gave the cashier his credit card. "I told her I'm taking you back to the hotel so she wouldn't worry." Worrying was the last emotion Beth would be feeling from that status update.

"Thanks." Ben escorted me across the street to the hotel. We made it past the throng of guests and into the elevator. He pressed the button for the eighteenth floor.

I opened the box of Corn Pops and shoved a handful of cereal into my mouth. "Very presumptuous to take me back to your room."

Ben stumbled over his words at my unserious observation. "I, uh . . . do you want to go to your room?"

"Oh no." I waved my hand dismissively, accidentally tossing cereal into the air like confetti. "There are dicks, dicks everywhere. Your brain will melt from all the penne!"

"Pasta?" Ben was so confused, I had to push him out of the elevator when it arrived on his floor.

"Pees knees!" I tried again. That didn't sound right either. "Never mind. You had to be there."

"I'll take your word for it." Ben welcomed me into his room, which did not have a penis balloon in sight. It was quite refreshing. "I'll order pizza?"

"You are a prince among men, Ben Yu." I sat down on the bed next to him as he ordered food on his phone. To tide me over for the main course, I tore off a roll of King's Hawaiian. I scoped out the room, trying to figure out their sleeping situation. I couldn't see Ben snuggling up with Mark, though the reverse was plausible. "Who are you sharing the room with?"

"Mark and Steven. Ethan's in the room next door with his chef friends. Al and Oscar," Ben added as an afterthought.

"You don't know them?"

"No. They know Ethan from before. They're the ones catering the wedding."

"Oh, the taco truck!" I could go for some tacos right now. "Can you make me some tacos?"

"Not at this precise moment."

I knew that. Where would he find a spit at this hour to make al pastor? I could see it, though. Ben sharpening his knives in a taco truck with the range erupting with flames. He'd wipe his sweaty forehead and unbutton his chef's coat, saying, "It's getting hot in here."

"You have quite the imagination," Ben said. The real Ben, not my fantasy version. Apparently, I'd verbalized my low-budget soft-core porn. "Do you want me to order tacos too?"

I shook my head. I must be sobering up if I turned down tacos. The image of Ben helming a food truck still floated in my brain. "Have you ever considered running your own food truck?"

Ben toed off his shoes and set them neatly against the wall. "Why do you ask that?"

He paced around the room, picking up things off the floor as he went. He gently laid my tangled wig on the desk and my sad, melted Klondike bars went into the minifridge. I saw it clearly now. Ben was nervous. The questions weren't walls he was putting up. They were gatekeepers. I used to think I couldn't pass through, but not today. "You have, haven't you?" Ben shrugged, which I took as a yes. "I think you'd be good at it."

"You'd be the only one," he said, organizing my snacks according to size and then switched to opened versus unopened.

I hugged him from behind, wrapping my arms around him like a sloth to a tree to get him to stop. "That can't be true." Ben fought this, keeping his body stiff, but after a few seconds he relaxed in my hold. "Tell me. What does your food truck serve?"

The answer was on the tip of Ben's tongue. "A version of my grandpa's Hainan chicken rice."

"Ooh yum!" Pizza sounded so boring now. "Why don't you do it?"

"Start-up costs. Saturated market. High rate of failure." Ben rattled off more depressing shit about running a business that I knew all too well, but that couldn't have been the whole story. I'd seen Ben work. He was smart and saw things through. There had to be another reason.

"What else?" Thanks to my heels, I was able to rest my face on his shoulder. It gave me front row seats to his jaw, working out the words.

"My grandparents took care of me when my parents had school board meetings or fundraisers to attend. I used to watch my grandpa cook and he would tell me how he was the most educated person in his family. But when he came to America, no one would hire him because his English wasn't good. That was why he opened his restaurant. If he had it his way, he would have loved to go to college and do the things my mom was able to do. It was a given that I'd do the same. Go to college and get a good job. Why choose backbreaking labor when I could work in an air-conditioned office and get a steady salary? So that's what I did and it was boring as hell. I know it would look like a big step backwards if I chose the harder path."

"But it would be a step forward for you. Isn't that what matters?"

A knock on the door interrupted our conversation. Pizza was here. I let go of Ben and kicked off my shoes next to his. I straightened them so that they were flush together. We resituated ourselves back on the bed, with a large margherita pizza in between us that had a nice blistery crust. It was nicer than what this situation called for. I could literally have eaten some cardboard dollar slice and it would have hit the spot.

"You could start small," I said as I bit into my slice and ate my words. This tasted like heaven.

"Small? How?"

I leaned back onto the soft pillows. "You could start by making me Hainan chicken." Ben's mouth twisted into a half smile as he copied me and lounged on the bed. "And then you could have a pop-up somewhere. Like at the farmers market? I could see you making rice bowls next to the jiānbǐng lady."

"I could," Ben said noncommittally, but he ruminated on it while he finished eating with a faraway look in his eyes.

"What are you afraid of?" I asked when he didn't say anything more.

Ben stared at the ceiling. "I want to be sure that it's a good idea first. I know what my family thinks of me. I don't want to be known as the fuckup in the family anymore." Ben offered me another slice before moving the pizza box to the TV stand. His hospitality was showing.

"Does it matter?" I asked as Ben plopped back into bed. "You're going to be a fuckup if you do nothing and you could still be a fuckup if you try and fail. But at least you're giving yourself a chance to do something you want to do."

"I—" Ben needed a second to follow my logic. "I hadn't thought about it that way. Wise words."

I turned on my stomach and bopped his nose. "It's the weed."

"No, it's not. It's you." Ben pushed the hair out of my face, resting his hand at the nape of my neck. "You have a way of getting people to tell you their deep dark secrets."

"It's the weed," I insisted, lying back down. I was no sage. I employed the same random button-smashing strategy I had for video games toward my conversations. I just poked at feelings until they spilled.

"What about you? What are you afraid of?"

I supposed that was fair. A secret for a secret. I didn't mind sharing. He knew most of my secrets already. "I'm afraid of being alone."

I could tell Ben was unprepared for my answer by the way he stopped mid-chew. This was why he shouldn't be going around asking pointed questions. It didn't bother me, though. This was the topic of many therapy sessions, so I didn't think much about it anymore. I accepted this part of me like it was my blood type or the shape of my nails. I wouldn't notice it for long periods of time until it would show up out of the blue like a pop-up ad.

"What do you mean?" Ben slid his arm into mine like a vine, weaving our fingers together, molding to the shape of me. "You're always surrounded by people. Your friends. Your family."

"You don't know my family. My parents couldn't be in the same room without fighting, so I kept to myself. Did my own thing." I learned if I stayed out of their way, they wouldn't make me take sides. If I did well in school and followed the rules, I could make things easier for everyone. When I stayed quiet, I didn't add to the noise. That was the only way I knew how to cope. "Sometimes I wonder if I've become too good at being alone."

"It doesn't mean you don't have people who love you." Ben stilled, with a certain alarm in his eyes, as if his brain was working overtime. I wondered if he was going back to reread his own sentence and he saw the word *love* highlighted in yellow.

"Thanks for the reminder." I chuckled, letting him off the hook before he agonized over it. I didn't want him to feel any pressure when he didn't owe me anything. I took chances on a lot of things, but not on love. Love was too precious to be thrown around carelessly. "But things change. People find jobs . . . get married . . . have kids. They all seem to move on." *Without me.* That part, I couldn't say out loud. "What will I have?"

Ben stayed quiet. I was afraid all this serious talk had brought down the mood, but then he pressed a reverent kiss on my forehead.

"What's that for?" I asked.

"I care about you, Elise."

"I care about you too," I repeated. The words felt awkward as I said them. They were a shell of how I felt, but they were safer to say.

Ben kissed me again. His mouth was soft on my lips, even as he deepened the kiss, as if he was trying to convince me of something I already knew. His arms enveloped me, and it was hard to imagine another place I'd rather be.

I slowly dragged the back of my nails against his stubble, tracing the edge of his jaw. Unlike the first time I tried this, Ben tilted his head, giving me more access. He palmed the back of my thigh, flirting with the hem of my dress. He gazed at me with soft hooded eyes that made me feel so wanted, I almost laughed in disbelief. My hair was matted down from my wig and half of my eyebrow was smeared on the back of my hand. I was a melting caricature of sexy. I told him as much.

"We don't have to if you don't want to, but I told you. I don't care about this stuff," he said, snapping the garter I'd forgotten about. "I like you just the way you are."

He said this so simply. No frills. No promises. If it had come from anyone but Ben, it would have sounded false. But because it was Ben, it made my chest swell, like it was making more room for him.

I pressed my mouth on his. Ben caught me, like he knew I was coming, and rolled me over until I was on top. He helped me out of my dress. I loved how his eyes danced when his hands explored my body, like there was more to discover. I impatiently tugged his clothes off him, which made him laugh. Then it was my turn when he produced a condom, a free one that he snagged at a community health event. He didn't know what was so funny when there was a loud PSA on the wrapper that declared, "Safe sex is hot, STDs are not."

"It's so you," I said. We managed to stop laughing when I lowered myself on him, exhaling together when I took all of him in. I loved watching him fall apart as I moved, that I could make him feel as good as he made me feel. I slowed down, trying to make it last as long as I could, but it was too late. My orgasm coursed through my body. My back hit the cool sheets and Ben buried himself in me, finding his own release. I didn't know where my pleasure began or ended. I didn't know how to describe it, other than it felt like pure color.

Chapter Twenty-Three

I was going to kill Ben. His alarm went off at six A.M. My head felt like a cement block getting jackhammered. I was never, ever going to drink that much again.

"Rise and shine." Ben shut off his phone and stretched like a lazy cat. Lucky for him. He didn't have a stomach that gurgled like a witch's brew. I grunted a response. Ben cozied up to me. "What happened to Miss Inspirational Poster? You were Queen of the World last night."

"She should have quit while she was ahead." As much as I wanted to, I couldn't go back to sleep. Not when my own breath tasted like battery acid. For that reason, I had to turn away Ben and his morning wood. "I'm closed for business today."

Wait. I was waking up next to Ben . . . in a room that he shared with two other friends. My brain was like an orange getting pressed in a juicer, so it took a while to put this together. I threw the covers over my head and closed my eyes like it would make me disappear and magically transport me somewhere, preferably in clothes that didn't make me look like a Bratz doll.

"What are you doing?" Ben joined me between the sheets. If I didn't feel like a prune, I might have done something about the way he stared at my naked body.

"Stop it," I whispered. "What if someone sees?"

It took Ben a second to grasp what I meant. He popped his head out for some quick reconnaissance. "No one is here."

How was that possible? I peeked from the covers and the other queen bed was still untouched. I turned around and looked toward the bathroom. Huh. No one was here.

"Did the guys text you?" I asked.

"Nope." He sunk back into bed, completely unbothered that we'd lost our friends or vice versa.

"Why are you so nonchalant about this?" I wrapped myself in the sheet and scavenged the room for food. I was like a woman out of a Japanese horror movie, haunting for cold pizza.

"We'll find them soon." Ben assessed my ghastly state and asked a smart question. "What do you think about phở?"

I thought it was the best fucking idea ever. God bless phở restaurants that opened at eight A.M. Ben offered to pick it up because he was a gentleman and I simply refused to go. I considered myself confident, but I wasn't strong enough to wear my club outfit in broad daylight for aunties to judge me. While he was gone, I jumped in the shower and washed my sticky skin. After we finished eating, I was a brand-new woman.

We eventually found most of our friends, lying around in the bachelorette suite. Mark and Rebecca were in one bed while Beth and Ethan were in the other. It was almost noon and none of them were ready to wake up.

A penis balloon whacked Ben in the face. "You weren't kidding about the dicks," he whispered. I stifled my laugh as I tiptoed around the room to get a fresh set of clothes.

I went to the bathroom to change, but the door wouldn't budge more than an inch. I put more muscle into it, but I kept slamming into something that was blocking its way. I looked through the small sliver and gasped.

"Oh shit." Two bodies sprawled on the tiled floor. The thing I had been slamming the door into was Jesse's head. "Jesse! Are you okay?"

Jesse's body remained still and a chill ran through me. Shit shit shit. I'd killed my best friend! I was about to call 911 when Jesse's snore bellowed in the marble bathroom.

"I'm so sorry, Jess," I whispered, atoning into the door.

"You should be," Rebecca mumbled as she sat up. "We were worried sick about you."

"No, we weren't," Mark said, his face still buried in his pillow. "We were . . ." He rubbed his forehead. "What did we do last night?"

"The last thing I remember was Rebecca giving you a lap dance," Ethan said from the other bed. "An image I could have done without."

"Same here." Ben's mouth curled in distaste.

"What?" Mark got out of bed and sauntered into the middle of the room, where he shot Magic Mike pelvic thrusts in Ethan's and Ben's direction. "Like you two don't have the same moves."

Ben glared at Mark. "Shut up."

If Ben got mad at every annoying thing Mark did, he was in for a miserable existence. I found it best to ignore Mark whenever possible, but that might be hard for Ben since Mark was his brother-in-law.

Rebecca tried to detangle the rat's nest on her head. "Okay, guys. Get your asses out of here. It's girl time." She pointed at Mark and Ethan and Ben. "Take Steven with you." She squinted through her crusty eyes. "Where is he?"

"In here," his voice croaked from the bathroom.

"I guess I'll see you later, then." Ben stole a kiss when no one was looking and helped the guys pick themselves up and out of the room. I wished Ben could stay with me when I faced Rebecca, but he knew better than anyone that whatever Rebecca said goes.

Beth and Jesse were still sleeping, so Rebecca suggested that we pick up coffee and breakfast from Eggslut. I wasn't naïve. I knew this was her way to get a chance to talk. We took a seat while we waited for our orders.

Rebecca covered her tired eyes with sunglasses. They were dark like the coffee she was nursing. Her fingers rapped on the side of her cup while we waited for one of us to say something.

"Do you think we'll make it to the day club?"

My iced coffee stopped midway to my mouth. This was what she was going to open this conversation with?

"Beth's doctor friends already left for the buffet," Rebecca continued. "They said they'd make it back on time but it's getting late. I had a cabana reserved, but how much you want to bet that Mark has one too? If Beth's tired, we could stay in. Would it be boring if we hung back and watched movies together?"

"Rebecca . . ." Her damn sunglasses hid half of her face. I had no idea what she was thinking. I decided to tread carefully. "No, it wouldn't be boring."

"We haven't spent a lot of time together lately. Quality time, I mean." I agreed. Our time had been absorbed by wedding stuff. "I feel so out of the loop. Like you and Ben? When did that happen?"

Rebecca sounded more concerned than upset. Somehow, that made me feel worse. "Not that long ago. I'm sorry we didn't tell you—"

Rebecca held her hand up to stop me and then both hands were up, like she was surrendering. "You and Ben are both adults.

Whatever you two decide is up to you. I was just shocked to see you two last night." It sounded like Rebecca had practiced reciting this because it was the mature thing to say, but it was a little too good to be true.

"There has to be more than that," I pressed.

"Fine. It's weird," she admitted. "It'll take some getting used to. You are like my sister and Ben is my brother. It feels incestuous."

I grimaced. "Ugh. Don't put it that way."

"Well, what do you want me to say? Ben is . . ." She clenched her teeth, holding back her words. "Ben is Ben."

"What is that supposed to mean?"

Rebecca took off her sunglasses. There was nothing scarier than two bare-faced women having a serious conversation before they finished their morning coffee. "Ben and I are opposites. He is quiet and moody and keeps to himself. I haven't ever been able to rely on him, so I let him be. Let him do his own thing. But for you . . ." Rebecca waited until I met her dark brown eyes. I thought I was about to face my judgment, but I found something else in her expression. Maybe I was reading into it, but it felt like a toss-up between wariness and hope. I couldn't tell which side of the coin Rebecca was on.

". . . he does seem happier around you . . ." Hope. It was hope.

". . . but . . ." No no no. Go back to hope!

Rebecca sighed. "Don't let him sidetrack you. If I held my breath every time I waited for Ben to come around—"

Our breakfast order was called. We both stood to get our food. Rebecca didn't finish her sentence and didn't bring it up again as we returned to the room. I couldn't stop thinking about the conversation, even as we rejoined our group and binged rom-coms instead of braving the desert heat. The person Rebecca had talked about wasn't anything like the Ben I knew. Ben wasn't the type of person who did anything carelessly, even if he wasn't perfect in his execution. Ben acknowledged that he wished he could have handled things differently with his family. I wished I had spoken up about it with Rebecca. But that was their history. It wasn't a problem I was meant to fix.

WE ARRIVED BACK home on Sunday. With Vegas behind me, I felt the crunch on time. The countdown was officially on for Beth and Ethan's wedding. I had six days to get her wedding together. Flowers had a short vase life, so the arrangements had to wait until Thursday.

On Monday, I went into the studio and started organizing all the supplies I needed for the wedding, so I could load them into my truck easily when it was go time. I opened my walk-in refrigerator and stared into the space as I sipped my tea. How was I going to fit all the flowers coming in?

"Are you having deep thoughts about flowers?"

"Shit." I spilled my hot tea at the sound of Ben's voice. Two years and I'd never thought to put a bell or something to alert me when someone walked in. My clients weren't usually this quiet, though. I set my mug down and quickly ran my hands under cold water in the sink. "I swear I'm not usually this clumsy."

"I'll believe it when I see it." Ben came around my workbench and dried my hands with a towel. He inspected my burned fingers and then glared at my mug, like it was to blame. If he wasn't already displeased, Ben found the pile of election mailers that were stuffed in the corner. He sorted them, keeping the ones for his mom and throwing the rest into my recycle bin.

"All lies," he said.

"You're biased," I reminded him.

"True, but it's getting ugly. Don't read that crap."

Too late. It was unavoidable when the glossy card stock used bold font to declare that Donna Yu was not to be trusted, that she catered to special interests. It sounded like the same kind of mud-slinging that happened every election cycle, so I didn't find it out of the ordinary. But what did I know? I wasn't in the thick of it like Ben was. "What brings you in today?"

Ben watched me box spools of ribbon. "I can't visit just because?"

"You can," I said before he took it the wrong way. He was welcome to drop by, but there had always been a reason before. What a novelty, seeing each other just because. It sent my heart into a tailspin. I should lay off caffeine for a while, I realized.

"There's something I wanted to ask you," Ben said, taking both of my hands into his. My heart rate suddenly spiked. What was so serious that required this formality? "Do you want to come over tonight?"

I raised an eyebrow at him and batted his hands away. "You could have texted that."

Ben reached for my hand again, lacing our fingers together. "I wanted to see you. I haven't seen you since Saturday." A frown appeared on his face. I hadn't seen one of those in a while. "How did it go with Rebecca?"

"It was fine. Better than expected. Didn't you talk to her?"

"I did."

"And . . . ?" Something told me she wasn't as kind to him as she was to me.

"And same. It went as well as it could have."

"Meaning?"

"Who's interrogating who now?" Ben laughed. He squeezed my hand to reassure me, I thought. "She's very protective of you." His frown made a brief reappearance, but he changed the subject. "So . . . tonight?"

I wished he'd tell me, but I reminded myself to be patient. I could try again later. "Are you going to make me dinner?"

"That's the plan," he said. If that already didn't sound perfect, he added, "And breakfast too, if you want."

If I want. I wanted a lot of things. More than I was ready to admit yet. "I like eggs over easy."

"Noted." Ben's face broke into a smile and you'd think I'd never seen teeth in my life. It transformed his face into that of someone I'd never met before, but hoped I had a chance to.

I sent Ben off to work with a kiss, stupidly excited for dinner.

Just because.

Just Ben and me.

It had a nice ring to it.

Chapter Twenty-Four

I went home to pack an overnight bag. As I walked through the door, my mom sat down for dinner.

Ma perked up at my appearance. "You're home early."

A pang of guilt struck me because my first thought was about the fish-ball noodle soup she was eating. Even though it was just the two of us, she still made this dish in big batches, so there would be leftovers the next day. But what really made me feel bad was that it had been weeks since I'd come home before dinner. With all the late nights and busy weekends, my house had become a place to sleep and do laundry and not much else. I wrestled with the idea of canceling on Ben, but he was expecting me. "I'm going out tonight."

"With your friends or someone else?"

"Do you remember Ben? From Jesse's wedding?"

"Mmm." She slurped a spoonful of broth. "I remember him. At the wedding, Jesse's aunts kept asking me if you were dating that boy. I said, I don't know. One of them said they saw you kissing and I said again, I don't know. That was three weeks ago. I still don't know."

I cringed that my mom knew about the kiss this whole time. I was ashamed to say that I hadn't put much thought into telling her about Ben. Most of the men I dated before weren't worth introducing to her in the first place. Since she'd met him already, maybe it wouldn't be as big a deal as I was making it out to be. "Do you want me to invite him over sometime?"

My mom thought for a second as she loosened her noodles with her chopsticks. "Okay. After I finish cleaning the house."

I had no idea what my mom was talking about. She had always kept our modest little house tidy. I'd lived in this house my entire life and it hadn't changed in twenty-eight years. The same leather sofa, which was too soft to sit on anymore. The same Chinese mother-of-pearl art, depicting the rivers and mountains of our ancestors' time. The same family photos, even the ones with my dad. I wasn't sure why she still kept them, but it was nice to think of a time when the three of us appeared happy together.

My mom picked up on my confusion. "I want to renovate the house soon. Everything is so old, no? I was going to ask you to help me. You're good at picking colors."

I hoped my mom liked sage green as much as I did. "I didn't know you wanted to update the house."

"It's been long enough." Ma casually picked something out of her teeth with her nail like she hadn't dropped huge news on me. "I want to make it a place I can enjoy."

"What about me?" I lived here too. Maybe my mom would let me pick out the new furniture as well.

Ma shrugged. "You'll find a husband someday and have your own place. You don't expect to live here forever, do you?"

Actually, that was my plan. The housing market was rough. "I thought you never wanted me to get married."

"Well, no husband is better than a bad husband," she said like she had many times over the years. "But if he's a good person, why not? Ben seems like a good person."

"He is," I confirmed. My cheeks warmed. I didn't think it mattered to me that my mom liked Ben, but it was nice.

I recounted the story for Ben as we were about to eat. He made Hainan chicken, which filled his apartment with a delicious aroma that had me salivating the second I walked in. The drool kept coming because Ben had his sleeves rolled up as he sliced and diced his garnishes. The man had me fanning myself over scallions.

Ben hid his smile poorly as he plated a heaping mound of rice. "Your mom likes me."

His ego inflated before my eyes. It got worse when he presented my plate. There were glistening slices of chicken with rice, accompanied with a bowl of soup and three different sauces. I knew he was showing off when I saw the cucumber slices that he rolled together to make a carnation.

"You like it?" he asked unnecessarily as I went in for my second and third bites.

I didn't bother with the spoon and sipped my broth straight from the bowl. The steaming soup delighted my taste buds with its clean, ginger flavor. "This is insanely good. Is this your grandpa's recipe?"

"More or less." Ben was being modest.

"What changes did you make?" I asked.

Ben shied away from answering, even after repeated questioning. "It's a secret."

"Is this like *Kung Fu Panda* where you say there's a secret ingredient but there really isn't one?" Ben laughed but remained mum. I drizzled my chicken with sweet soy sauce and ginger-scallion oil. "Why won't you tell me? I'm not going to tell anyone. I wouldn't know how to replicate it either."

"I'm still fine-tuning the recipe." Ben delicately dipped his spoon into his broth and tasted it with great concentration like it was wine. "It's not where I want it yet."

I wasn't sure what Ben was on if he didn't think this was perfect. I was sitting over here, having a transcendent experience over poached chicken. "Have you put more thought into doing a pop-up?"

"I have." He said this lightly, but his frown gave him away. "Still working through the funding and the logistics of making enough for a crowd. I was thinking about the Saturday three weeks after Beth and Ethan's wedding. I don't have campaign events that weekend."

I gasped. If Ben had thought that far ahead, he was seriously considering it. "Can I be your first customer?"

"If it happens, yes." Ben's brand of optimism was cautious, like a baby giraffe taking its wobbling first steps.

"It will," I said more definitively. "I believe in you."

Ben pointed his chopsticks at me. "There's the inspirational poster talk again. Did you partake in some recreational marijuana tonight, Elise Ngo?"

I thought the interrogation phase of our relationship was over. "Excuse me. I'd like to speak to my lawyer."

Ben snorted but settled into an amiable silence. After a few beats, he said, "Thanks."

"For what?"

"For encouraging me."

I reached across the table and gave his hand a squeeze. "It was just a nudge."

"It was a good nudge," he said. "I hadn't given much thought about what I'd do after the campaign. If I didn't have anything lined up, I probably would have gone up to Sacramento to help my mom."

"Oh." I put my chopsticks down. Ben had never mentioned anything like that before. "I didn't know that was something you'd consider."

"It wouldn't have been my first choice."

I felt a little brave. "I want you to stay. For purely selfish reasons."

"Yeah?" There was a twinkle in Ben's eyes. His ego was a hot air balloon now. "Like what?"

"You could be my personal chef."

Ben waved his arm over the table. "Does this past muster?"

Again with the compliment fishing. In a few more bites, I could lick this plate clean. "And you're good at carrying things."

"Are you saying you only want me for my body?"

Was that the worst thing in the world? "Not only, but mostly."

Ben's eyebrows cinched together, deepening his signature frown, and I wondered if I'd said something wrong. He had to know that wasn't the only reason, right?

Ben sighed deeply and pushed away from the dining table. He didn't say anything as he unrolled his sleeves, covering his beautiful forearms. His dark eyes pinned me to my seat and just as I thought I'd really put my foot in my mouth this time, Ben started to unbutton his shirt.

What was going on?

"Oh my," he said, his face turning a rosy pink. He shuffled out of his dress shirt and pulled his undershirt over his head. "It's getting hot in here."

I might have ascended out of my body because I couldn't move from my seat. Ben was acting out my sexy chef fantasy, twirling his shirt over his head and tossing it into the middle of the living room. He committed to the role, pulling me onto his lap, where he still had his half apron on. I palmed the pink patches that appeared on Ben's chest. He was blushing so hard, he was going to turn himself into a raspberry. This silly side of him was too much for me to handle.

Ben dug his hands into my hair, about to bring me in for a kiss, and I did what any normal person would do when faced with a shirtless, hot man. I spurted laughter right into his face.

Ben bit his lip to stifle his own laughter, breaking character. "I thought this was what you wanted."

I did on some subconscious horny level, but I liked the real Ben more. "I . . . want . . ."

Ben watched me fight for words through my laughter with a myriad of expressions. Since the day we met, I'd gotten to know most of his frowns. The single, raised eyebrow frown meant he was confused. The one with the pursed lips meant he was refraining from giving his real opinion. When the frown was paired with narrowed eyes, watch out. He was definitely pissed. But this face was something else. It was smooth, not a worry line in sight. His amused smile settled into contentment. His deep brown eyes soaked me in, waiting for more. It was the look of adoration I saw in rom-coms or between my brides and grooms. I'd never had it directed at me and the intense rush of feelings made me indecisive.

I wanted to jump into his arms, but I was already there.

I wanted to kiss him, but I couldn't stop staring. All my life, I'd waited for someone to look at me like this and I wanted time to stop long enough for me to memorize it.

I wanted to say, *I think I'm falling in love with you*, but I wasn't sure how. I'd never said it before. I'd seen countless brides and grooms openly declare their love in front of their closest friends and family. I couldn't even bring myself to say the words in private. Maybe I didn't know anything about love at all and I had no business saying it. I didn't want to get this wrong.

I took the easy way out. "I want you."

Ben's head tilted back in surprise. "Are you saying my bad striptease worked?"

I swallowed my disappointment and smiled. This was what I got for leaving my words up for interpretation. "More or less."

"How should I spice it up next time?" He smirked at his own pun. "A spatula? Potholders? To handle these hot buns?" Ben put both hands on my ass, giving it a squeeze, and I couldn't help laughing. It brought me out of my head and into the present.

I slipped my hands around his face and kissed him until there was nothing left to think about, no words left to say. Everything I needed to know was right in front of me.

THE WAKE-UP CALL at Ben's apartment was the smell of coffee. I stretched and contemplated taking a shower, but I was sore and lazy. Instead, I helped myself to one of Ben's enormous campaign T-shirts. I was expecting the slogan to read "A Vote for Yu Is a Vote for You," but it ended up being something more tried and true: "Donna Yu: Effective Leadership for Californians."

"Good mor—" I stumbled when I saw Rebecca and Donna Yu sitting at the dining table with a stoic Ben. There was no breakfast in sight. Only laptops and silenced cell phones that kept lighting up, beckoning for attention.

"You're going to need pants," Rebecca said without preamble. "We have a situation on our hands."

Chapter Twenty-Five

Well, this was awkward.

I returned to the dining table after changing into a shirt and pants that didn't scream "I had sex with Ben last night." I took a seat and waited for someone to tell me what was going on. Rebecca flicked her eyes at Ben, who replied with an arched eyebrow. While they were stuck in their silent fight, Donna greeted me with a polite but uneasy smile. The situation was dire because Donna was sitting here in athleisure wear without makeup, without the veneer of her public persona.

"Elise," Donna said in exasperation, when no one else offered to clue me in. "There's no good way to say this. We're caught in the middle of a scandal. My campaign manager, Emilio, received a tip from a journalist friend of his and called me first thing this morning."

"About the election?" I asked. What more could they say about Donna Yu? "What are they saying about you?"

"It's not my mom," Rebecca said. "It's me." She turned her laptop so I could read the email forwarded to her from Emilio. The headline read, "Assemblywoman's Embroiled Campaign Sparks Investigation." The first few lines read like a gossip rag, detailing accusations exchanged between the Donna Yu and Shawn Tam campaigns. I didn't see how any of this applied to Rebecca until I saw a picture of her in her wedding gown, standing next to Veronica Reed.

> Last week, a whistleblower filed a complaint about Assemblywoman Yu's recent fundraising activities. In June, Assemblywoman Yu's daughter, Rebecca, married entrepreneur Mark Kim. It is alleged that guests were encouraged to make a donation to the California Conservation Center, where Rebecca Yu-Kim is employed. It's rumored that donations exceeded the $4,900 contribution limit, bringing into question how else Assemblywoman Yu is circumventing election rules to curry funds from special interests. Yu-Kim is pictured here with Veronica Reed, who is president of the California Hospital Association (CHA). The CHA recently endorsed Assemblywoman Yu.

I looked up from the screen. "Rebecca, is this true?"

Rebecca waved away this question like it was an annoying fly. "Of course not. Anything can be alleged these days. Even if it were true, it isn't illegal. You should see some of the other kinds of fundraisers. You can join an assembly member for spin class for two thousand dollars."

"It's not illegal but it doesn't look great to the public," Ben interjected, which drew more ire from Rebecca.

I kept a level tone to prevent this conversation from escalating. "If it's not true, then why would they say this?"

"It's a distraction," Donna replied. "The press gets to put out this misleading headline to get their clicks. Meanwhile, this dominates the narrative of my campaign and Shawn Tam gets to reap the benefits as my fundraising activities get investigated."

"What are you going to do?" I asked Rebecca. "Are you going to be okay?"

"You haven't read the rest," Rebecca said, prompting me to scroll farther down.

The family connections don't stop there. One of the remaining campaign staff members is Benjamin Yu, Assemblywoman Yu's son. The youngest Yu joined the campaign team recently as the assistant to campaign manager Emilio Suarez. It was reported that a recent fundraiser, handled by Yu, ended in disaster. More notable is his choice to hire Elise Ngo of Elise Ngo Floral Design. Ngo was the vendor for the Yu-Kim wedding and multiple Yu campaign events. Evidence acquired by this paper indicates that this may be due in part to Ngo and Yu's romantic relationship.

Below this paragraph was a picture of Ben kissing me in the farmers market. The picture was grainy, as if it was taken from far away. That had to be the case because no phone this day and age could take such a bad photo, unless a filter was added to make it extra sleazy. This was getting blown way out of proportion.

"Ben." If he kept clenching his jaw like that, he was going to break all of his teeth. "Say something."

"I told you," Ben said, directing the barbed words at Rebecca. "You should have kept the wedding small."

"Not this again," Rebecca complained. "This isn't relevant."

"It is. I warned you that this could possibly happen. It blurred the lines between our public and personal lives and the press ran with it."

"It's only one website," I said, trying to be helpful. "And look at how many sketchy ads there are. No one's going to take this seriously."

"It's only a matter of time before other outlets report it too," Ben said. "This site is one of many under the same parent company that owns *Wedding Style*. That's how they have the photo from Becks's wedding." He swiped over to a different email that contained photos of me and my *Wedding Style* entries. "When you signed the release, it gave them permission to use your photos as they pleased. Now it's front-page news."

This I didn't know. I should've read the fine print more closely.

This was the least of Rebecca's concerns. She went on the offensive. "Don't act like this is all on me. If anyone is guilty of blurring the lines, it's you and now you got Elise involved too."

I froze. Rebecca was speaking as if there weren't two of us involved in our relationship. "It's not like we planned any of this, Rebecca."

"I'm not blaming you," Rebecca said, missing my point. "Ben knew getting involved with anyone attached to the campaign was breeding ground for a sex scandal."

Sex scandal?! "You're overreacting. It's just a kiss."

"You'd think so, but people get weird when it comes to romance. Once you smush body parts together, suddenly the public thinks you lack morals."

"Well, neither of you did anything wrong, right?" I asked. I was reaching for any inkling of hope here. "Your names will be cleared."

"It doesn't matter. In the court of public opinion, the damage will be done," Ben said. "Once voters lose trust, it's over."

"But—"

Rebecca placed her hand on my arm. "I know you want to defend Ben, but I'm not saying anything he doesn't know already. This is what it's like in politics. If it can be spun in a negative light, it will. Ben knew this, but he failed to follow protocol." Ben glared at Rebecca but she was impervious to his feelings. "No one on the campaign was supposed to have any kind of relationship with third-party contractors to avoid scandals like these. It's common sense." Rebecca swiped her phone for new notifications. "It doesn't matter," she conceded. "We need to put out a response quickly to get ahead of this."

"Emilio is going to get back to me to see if we can spin this somehow." Donna, who had been letting her calls go to voicemail, saw a text message on her phone she couldn't ignore. "I'm needed at the office." She stood and hugged Rebecca and Ben. "I'll keep you posted." Donna excused herself and left.

Ben shut his laptop. "No. We wait this out. Responding would blow this up bigger than it needs to be."

Rebecca became incensed. "We can't sit around while the press and Shawn Tam's campaign take control of the narrative. There are going to be headlines claiming corruption and you want to sit back and ride this out? Are you out of your mind?"

"There's too much at stake," Ben insisted. "We're only three months away from the election."

"That's exactly my point. We don't have time to lose." Rebecca scrolled through Shawn Tam's social media profile. "There's gotta be dirt on Shawn Tam's ass."

Ben covered Rebecca's phone screen with his hand. "We promised to run a low-key campaign without stooping to slander. Voters are sick of it. We can't go back on that now."

"Who said anything about slander? There has to be legit gossip somewhere."

"Focus, Becks. Now we're dealing with the FPPC," Ben said, trying to reason with her. I googled FPPC so I could keep up. Fair Political Practices Commission. "Look at the claims in the article. Conflicts of interest. Improper use of campaign funds. This is serious."

"We have to play a little dirty here, Ben." Rebecca gave up on her phone and stole Ben's laptop for her snooping. It was like they were fighting over toys. "We can't play by the rules when there will be tweets and TikToks taking all of this out of context. Constituents are not going to bother looking for the truth. We have to buy time to repair it by putting the attention on something else."

I sat still, disassociating, while Ben and Rebecca continued to argue back and forth. I didn't know how to stop the onslaught of words coming out of both of their mouths. Rebecca, defending her choices, like I knew she would. Every argument she made sounded like a hill she would die on. Ben was a strong opponent, throwing out every worst-case scenario that was materializing in real time. I felt my body curl into itself. I didn't belong here.

"And what about Elise?"

Hearing my own name stopped me from withering away. It was a gut punch to hear Rebecca and Ben talk about me as if I weren't sitting in between them, like I didn't have something to lose here as well. The ramifications of this mess started to sink in. My name and my studio were now attached to the scandal. The allegations weren't true, but if Rebecca was right, then no one at this table was going to suffer real consequences but me. Rebecca would still have her job. Ben was never going to work on the campaign long-term anyway. I was the one with the most to lose. I stood from the table and excused myself.

"Where are you going, E?" Rebecca asked.

"The studio," I mumbled. "I have work to do."

"Maybe you should stay here for a bit," Ben said. "At least until we find out more from Emilio."

"Stay, Elise. I'll be here too," Rebecca said. "I told my boss and she asked me to take PTO while the investigation is ongoing."

Blindsided by the news, Ben resorted to sarcasm. "Thanks for asking."

Rebecca stuck her tongue out at him like this was a playground fight. "Emilio advised me to hide here since you have no digital footprint. No one knows where you live."

"And I want to keep it that way," Ben said. "I don't want private investigators lurking around here."

"You're being too paranoid, Ben."

"You're sleeping on the couch."

"I'm not sleeping on that lumpy-ass sofa." Rebecca looked at me from the corner of her eye. "But do me a favor and put on new sheets for me."

While they bickered, I gathered my things. Things got so heated, they almost didn't see me leave.

"Elise," Ben called out as I was about to close the door behind me. He ran out and caught me before I took off. "I'm sorry about all of this."

"It's okay," I lied. I took a deep breath and clenched my teeth, hoping it resembled a smile. "Both of you have a lot to discuss and I have so much left to do. We can touch base later."

"Touch base later?" Ben ran his hands through his hair. "Elise. I know this is a shitstorm and it's a lot, but I need you here."

"What about what *I* need?" I couldn't believe I had to say that. Had he suddenly forgotten about me? "I don't have the luxury to hide. I don't have PTO. If I don't work, I don't get paid. If I don't get paid, I'll have to close my studio. I'm barely surviving. I didn't think I had to spell this out to you. You knew this."

Ben's face fell. "I'm sorry. I—"

The door opened behind him. It was Rebecca. It was obvious she'd heard the whole thing because she tucked her hair behind her ear and crossed her arms like she was a superhero, ready to jump into action. "How long has this been happening?"

Great. Just what I needed—my friends finding out I'd been hiding this from them. That I'd been pretending not to be a big, massive failure.

Ben and Rebecca waited for me. Both of them wanted something different from me and I didn't have anything left to give. This time, I had to do what felt right to me.

"I need to go," I said. "I need some time to think."

Chapter Twenty-Six

There were four people loitering in front of my studio when I drove into the parking lot. They didn't look like anyone from the neighborhood. When one of them turned at the sound of my truck, making eye contact with me, I felt the hairs on the back of my neck stand up. I drove past my usual parking spot and parked behind my studio to escape attention. I should have known it was an impossible task when my name was plastered along the side of the truck.

"Excuse me!" someone called out. "Do you work here?"

I quickly ran to the back door. I regretted ignoring Ben's advice. I should have waited until they figured out a game plan because I was out of my depth. What did people want with me? I wasn't part of the campaign. My involvement was limited to flowers and kissing someone I shouldn't have, but that was none of their business.

I should have gone home. Oh shit. What if they were also at my house? I needed to warn my mom. Why couldn't I get these damn keys to work?!

A man turned the corner, holding out his phone like he was recording me. "Are you Elise Nah-go?"

Hearing my last name mispronounced was just the thing I needed to calm my trembling hands. Whoever this guy was, he was not on my side. He couldn't have bothered to google the proper pronunciation of the person he wanted to interview. I slipped inside before anyone else could hurl questions at me. I locked the door and set a chair underneath the doorknob as a precaution. I didn't know if it worked, but I'd seen it on TV enough to give it a try.

The landline for the studio rang. I hesitated to pick it up. The blinds for the storefront's windows were thankfully pulled down, obscuring the loiterers outside from seeing in. But I could see their shadows, pacing back and forth with their cell phones. I let my phone ring, exhaling when it stopped, only for it to ring again.

I had to think about this. The only people who would call the landline were prospective customers who found me online and robocalls. I didn't want to lose potential clients, but I didn't want to spend the day hearing the phone ring from reporters looking for a comment. I turned up the volume on my radio. It was the only way I could focus or else I'd hear the jarring sounds of my front door trying to be opened. I disconnected the line and collected my tools so I could finish prepping for Beth's wedding while I hid in the back. I had to. I couldn't get anything done when I could see people lurking around, waiting for me, like I was being hunted.

I wish I had gone home, but I still had to finish the ceiling installation for Beth's wedding. I tore open boxes of artificial white snapdragons and green vines and began weaving them into a grid-wall panel with fishing wire. It was hell on my fingers, but the repetitive work helped me tune everything out.

I powered through the first panel, but as I worked on the second and the third, the fuel burning through my veins wasn't adrenaline. It was simmering rage. I was behind schedule and I felt like I was letting Beth down. I'd worked so hard to keep this wedding going and I couldn't let it get derailed over fake accusations that had real-life repercussions for me. Effective leadership, my ass.

It was dark outside by the time I finished. I propped the panels against the wall for the time being. The flowers and greenery hung limp for now, but once the panel was placed on the ceiling, it would look beautiful. I stretched my arms, feeling aches all over my body. My fingertips throbbed from pulling fishing wire into tight knots. Anger was exhausting. I switched off the radio, wondering what I had to eat at my house because somehow, I had forgotten to eat. It had to wait because multiple sounds called my attention.

My cell phone rang as someone knocked on my front door. Someone was still trying to come in? At this hour?

I glanced at the screen. It was Ben. I swiped the call away. He could wait. My bed could not. I hid in the back until it was quiet again. I peered into the studio. There were no silhouettes of bodies behind the shaded windows. I dug into my purse and gripped my keys, lacing them through my fingers like Wolverine for protection. I resented that I had to come up with a plan for my own safety, that it was up to me to protect myself. With the second wave of rage, I found the courage to leave the studio.

I unlocked the back door quietly and slowly turned the knob to peek outside. I didn't see anyone around my truck, so I plotted the direct route in my head and shot out the door, locking it as fast as I could. Which turned out to be not very fast since I had claws for hands.

"Elise?"

I dropped my keys. I dropped my fucking keys. For all my rage and supposed bravery, I'd let go of the only weapon at my disposal, which I wasn't sure would even work, if I was being honest. In the end, I was a coward and I was so fucking mad at myself for it.

"Elise Ngo?"

I picked up my keys and locked the door. "I'm sorry. I'm closed." I turned around to get to my truck.

The man held his hands up to show he wasn't a threat but he sidestepped, blocking my path. "I wanted to ask you a few questions."

"Who do you work for?" I sounded like Ben, asking this, but if this man was from a reputable media outlet, he would tell me.

"How long have you been working with the Donna Yu campaign?" he asked, ignoring my question.

My heart raced. "No comment." I pivoted around him, but the man's arm darted in front of me. My first instinct was to scream.

The man was unfazed. "What do you know about the corruption in the Yu campaign?"

Corruption? I was way out of my league.

"Can you get out of my way, please?" I hated that my voice came out small. Even in the face of a man who didn't respect me—not my time, not my space, not my boundaries—I still had to ask politely for my safety.

"Just a few questions," the man said.

I took note of his bland business casual attire, which I couldn't see too well in the dark. He wore a smile, but I knew he was not my friend. I hunched, crossing my arms in front of me. I wanted to kick this man in the shins, but my legs were glued to the ground.

"Go away before I call the police." Ben's voice cut through the air, loud and clear. I didn't know where he'd come from, but he stood in front of me, at the full extent of his height.

"Are you Ben Yu?" the man asked. "I have some questions—"

"I'm calling right now," Ben said, dialing his phone.

The man waited like he didn't care. He must have thought Ben was bluffing, but Ben's volume was on loud. When we all heard someone from Arcadia Police Department answering the call, the man backed away. He huffed, shrugging this off like it was nothing, which gave me a sinking feeling in my stomach.

Ben followed the guy and made sure he was gone before coming back to me. "Are you okay?"

I sunk against my truck. "Do I look okay?"

Ben wrapped his arms around me, holding me steady. "I tried calling you. You didn't pick up my calls."

I checked my phone. Eleven missed calls from Ben. "You could have texted."

"I didn't want to leave a trail."

Wow. That was what this was coming down to. He was just looking out for himself. "I wouldn't have screenshotted anything to sell to the *LA Times,* if that's what you're worried about."

"No, not you. Other people. Once the investigation starts, they might pull all our records, including our phone calls and texts. It's hard to dispute something in writing."

"Good thing we haven't sexted." I said this lightly, but it still sounded defensive. I understood where Ben was coming from, but I was still reeling. "Aren't you afraid people are going to see us like this?"

I said this sarcastically, but Ben let go of me. It gutted me. "Let me take you home. The campaign decided on a plan and I need to go over it with you."

I didn't want to talk, but I didn't feel safe going home by myself, so I let him drive.

"My mom and the campaign staff met this afternoon," Ben said, as soon as we got into his car. "They decided that the best course of action is to let the investigation go through. We're going to cooperate so it goes as quickly as possible. In the meantime, we need to lay low. Don't make any comments. Ignore it the best you can." Ben's professional tone rankled.

"What does that mean for us?"

"We should keep our distance for now." Ben rubbed the back of his neck. "It's probably best if you withdraw from the *Wedding Style* contest too."

My skin was hot, seeping with anger. I couldn't believe I did all of that for nothing. "How are we going to do that with the wedding coming up? I'm the maid of honor and you're the *best man*."

"Elise. I'm sorry." Ben couldn't look at me as he said this. Instead, he was busy searching my neighborhood for any suspicious activity before pulling into my driveway. "I know this sucks, but this is the best option we have."

"So you're going to ditch me four days before the wedding?" I couldn't believe this. I'd let myself trust Ben and now he was ditching me before the most important wedding I'd ever had to design.

"It's not that simple. There are much bigger things at play here. If I had a choice—"

"You do have a choice!" I was trying so hard to keep it together, but I didn't like being spoken to like I was stupid. "What do you really have to lose here? So there will be a few articles about this and sure, it'll make a dent in your reputation. But what happens when something else lights the internet on fire? People will forget about this stupid scandal and you'll still go on with your life. You will still get hired with your education and your fucking connections. I don't have any of that to fall back on. You know what will happen to me? My studio can't survive this."

Ben was quiet. He was probably stunned at my outburst because so was I. When Ben spoke again, his voice was soft. "We'll figure this out."

"How? You spent the whole day coming up with a plan to save this campaign but what about me? What are you or your mom or Rebecca going to do when I'm out of business? Who's going to bail me out?" I took Ben's silence as confirmation. "Yeah, that's what I thought."

I got out of Ben's car and dragged my aching body up to my porch.

Ben followed me but stood a safe distance away as I unlocked my door. "Elise. I'll figure something out. I promise."

"Oh, you promise?" My laugh was sad and empty. "Do you know what it was like for me to see you and Rebecca argue over this, trying to save your own asses while I was hung out to dry?" Ben opened his mouth, ready to make his rebuttal, but I didn't want to hear it. I held up my hand to save him the trouble. "I don't want to be treated like an afterthought, Ben."

I went inside my house and locked the door behind me, falling slack against it. I was proud that I stood up for myself. I'd said what I needed to say. I held on to this thought with all my might because it was the only thing I could control while everything fell by the wayside.

Chapter Twenty-Seven

I pounded on my horn, which drew ire from the other florists. It was five-thirty on Wednesday morning, after a sleepless night and wallowing in my dinner of pita chips and hummus. It was much too early for road rage over a loading zone parking spot. It was too early for doing anything, really. But I'd decided to pick up the flowers for Beth's wedding instead of having them delivered, as a cost-saving measure. This was why I was stuck in the middle of the Flower District getting flipped off. When the truck in front of me finally pulled away, I parked my truck and jogged into the California Flower Mall, running past a rainbow of roses, tulips, peonies, and carnations to procure my order.

Buckets of peach roses, pink carnations, and white gardenias were loaded onto my truck. Pre-wedding anticipation zipped through my body, tingling the tips of my fingers. It was a welcome feeling, covering up the disappointment from my last conversation with Ben. Tears began to build in my eyes, but I squeezed them shut. I couldn't think about that right now. There were centerpieces to be made and bouquets to assemble with no one available to help me with either.

I returned to the studio at seven. The parking lot was empty when I arrived, and I entered the studio unseen. To keep journalists and other unwelcome visitors away, I kept the blinds drawn and the "Closed" sign up while I worked in the back. Since the flowers had to be done last, I finally sat down to write my maid of honor speech.

I opened my notebook and put pen to paper, ready for the words to flow. And then, I waited. Nothing was coming to me. I sipped my tea, hoping some caffeine would wake my brain up and shield me from the creeping sense of regret that came with procrastination. Still, the page was blank. How was it that I'd been to so many weddings, knew all the dos and don'ts of MOH speeches, and I was drawing a blank?

I had to write something. Anything.

Hi. For those of you who don't know me, my name is Elise, Beth's maid of honor.

Okay, this was a fine start. A bit expected, but I could go back and revise it if I wanted.

Beth is my best friend. Beth, the bride. The person getting married. The person who will kill me if she knew I was writing this last minute but she won't because she is professionally obligated to do no harm.

Fuck. Who knew writing was so hard?

I scribbled over every word until it was one big ink stain and shut my notebook. I needed some inspiration. I turned on my phone to look through some photos of us through the years, but I was stopped by an urgent text from Beth: CALL ME NOW ASAP

I pressed her number on speed dial, wondering if wedding day jitters had possessed Beth to text in all caps. She was not an all-caps kind of woman.

Beth picked up right away. "E. Are you at the studio?"

"Yes. What's going on?"

"You need to come with me. I'm parked next to your truck. We have a wedding emergency on our hands."

I didn't want to leave the studio, but I had to take the risk for Beth. She didn't take emergencies lightly. I darted out the back door and into Beth's car. I offered to drive, but she insisted. After a few minutes, she pulled into a nearby boba shop and that was when I knew that I was being kidnapped. I should have seen this coming. Beth was eerily calm for someone supposedly in crisis.

Customers were trickling in. There was a young family eating in a booth and another table full of teenagers, their faces in their phones. Seated at a corner table was Rebecca, disguised in a hat and sunglasses. She was chiding Jesse for digging into the Taiwanese sausage and popcorn chicken before everyone arrived.

"What is this?" I asked Beth. "An intervention?" I sighed. I didn't have time for this.

"Yes, for you." Noting my surprise, Beth pushed me toward the table. "Come on. We ordered for you already."

I crossed the short distance, past the handwritten signs advertising new specials taped along the counter and toward the aroma of fried Thai basil. Some catchy Post Malone song was playing overhead. It sounded upbeat, but it was probably sad. A waitress dropped off our drinks as I took the seat across from Jesse and next to Beth. Rebecca distributed drinks to their rightful owners.

Matcha milk tea, no boba, half sweet for Beth.

Hokkaido milk tea with boba, 0 percent sweet (a crime against humanity), for Jesse.

Peach green mango iced tea, bright orange gems of mango jelly, 25 percent sweet, for Rebecca.

"Here." She pushed a tall cup of milk tea, topped with egg pudding, to me. "One hundred percent sweet, just the way you like it."

"Let's get this over with," I said, taking a delicious sip. I was going to need all the sugar for what was to come.

"Fine," Rebecca said, giving her drink a quick shake. "I think we should start with the elephant in the room." She removed her sunglasses and set her big brown eyes on me. "Elise. I'm sorry."

I blinked as I processed Rebecca's words. She rarely apologized for anything. "For what?"

"The scandal. I got so sucked into the whirlwind of PR and reading articles about myself that I didn't stop to think about how you were doing. I didn't think you'd take any heat from all of this."

Ben must have told her. I wasn't sure how I felt about them talking about me in my absence. "It's okay—"

"No, it's not," Rebecca insisted. "I've seen scandals play out before and I should have been there for you."

"Thanks," I said, suddenly aware we were having this conversation out in public. "We could have done this over the phone."

"No," Rebecca said. "Ben watched me like a hawk every time I reached for my phone." She stabbed her skewer into a slice of garlic and sausage. "I couldn't even ask Beth a question without Ben looking over my shoulder. He's so paranoid that texts can be taken out of context."

"That's the other thing," Beth said. "You and Ben—"

She shot out our names together like an arrow aimed right at me.

"You don't have to worry about a thing," I said preemptively. "Ben and I can be cordial for a few hours at your wedding." We'd done it before and we could do it again.

"Oh." Beth looked unsure for a moment. I'd assumed news about our fight had traveled through the group. I'd thought there were no such things as secrets among us but maybe I was wrong. "Actually, I came to say that I want you to be there for rehearsal and to get ready with us in the morning. Is there any way you can do that?"

This was a normal request for a bridesmaid, but as her florist, I couldn't give up that precious time. How were the flowers going to get set up without me? "No. I can't."

Beth had stopped swirling the straw in her drink, now that the previously separated green and white layers combined into a swampy color. "Why not? You did Jesse's flowers the night before."

"That was different," I said. "Her ceremony was in the morning and my studio is close by. If I cut your flowers too early in this heat, they're not going to look as fresh by Saturday—"

"No offense, E, but I don't really care that much about the flowers," Beth blurted. She might as well have poured Roundup on my heart. "I let you design the flowers the way you wanted because I felt bad for asking you last minute. I thought it would make things easier for you. I never expected you to do so much. Don't get me wrong—your design is beautiful—but I would rather have you there as my maid of honor than my florist."

"I—" I sighed. I couldn't really argue with that. Beth was right. I knew Beth would have been happy with something simple, but I made it more elaborate so I could have nice pictures for *Wedding Style*. Entering the *Wedding Style* contest had muddled my priorities. I thought I could have my cake and eat it too. "I wish I could, but it's too late to find someone on short notice."

"What about your old assistant? Sarah?" Beth asked.

"I'd have to ask." I wiped the condensation off my cup with my fingers, leaving a puddle of water on the table. "But you would have to pay her."

"I would've paid more anyway if I hired a florist that didn't give me a best friend discount," Beth reasoned. This made sense, but it was not what we'd discussed. It defeated the purpose of helping her save money. I felt awful. She sensed that I was not satisfied with that answer and added, "I can ask my parents to chip in a little."

Rebecca gave me the auntie palm-down, "come here" gesture.

I was so busy feeling guilty that I unwittingly gave Rebecca my phone. She made me type my passcode and called Sarah. When I realized what I'd done, I tried to intercept it, but then Jesse fired off another question, distracting me.

"Does Sarah need helpers?" she asked. "Because I don't know if you know this, Elise, but I know some people. People with muscles."

"That's nice, but—"

"But what?" Beth asked. "What do you need, Elise? Whatever it is, I'm open. I just want you there."

Why was this becoming about me? "I—"

"Sarah said she's free Saturday morning to lead the setup," Rebecca announced with one hand covering the receiver as she continued to listen. "She said she can follow Elise's plan, no problem. As long as she can leave by one to get to another wedding."

I opened my mouth, but I was speechless. Things were happening too fast.

"Beth." I gave her one last chance to think this through. "I know I can finish the job in between events. I'll head over early tomorrow morning."

"Elise . . ." Beth hesitated but her eyes pleaded with me. "I need you there just as my maid of honor. The three of you are so important to me," she said, addressing the entire group. "And I want one last night with you guys before I get married." She clasped her hands over mine. "Does that sound dumb?"

"No." I squeezed Beth's hands in reply. It sounded really nice.

"Good," Beth replied, giving me her sweet angel eyes. "Because you're fired."

Never mind. Beth wasn't nice at all. I tried to free my hand but Beth wouldn't let go. "You have to let me do your bouquet." And the crowns. And the centerpieces.

"Just the bouquets," Beth said with her mouth and *Cut the crap* with her eyes.

"Fine." This was the worst intervention ever. I'd got called out and fired in one sitting. Beth went over the schedule with us, making sure we were ready to carpool early on Friday to avoid traffic on the way to Granada Ranch. The gang was on board, but all I could think about was my crunch time being cut in half. Our boba intervention turned into lunch when Jesse ordered wonton noodle soup. Then everyone else had to order their own plate. When the food arrived, we fell back into old habits, and started gossiping about people we used to know.

Rebecca alternated between our conversation, eating her minced pork and egg rice bowl, and checking her phone. She kept a cool expression, but the image of her bore a striking similarity to when she was the main character in the college debate scandal from ten years ago.

"How are you holding up?" I said. I hadn't kept up with the news, so I wasn't sure how the scandal had progressed in the last twenty-four hours.

"It is what it is." Instead of elaborating, Rebecca asked, "Why didn't you tell us that you might have to close the studio?"

What did she want me to say? Nobody liked to fess up to their own failings. "I was hoping I wouldn't have to."

"That's not an excuse," Rebecca said.

Beth was gentler in her response. "We would have helped," she offered, though I wouldn't know how they could have. "We would have paid you more. You know what? Write me a new invoice without the discount."

I grimaced. It felt gross to boil this down to dollar signs. This was why friends and money shouldn't mix. "No, it's fine. I was happy to do all of your weddings. It's fine," I insisted.

"Stop saying that when it's not true," Rebecca said. "It doesn't help you or us." Her cool face cracked and her eyes were sad. "If you don't want us to help you, then that's your call, but don't put us in a position where we're unknowingly making it worse." My stomach sunk. I hadn't thought about it that way. All along, I thought I could do everything myself—the work, the burden, the stress—without affecting them, but I was wrong. "We would have been there for you, even if it was just moral support."

My head dipped toward my empty bowl of beef noodle soup. I didn't know why it was so hard for me to ask for help when I knew they wouldn't think twice about it. That was what we did for each other since the beginning of our friendship. Why was it so hard now? I glanced up, saw my three best friends, and I knew.

I thought when all my friends got married and continued to soar in their lives, taking them far away from me, that I would at least have my studio. That if I didn't have my studio, then I wouldn't have anything. As I looked around the table, cornered by the three people who'd voluntarily stuck with me for the last ten years, I realized it was a stupid thing to believe. They would sooner kidnap me than let me run away.

"I'm sorry," I said. "I won't hide that kind of stuff from you guys anymore."

Jesse tapped her fist against her chest, exhaling a labored breath. "I think I ate too fast." Rebecca shot her a nasty look for interrupting the mood, but Jesse redeemed herself when she offered some tangible help by suggesting her gym's business advisor to look over my business plan. "He's good. He'll tell you what to do to turn things around."

I liked how Jesse talked about her business advisor as if I didn't know it was Steven. He reviewed many business plans in his work, so I should let him look at my books. I was scared to send Steven my sad Excel sheet, but I had to let go of my pride. It wasn't helping me anymore.

We split the check four ways. Beth was hesitant to drive me back to my studio. I had to promise her that I wouldn't overwork myself, but there were still things I had to do to make this easy for Sarah to take over.

"What else do you need to do?"

Everything. Beth arched her eyebrow like she knew what I was thinking.

"You gotta let me do the bouquets," I pleaded when she took a wrong turn. "And the crowns! Those have to come from me." My vision for Beth's personal flowers had been in my mind for months. I had to be the one who made them.

Beth turned the car around at the next traffic light, relenting. "Okay, but you have to promise me that's the last thing you'll do."

"Okay." I did a quick mental calculation. I had enough time to make as many centerpieces as I could, giving Sarah a head start, and then do personals last. I must have agreed too fast because Beth gave me a wary look. So, I reassured her again. "After those, I swear. I'll be done."

"You promise?"

I gave her my word.

Chapter Twenty-Eight

*B*eth always thought the phrase "best-laid plans" meant that it was good to have things planned out to a T. Her itinerary for her wedding weekend included ten-minute breaks for chatting, using the restroom, and buffer time in case things ran late. To date, this was how she'd managed the major events in her life. She graduated high school and college on time. She always hoped she would marry someone before turning thirty, which she would accomplish two years early. But nothing prepared her for the sheer clusterfuck that was the day before the wedding.

> **BETH:** My dry cleaner lost my dress!

> **REBECCA:** wtf. Do you want me to make a call?

> **BETH:** No. They're searching. I'm hoping it will turn up

> **JESSE:** Finished loading stuff into Elise's truck

> **JESSE:** What is this donut wall thing?

> **BETH:** Omg! Who's picking up the donuts?

REBECCA: Calm down. One of the guys will. It's on the itinerary

ELISE: Shit. Sorry catching up

BETH: Tell me all of you packed your dresses

REBECCA: Check!

ELISE: Yes

JESSE: Uh . . . I have to go home real quick

BETH: OMG! Now my parents want to do a small tea ceremony at the ranch

BETH: Where can I find teacups? Do they have special wedding teacups or something?

JESSE: You can borrow mine!

ELISE: And I have tea!

BETH: 😭😭😭

ELISE: It will be okay! Hang in there!

Each of us scrambled to get things done. I had to drop off the keys to my studio and truck for Sarah. Jesse had to pack . . . well . . . everything. Rebecca went to Beth's aid, taking over her phone calls so Beth wouldn't implode from the sudden pressure of the big day. In the end, we gave up on trying to leave early. The sky was dark when we arrived at Granada Ranch. The only lights on were the ones from the house.

"I'm sorry we made you wait," Beth said when Esmeralda greeted us at the door.

"Don't be," Esmeralda replied. "The guys were here earlier to set up the lights outside."

"I didn't see them here," I said, scanning the room, hoping it wasn't too obvious that I was looking for one particular guy.

"They left for dinner," Esmeralda said, turning over her watch. "A late dinner. I'll let you get settled and I'll be out of your hair. I'll be back in the morning to oversee the space and take care of anything that may arise."

"How much do you want to bet that the guys are out drinking?" Rebecca said as we climbed the stairs. Given that Mark was involved, her question was a rhetorical one.

We took two rooms upstairs, but congregated in the honeymoon suite in our finest pajamas for our girls' night in. Knowing that the nearest store was a fifteen-minute drive down the hill, we'd each brought our own snacks and drinks. Rebecca was the only one who brought champagne and had no problem breaking into it.

"What?" she asked when we all rolled our eyes. "It's a wedding. There has to be champagne." Nobody brought glasses, though, so we had our Moët in red Solo cups. After a quick toast, Rebecca dug out what appeared to be a black shoebox from her suitcase. "I brought something else."

"A vibrator?" Jesse asked.

"Really, Jess?" I said.

"What? Beth didn't have a bridal shower and that's when you get these types of things."

"What kind of bridal showers do you go to?" Beth asked.

"You guys are boring," Jesse said. "Who needs a blender when you can have orgasms?"

"Okay, you guys are ruining this," Rebecca said. She shushed us and unveiled her real gift. A brand-new, rose-gold wireless karaoke microphone.

Rebecca connected it to her phone and wasted no time in kicking things off with her rendition of "Diamonds" by Rihanna. Jesse went with her karaoke standby, "Wrecking Ball," which wouldn't be complete without licking the microphone. Another round of drinks came by—Rebecca's infamous pink drink.

Beth used an antibacterial wipe to rid Jesse's germs from the microphone before choosing the next song. "This next song," her tipsy voice echoing, "is dedicated to my maid of honor, Elise."

I loved Beth, but she couldn't sing on-key if her life depended on it. "Why are you singing me 'Call Me Maybe'? I call you all the time." I picked up a cookie from our pile of snacks in the middle of the bed but thought better of it. I couldn't trust cookies these days.

Jesse plopped down next to me. "I think she's trying to send you a subliminal message."

"And what's that?" I asked. "Call me maybe" was pretty overt messaging to me.

Jesse slipped out a folded sheet of paper from inside her shirt somewhere. The paper was warm when she handed it to me and I didn't ask why. I didn't need to know. "Here, E. Finally, one for you."

"What is this?" I unfolded it to find a picture of Ben at Jesse's wedding cropped in the top right corner. Beneath his photo was Jesse's assessment on the Boyfriend Test. She approved Ben on the grounds of "following you around my wedding like a simp." She added two points for Ben because "he annoys Rebecca and that's fun to watch." Before I could analyze the meaning of all of this, Beth tossed in her final verdict of Ben. I already knew he was approved before looking at it, but her notes were inconceivably less mature. "Please kiss and make up already."

"You guys . . . " My eyes snagged on the picture Beth had used. Ben was in his chef's jacket and damn if he didn't look good in it. I had to stop myself from staring at it before I forgot why I was mad at him. He was the one who wanted to keep a low profile and he was sticking to it. I hadn't seen Ben in three days and he only texted through the wedding party group chat. "I don't know what you've heard, but *he* was the one who decided to take a break." I threw the Boyfriend Test aside and ignored everyone's intervention mode. I held my hand out for the microphone. "Let's get back to our girls' night in."

"What do you think we're doing?" Jesse said. "You know gossip is part of the schedule and the hottest goss around town is you."

"You need to get out more." I fixed my attention on my Korean face mask, praying for a little privacy now and glass skin tomorrow.

Jesse ignored my sarcasm. "Give us a break. You hid this relationship from us and you expect us to forget about it. Tell us everything!" she demanded. "Don't skip any details."

"What do you want me to say?"

Beth turned down the music. "For starters, was it love at first sight?"

"Of course not. He was so rude." But, knowing what I knew now about Ben, I could see he'd been uncomfortable. The big crowd of strangers, having to put on a smile he didn't mean. I didn't blame Ben for being anxious.

"So when did you know that there was something there?"

"Um . . . " I bit down my smile. They told me not to skip any details, so I said, "When we were stuck here . . . in this room together."

Jesse's jaw dropped. "Did you guys do it in this bed?"

"Ew!" Rebecca shot up from the bed and shook imaginary cooties off her clothes. "I didn't need to know!" This was what they deserved for being so nosy.

"Nothing happened!" Not in the way they were thinking, at least. "I don't know how to explain it. Something just changed after that weekend. I saw him differently." I confirmed that we kissed at Jesse's wedding since the entire Lo family knew about it already and outlined parts of our whirlwind summer. I watched Rebecca's face carefully as I shared information. She held a neutral expression but I sensed the cringe. I kept the details to a minimum. Ben probably would have preferred it that way too. "I'm sorry I didn't tell you guys earlier."

"Did you really think you could hide it from us when you sucked face at my wedding?" Jesse so eloquently countered. I shot her a dirty look but it bounced right off her.

"And where are things now between you two?" Rebecca asked.

"I think you know already."

"I want to hear it from you."

This wasn't Rebecca wanting to hear both sides. She was putting me in the hot seat. What was I supposed to say? I hated how the last conversation between Ben and me had gone down. It was the worst versions of ourselves coming head-to-head and in the end, there were no winners. In the days since, I'd wondered if it wouldn't have hurt so much if I hadn't trusted him to take care of my heart as if it were his own. That was my mistake to bear.

"We're . . ." I shrugged. ". . . on hold."

"Until when?" Rebecca inquired. "You're going to see each other tomorrow." I swallowed at the thought.

"We'll manage." Ben was good at hiding his feelings and so was I.

"Do you want to get back together?"

"I don't think that's up to me," I said. Ben had made his priorities clear.

"I think it is."

Rebecca handed me her phone and a video from @angelcitymag began to play. It was Ben, holding a press conference. In the background was my studio.

My heart was pounding. I sat up from the bed. "Why is Ben standing in the parking lot?"

"Believe me. Politicians have had press conferences in worse places." Rebecca shushed me. "Listen to the video."

I replayed the video to start from the beginning and increased the volume.

"Thank you all for coming on short notice." Ben took an audible, shaky breath before he proceeded to thank members of the press from behind a podium. A flurry of camera flashes stunned him momentarily until he lowered his eyes to the sea of microphones in front of him. "I'll keep this brief. My name is Benjamin Yu. Over the last few days, my mother, Assemblywoman Donna Yu, has faced unfounded claims regarding her fundraising. I want to be clear that all fundraising activities were in line with California laws and we are cooperating with the third-party investigation to confirm this fact. However, I am here before you because one claim that came to light was an alleged romantic relationship between myself and a vendor for our campaign. That part is true." Murmurs swelled from the audience. "Despite no wrongdoing from either party, I believe it's best to resign from the campaign to refocus on what really matters."

Ben was then replaced by Emilio, who transitioned into a campaign spiel. "Donna Yu remains a steadfast advocate for the communities in District 49 and . . ."

I paused the video. "Why did Ben resign?"

"Why do you think?"

"He didn't want to work on the campaign anymore?" I guessed.

Rebecca cut me a look to stop the shit, like I couldn't be that dense. "This was the compromise we came to. We put out a statement and he resigned to minimize the connection between your relationship and the scandal. It puts the focus squarely on the finances."

That didn't make any sense. "Then why is this announcement made in front of my studio?"

"Ben said something about getting you exposure." I'd heard the saying that bad press is good press, but it didn't feel that way. "I told him to run this by you," Rebecca continued, "but unfortunately, we were working on limited time. We had to make quick decisions."

"When did this happen?" I went over the last few days. I'd gone to my studio early, even beating the old ladies who ran the Taiwanese breakfast joint next door, and left as late as I could before my friends badgered me out. The only time left was . . . "Are you serious? Is that why we had an intervention?"

"No, we had an intervention because you were being a butt," Jesse said. "And then we had lunch because we were hungry. It just so happened a news crew stormed your studio that same day." I couldn't believe they coordinated this together.

"Fine. I admit it. I was being a butt. I lied. I hid this thing with Ben. But what now? What good did this do? He hasn't tried to reach out once." Beth gave me those moony eyes and I already knew what she was thinking. "No. Don't tell me to be patient with him. I've been patient with him."

"He had to wait," Rebecca said. "We weren't sure if this would work unless we gave it some time. If the press caught the two of you together, it would have been all for nothing. And look." Rebecca pointed at the bottom of the screen. The video had amassed ten thousand views in the last few days. People loved a good scandal, didn't they?

I didn't know what to think anymore. "Since when were you on his side?"

Rebecca let her cool façade melt away. "It took a lot for Ben to stand up there and resign in front of everyone. For once, he tackled a problem head-on and it was all because of you."

I didn't think I deserved that much credit, but my optimism flickered. If what Rebecca said was even partly true, then shouldn't I give Ben a second chance? I tried to replay our last conversation again. I couldn't remember it word for word, but I recalled his sense of urgency. He'd wanted me to give him time, but I was so upset, I didn't. He wanted us to figure this out together, but I wouldn't listen. Now he'd gone and resigned for the world to see, knowing he couldn't take it back. It's not what I would have wanted for him, but this was him trying. I should've tried for him too.

I peeled off my mask, crumpling it in my hand. I climbed out of bed to throw it away and glanced out the window on my way back to bed. The lights below were on, but there was no sign of the guys. Whatever I had to say would have to wait until tomorrow.

The big day.

Chapter Twenty-Nine

You are cordially invited to the wedding celebration of
Beth Chan
and
Ethan Scott
Granada Ranch
Saturday, August 5th
Four o'clock in the afternoon
Reception to follow

It was ten-fifteen and no one was awake. It was so quiet, I heard the grass rustling outside. When Sarah drove up in my truck, you would have thought the earth was shaking. I put on my tank top and jeans and sneaked downstairs.

Sarah rolled up to the rear door and appeared before me in all black like a goth witch. She was a welcome sight. She jumped down and gave me a hug. "You're not supposed to be here." I wasn't scared of my friends. Our pre-party had lasted until two A.M. and they were sleeping like logs.

"Good to see you too," I said. "Thanks for coming." I wouldn't have handed over this wedding to anyone else. Sarah had been my assistant for over a year before I let her go, so I was confident that she could execute the vision. She was a great designer and she could decipher my messy notes. "Did you have any trouble getting here?"

Sarah climbed back up to the truck and slid my tool bag across the trailer. "How could I? You marked everything that needed to be transported and texted detailed directions like I don't know how to use Google Maps." She carried a bucket of roses over to me and knelt by the edge of the door. "One day, you'll learn to delegate."

"One day," I said, but not today. I was working on borrowed time. Wedding day adrenaline kicked in and at any moment, I could possibly run into a man who'd ghosted me and grand-gestured me within a matter of days. To say I was on edge was an understatement.

My fingers itched for flowers. I kept my word and only worked on the crowns and bouquets. I dotted Beth's mostly white arrangement with peach and pink blooms, interspersing greenery in the mix. Every so often, I looked around, waiting for Ben to pop out of nowhere to buzz around me like a bee, asking me what I was doing there. He never came. I was starting the last flower crown when I received my first warning text from Rebecca.

REBECCA: Where are you?

I hid behind the truck bed to avoid being seen. Ten minutes later, my phone pinged with another text.

JESSE: Get your ass in here

JESSE: Rebecca is attacking me with a curling iron

I twirled floral tape around as fast as I could. Why were they rushing me? They were the ones who woke up late.

BETH: Put the flowers down

BETH: We have a wedding emergency

I ignored it. I fell for that once. I wasn't going to fall for it again.

BETH: My parents are lost

Okay, never mind. That was a real problem. I dropped everything I was doing. I packed the crowns to take with me, praying that it would help everyone stop and smell the roses (figuratively and literally). I said goodbye to Sarah and reminded her to text me if she needed help.

"You're not my boss anymore," she said, half joking.

I would have laughed if it didn't sting a little. I missed having Sarah around the studio. "Can I call you if I book more jobs?" I checked my phone. There were some rude DMs, which I immediately swiped away, but there were some encouraging ones too, inquiring about my availability for weddings next year. Some of them had to be legit. "I need all the help I can get."

"I noticed." Sarah smirked as she unloaded the ladder. "If you get more jobs, then yeah. Call me."

Slowly but surely, Elise Ngo Floral Design was coming back to life.

BETH LOOKED LIKE she was about to cry when I walked into the bedroom.

"Elise." Her eyes twitched. "My parents were stuck in traffic, so they took the next exit and now they're lost." Beth threw her hands to the sky. "I reminded them to leave the house early. You'd think they would apprehend the importance of being on time to their daughter's wedding."

Comprehend was on the tip of my tongue but I held it back. It was not the time to correct her. "Let me talk to them on the phone."

Rebecca stepped in. "I'll do it. You need to get ready."

The team spirit was alive for a second until I jumped in the shower.

Rebecca groaned. "Not again!"

"I'm sorry!" I shouted as I lathered furiously. "Don't worry! I can get ready fast!"

These were the fibs I had to tell to keep everyone happy before showtime. I never had moral qualms about these little white lies because we weren't the only ones behind schedule. When Esmeralda stopped by to check in, she alerted us that the groomsmen were, as expected, hungover and dealing with their own "fashion emergency."

"Everything's fine," Esmeralda said, but then she added, "It will be fine." Meaning, whatever the issue was, it hadn't been fixed yet.

Beth began to fret like it was exam day. I held her hand while brushing my hair with the other. She couldn't disappear today, of all days. "Trust the process. Everything will come together and no one will know all this shit was going on behind the scenes. Your only job today is to smile and have fun, okay?" I offered her my mug of chamomile tea.

"None of this mushy business," Jesse interjected. It was hard to take Jesse seriously most days, but even more so when she was glam from the neck up but looked like she was about to run the Ironman from the neck down. Jesse poured Beth a stronger beverage. "Drink this and relax."

I finished getting ready while Rebecca stayed on the phone with Beth's parents. Despite wearing different colors, we matched somewhat. I had my lilac wrap dress. Jesse wore a powder-blue tea-length ruffly frock and Rebecca had donned a silver, red-carpet-worthy, one-shoulder gown that she toned down with simple, sleek hair and dainty accessories. Beth's parents eventually arrived at three-fifteen, giving them enough time for a quick tea ceremony.

To keep things moving, Beth let Ethan pick her up without door games or acts of chivalry. We let him into the room and he greeted his bride with a hug and a kiss.

"You're not supposed to kiss the bride until you're husband and wife," I said.

"I hate to break it to you, but we live together. We've done a lot of premarital kissing," Ethan said, dipping her for another smooch. It was like a scene out of a classic movie, with Ethan in his dove-gray tuxedo and black lapels and Beth floating in her gauzy vintage dress.

When it was time, Esmeralda led us to the venue. I picked up my dress as we trekked down the dirt path. My stomach was full of knots. I hadn't seen Ben all morning and suddenly there he was, in his dark suit talking to Steven. They turned as the bridal party approached them and when Ben's eyes locked on mine, I couldn't turn away. With each step, I held on to the anticipation buzzing between us. I took some solace watching Ben as he fiddled with his cuff links and readjusted his tie. He was nervous too.

He helped Rebecca step over a muddy patch. Both of them exchanged a grateful glance before she joined hands with Mark. Jesse followed behind, giving Ben a big slap on the shoulder as she passed by him for Steven. Then, it was my turn.

"There you are," he said with a voice as light as a feather. We coupled up for the processional. He handed me my bouquet and I swear I didn't feel my feet touch the ground. Good thing there was a soon-to-be doctor in the house.

"Here I am." The words came out shaky and lacked the same warmth as his. The light in Ben's eyes dimmed and I wanted to kick myself. I pulled myself together as we took our places in front of Beth, toward the end of the line. The processional music began to play and I put my maid of honor face on. I kept my eyes forward and weaved my arm into the crook of Ben's, finding comfort in how easily we fit together.

We waited for our turn to enter the indoor pen, now transformed into a wedding chapel. Ben ducked his head and whispered, "Can I say you look beautiful?"

My eyes caught on his lavender tie. It wasn't the same shade as my dress, but close enough. "You just did." Ben's lips twisted at my cheeky reply, so I added, "Thank you."

"Can we meet later?" His Adam's apple bobbed. "By the deck? After the ceremony?"

"We have to take pictures," I reminded him.

"After then. Before the reception?"

I nodded, confirming our plans, right before we stepped inside.

We followed the path of petals and candles to the end of the dance floor, where Ethan and an officiant waited. Sunlight streaked into the venue, dappling everything in gold. The flowers were gorgeous, if I could say so myself. Sarah had executed my vision perfectly. It was like walking into a fairy tale.

I waited until the last second to let go of Ben to take my place. If anyone had asked, I would swear on my grave that I poured every ounce of attention on my best friend getting married to the love of her life. I kept my eyes on Beth and Ethan. Ethan and Beth. But Ben lingered in my periphery. I felt his eyes on me as the officiant blathered on and on about love being patient and love being kind and every kind of cliché. I wanted to tell him to get on with it. I had a date with the best man.

If the wedding gods were listening today, they weren't listening to me. After the officiant pronounced Ethan and Beth as husband and wife, the photographer made us go out into the fields to take a million pictures. Beth was adamant about having this wedding run on time, that we go straight from pictures to the reception, where Ben and I were seated side by side at the head table with the rest of the wedding party. We were once again surrounded by people.

Ben and I ate our tacos silently as we faced out toward the guests. We were back to playing a game of emotional chicken. To bide the time, I took a closer look at the flowers and the venue, cross-checking against the plan I gave Sarah. The ceiling installation wasn't as full as I would have liked. The donut wall was missing. They were minor details that I knew were different, but guests wouldn't have noticed.

Ben followed my line of sight. "I'm sorry. I couldn't pick up the donuts."

I wasn't the one he should apologize to. It wasn't my wedding. "It's okay. There was so much to do before the wedding." Something was bound to slip through the cracks.

"It was a conflict of interest," he said, scooting closer so he could whisper. "Jas, from *Angel City Magazine*?" He asked like it would ring a bell, but my mind was thinking about how our thighs were pressed together. "She reached out to me for an interview about the campaign and she mentioned in her email that she knew you. She forwarded me the email you'd sent her about featuring your studio and explained how you ordered donuts from her parents' shop. I knew she would be sympathetic and that's when Rebecca and I compromised on putting a message out."

Okay. So we were going to have our conversation here, among our closest friends. Cool cool cool. "Did you have to film it in front of my studio, though?"

"That was Jas's idea. Something about the algorithm and that any mention of your studio would bring related links about you, like your social media. That way, you'd get more views." Ben watched my face. "Wasn't that what you wanted?"

"No." This wasn't about good intentions or grand gestures. I didn't want Ben to do something he hated for me. I needed him to fulfill his original promise. That we'd figure things out together.

Ben slunk into his seat, putting more distance between us, and I found myself wishing that I weren't at a wedding for the first time in my life. It was hard to have a serious conversation when I overheard a request for "Cha Cha Slide." I was about to ask Ben to step outside with me, but then someone clinked their glass. Without an official emcee, Mark took it upon himself to make announcements. "Ladies and gentlemen and fine folks. May I have your attention?" Guests hushed. "It's time for toasts from our best man, Ben Yu, and maid of honor, Elise Ngo."

Perfect timing. Just perfect. If I believed in fate, I would think the universe was thwarting us at every turn or worse, it was trying to torture me into patience.

Ben stood to mild applause, withdrawing an index card from his jacket as Mark handed him a familiar rose-gold microphone. "Hello. I'm Ben Yu. Some of you may know me as Tom." Someone from the crowd yelled, "Yeah buddy!" Ben took a pregnant pause, which made me wonder if he'd lost his place. But then I saw his hand trembling. The interruption seemed to have made him ultra-aware that people were watching him. His eyes darted between his index card and the audience. A sheen of sweat broke out on his forehead. I had to do something before he completely shut down.

I reached up and rested my hand on his tense forearm. We exchanged glances.

It's okay. I'm here.

I wasn't sure if he got the message, but he nodded anyway. His body relaxed and he took a deep breath as he faced the crowd once again. "I'm honored to be up here as Ethan's best man. If I'm being honest, I'm surprised I'm up here. There are many people in this room who could've been standing right here giving this speech. Ethan has that special ability to befriend people the second you meet him. I've never told him this before, but I was leery of people like him. But then, I got to know him." Ben recounted the story about how Ethan saved him in the kitchen. "I knew then that he was the real deal. The first time Ethan greeted me with a 'Boss Man,' I was done for. I may have fallen for him that day."

"The feeling is mutual, Boss Man!" Ethan shouted.

Ben put a hand on his heart. "I shared that story not because it's unique. Anyone who has worked with Ethan has a story like that. He readily shares his passion for cookery and food. He is a rare mentor and friend in this business." Ben turned to face Beth, who was a couple seats over. "If everyone can raise their glasses, I want to toast to Ethan and Beth. I cannot think of two more wonderful people and I wish the both of you many happy years ahead. Cheers."

Ethan stood and clapped a hug around Ben.

Then it was my turn. Ben gave me the microphone. I took one look at the sad bullet points I'd saved in my notes app and decided to wing it. This could go badly, but I was full of emotion. If there ever was a time to speak from the heart, wouldn't it be here, where we had gathered to celebrate love?

I stood, tilting the microphone until the feedback disappeared. "Um, hello. My name is Elise and I'm the maid of honor." Jesse and Rebecca wooed. They were the best cheerleaders. "Unlike Ben, I know why I'm here. I met Beth in college. We were roommates. Thank you, Pepperdine Student Housing." The audience laughed, giving me a confidence boost. "Isn't it funny how life works that way sometimes? It was pure luck that we were paired together, like we were two names pulled from a hat. And every day since, I've been so thankful because I can't imagine my life before her." I turned to Beth and listed all the wonderful things about her. "Beth has the biggest heart and she's hella smart. She always wants the best for others. When I dropped out of school and decided to open my own floral studio, Beth was the first person I told. She was and still is my biggest supporter. And I must say, I've been to a lot of weddings. I used to think finding our person and getting married was the pinnacle of love and devotion, but there's something to be said about the kind of friends that choose you and love you as you are. Beth has seen me at my best and gives me the benefit of the doubt when I'm at my worst. She showed me that was what we did for people we loved."

I felt Ben watching me and like a magnet, my eyes slid until they fixed on his. I cleared my throat to get back on track. This was not about him. Not right now. I refocused on Beth. "I'm starting to think I should have married her." Guests laughed and I fanned the flames when I blew her a kiss. "But no. It is Ethan who won Beth's heart. I remember the day she called, gushing over the best first date she ever had. She made me believe in dating apps for a week before I quit again."

I chuckled. "So, I think I'm supposed to end this with some marriage advice. I've never been married so there's no reason that you should listen to me. But as Beth's best friend, I should warn you, Ethan, that unfortunately, Beth is usually right. We've established that she's the smart one, but that isn't true one hundred percent of the time. Once she almost set our dorm room on fire when she microwaved mac and cheese that was covered in foil. So, my only advice is to keep Beth away from the kitchen, but I think you've got that covered."

Beth threw her arms around me and, miraculously, there were no tears. Just joy shared between two friends. We raised our glasses to another toast and with that, it sunk in that the last of my friends was married.

It was the end of an era and the start of a new one.

Chapter Thirty

I loved Beth, but I was tired of smiling. How many more pictures of the bridal party did we need?

"One more!" the photographer shouted from behind his lens.

"Thank god." I needed a break. The flash had me seeing stars. "I'm going to get some air."

"Don't forget," Beth called after me. "Cake cutting is next."

"I wouldn't miss it." I picked up a Corona from the bar and strolled outside into the garden, taking leisurely swigs. The sun hadn't fully surrendered to the night yet, but it was dark enough for the solar pathway lights to glow. I stole a moment to browse through my notifications. There were more rude DMs that I immediately swiped away, but there were more client inquiries coming in too. I didn't know how serious they were, but it was better than nothing. I turned off my phone. It could wait until tomorrow.

I was about to turn back when a shadowy figure approached. I knew that slightly hunched, hands-in-the-pockets stride anywhere.

"Are you supposed to be here?" I asked Ben.

"How the tables have turned." His lips tipped into a half smile. "May I join you?"

"I guess. We were supposed to meet earlier," I reminded him, "before the wedding got in the way."

"Remind me why you like weddings again."

It was hard to remember when I finally had Ben to myself. "What did you want to tell me?" I was feeling bold. I'd waited long enough. "There's no one around to hear except me."

"That's even worse."

A breeze ushered in the desert chill. I crossed my arms, trying to stay warm. "Why?"

"Because," Ben put his jacket around my shoulders, "out of all the people here, it's your opinion I fear the most. I've been selfish. I should've consulted with you when the scandal broke. I see now how my actions hurt you. For that, I'm truly sorry."

"Oh." His apology was good, but it sounded like someone on the PR team wrote it for him. "Thanks."

"Wait. I'm not done." Ben inched closer as he slid his hands over my arms, one landing on my dandelion tattoo. "I wish I could be more like you. Generous and kind and fearless. In these last few months, you've showed me that I could be a better version of myself. If you'd give me a chance, I want to be that person for you every day."

That sounded almost perfect to me, but I needed him to give me something more.

"Promise me something?" Worry lines set up camp in between Ben's eyebrows. I smoothed them away with my thumb. "Promise me that as long as we're together, we'll be a team."

"Okay, MVP." Ben reeled me in for a kiss when a loud voice startled him.

"E! Time for cake!" Jesse was nowhere to be seen, but her striking voice made her sound closer than she was.

"I changed my mind. I hate weddings." There. I said it. "People should elope more."

Ben chuckled but choked on it when I jumped up and pressed

my lips to his. I was too eager, but then, Ben didn't seem to mind. Our bodies intertwined as he coaxed my lips open for a deeper kiss, making a sound that was like a sigh. Relief.

"Fai di la!" Jesse's voice echoed across the canyon.

I groaned as I peeled myself off Ben. Who thought it was a good idea to give Jesse a microphone? "Let's stop meeting like this. Can we go somewhere later? Far, far away from here?"

"Yes, please." Ben kissed my forehead before taking my hand. "Come on. We should head back."

We returned to the reception and I could tell immediately that something wasn't right. The cake was untouched and Ethan was speaking to a murmuring crowd. The seats at the head table were empty. I looked for Beth and found her pointing at me from a seat at the edge of the dance floor.

"Ah, finally. Our maid of honor is back," Ethan announced. "Elise, if I can have you next to Rebecca, we can get started."

"What's going on?" I asked Ben, as he escorted me to my seat.

Ben took my beer and gulped it down. He winced as he returned the bottle to me. "For the record, I suggested Backstreet Boys, but Ethan said it wasn't his style."

"What?" I asked, but music swelled over the crowd.

"If you know Beth, you know that she loves to sing. This one is for her." Ethan sang the opening bars to Frankie Valli's "Can't Take My Eyes Off You" directly to his bride. My eyes went directly to another man who was bouncing into his dance steps with the other groomsmen like they were backup singers for a Motown group. Ben shook his head at me like he hated it but his face broke into a smile when Mark twirled into him, dancing all up on Ben like he was Patrick Swayze. Mark, the ham that he was, then galloped away Gangnam Style, befitting of our arena. The whole groomsmen dance was a train wreck, but

Ethan wasn't concerned about anything happening behind him. He only had eyes for Beth.

Halfway through the song, each of our men stopped their so-called choreography and invited us up to the dance floor. I rested my hands at the nape of Ben's neck and tried to keep up with the song.

"When? How?" I shouted over the upbeat verse.

"YouTube videos," Ben said as he put a little more oomph into his side steps. "We snuck in a practice here and there. It was hard to keep it a secret. I almost blurted it out the day you were at Beth's apartment. Then Steven ripped his pants when we had a dress rehearsal this morning."

I spotted Steven on the other side of the dance floor and the poor stitchwork along his thigh. "Oh my god. Are those staples?"

Ben's arm tightened around my waist. "Sorry we were late this morning."

"I forgive you." It was worth it. I rested my head on his shoulder. "I can't believe you did this."

"Love makes you do foolish things sometimes."

Love? The word reverberated to the beat of my heart. "Is that the beer talking?"

"No." Ben kept slow dancing, even as the song ended and a new one began. I didn't care. Ben's eyes shined, like he had found what he'd been searching for. Everything else faded away and all I heard were the words coming out of Ben's mouth. "I love you, Elise."

Whenever I'd imagined my dream wedding, I thought of a night like this. Me, in my finest dress, surrounded by my closest friends. The only thing missing was the kind of imperfect man who was perfect for me. Here he was, standing in front of me the whole time.

"I love you too, Ben."

I'd changed my mind. I fucking loved weddings.

Epilogue

"Let's stop for a second."

Sarah and I paused to regroup. We were in Newport Beach setting up for a sunset wedding. It was going to be beautiful, if we could keep the gold hexagon "arch" our couple requested from sinking into the sand.

I walked backward to get a better look at the situation. "We might need to move it forward where the sand isn't so soft. It's leaning on the left."

"I despise beach weddings," Sarah muttered as she grabbed a side to straighten it out.

"How dare you." How could she hate this? It was November and the sun was shining, warm and bright. I jogged back to help her. I braced the arch with some sandbags, which I covered with an arrangement of white roses, plumeria, and palm fronds. "Isn't it a gorgeous day for a wedding?"

"You say that about every wedding." Sarah hammered in stakes to keep the arch steady. When we were sure it wouldn't float into the Pacific Ocean, we climbed up the pier, stomping sand off our boots to head out for the night.

"I'll come back tomorrow to pick up the rentals," I said before Sarah and I split ways. "See you next week!"

"Is it the Escanilla-Lim engagement party?" Sarah groaned. "You sure you want to do their wedding, Elise? I could tell just by looking at this guy that he's going to be a groomzilla."

I already knew that. Everything was more, more, more with this groom. He texted me new inspiration pictures every day ever since he hired me, but I couldn't say no. This couple was referred to me by several aunties. And with his budget, I didn't want to say no. If the engagement party was going to be this extravagant, I could only imagine what he'd want for his actual wedding day. "Don't forget to bring your winning attitude."

Sarah scoffed. "Don't forget to bring your man."

"He'll be there."

When Ben resigned, it opened his schedule to pursue his pop-up. He made his apartment a test kitchen for weeks before reserving a spot at the farmers market. I had to tell him I couldn't eat Hainan chicken for the sixteenth day in a row. That was my Hainan chicken limit, apparently. When he wasn't cooking, he volunteered to help me around the studio. I told him he wasn't obligated to help when I couldn't pay him yet. To which he said, "I'll leave if you don't want me here, but I like being here."

How was I supposed to turn him away after that?

I drove to Ben's apartment. I was staying there while my mom renovated our house. When I walked through the door, Ben was at the sink, washing dishes.

I greeted him with a back hug and picked up a towel to help dry. "So, who do you think will win?"

The scandal had been resolved after about three weeks, when the investigation cleared everyone from Donna Yu's office. The clickbait headlines still resulted in a drop in Donna's lead, but it wasn't long before an "anonymous" tip revealed that Shawn Tam was a few credits short of his MBA. Shawn got clowned on social media for a few days before it died down. The election was as tight as ever.

Ben dropped a kiss on my temple. "I don't know. Rebecca will tell us on Tuesday."

After Beth and Ethan's wedding, Ben and my weekends were getting more and more booked for work—thanks to all the media coverage and referrals. I always worried that my friends would get too busy for me, but I ended up being the busy one. It was okay because my friends tried their best to accommodate our schedule, meeting us on weeknights. We made time for each other. Ben folded easily into our group and with each outing, Rebecca and Ben gradually rebuilt their sibling bond.

"She did say she had big news," I said, putting away a stack of plates. "Do you think she's pregnant?"

"No," Ben said, drying off his hands. "Mark wouldn't be able to keep that to himself."

"Can you imagine Mark as a father?" I pointed at Ben when he made a face. "You're mean. That's your brother-in-law!"

Ben threw down his towel and chased me out of the kitchen. "You're mean. You're the one who brought it up."

I laughed as I dodged him, running around the couch. But then he switched directions and caught me. I screamed and accidentally kicked him in the nuts. I was happy my reflexes still worked, but Ben wasn't as thrilled.

Ben clutched his groin, writhing in pain on the floor. "I knew you were trouble when I met you."

"Ha-ha." I joined him on the floor and wrapped my arms around him, tucking him under my chin. "You should have had me arrested."

"You know what I was thinking?" Ben said in between ragged breaths. "If we ever got married, Mark would be *your* brother-in-law."

I gasped. The horror.

"Why do you hurt me like that?" I said, even though my heart fluttered as it did whenever Ben brought up marriage. It was easy for us to talk about it since we'd spent the beginning of our relationship at weddings, but we weren't in a rush. We liked how our lives were right now, getting to know each other day by day, turning the days into weeks and months. I was having the time of my life, lying on the floor, having and holding the one I loved.

Acknowledgments

I was so excited when I got the green light for this book. For a long time I've wanted to write a story about weddings that also celebrated friendships. However, when it was time to put pen to paper, I came down with a severe case of writer's block. This book was hard to write, so I'm grateful for the following people who cheered me along this journey.

Thank you to my agent, Laura Bradford, for guiding me through this tough year.

To my editor, May Chen—my books are better because of you. Thank you to all the hardworking folks at Avon/HarperCollins who touched this book, giving it that extra love and sparkle before it hits the shelves, including Allie Roche, Diahann Sturge, Karen Richardson, Yeon Kim, Jennifer Hart, Elsie Lyons, Brittany Di-Mare, Pamela Barricklow, Marie Rossi, Jessica Rozler, and Hope Breeman. Jes Lyons, I'm always excited to see an email from you. Debs Lim, thank you for this gorgeous cover! I immediately fell in love!

Joyce and Laura, I am indebted to both of you for reading early drafts during your own eventful year! Both of you kept me going when I wasn't sure I had any more to give.

Thank you to my writer friends for being real with me in

the group chats. Suzanne Park, Michelle Quach, and Carolyn Huynh—I can't wait for our next four-hour lunch meeting. Alicia Thompson, you always make me laugh. Joanne Machin, thanks for reading early chapters of this book! Much love to Sloth and Steady Writers—Linh, Daphne, Evalyn, Karra, and Cecile—for your continuous support. Thanks to the Asian Romance Authors Slack group for uplifting our community.

Shout-out to Amanda at Bookish Brews for championing books by marginalized authors. Thank you to Jes Vu for your kindness. To Jess Ju for immediately getting the 888 wedding experience and reminding me why I wanted to write this book. To Natalie Naudus and Reuben Uy for bringing my books to life with your voice, humor, and talent.

Since this is a book about friendship, I have to thank my wonderful friends, who've been there for me through the seasons of my life. To my Superfriends, I love you for life. To the Goof Troop, you're all so freaking amazing. Thanks to Portia for letting me pick your brain! Thanks to Allen for being my one-man street team, lol.

Thank you to the Asian American leaders and organizers, past and present, for tirelessly advocating for our community, especially during these difficult times. You inspire me.

Honorable mention to my regular boba shop for supplying enough sugar and popcorn chicken to get me through this book. Much love to Teresa Teng.

To my family, who showed up for me time and time again. Thank you to Phuong for being so generous with your knowledge. Thank you to Plumeria Design Studio (RIP) for the apprenticeship. Thanks to Sue for giving me my first shot at being a bridesmaid. To everyone who watched the kids when it was crunch time, I couldn't have done this without you. Thanks to

Ma for feeding me when I wrote at the house and to Ba for teaching me that sometimes you have to be the first volunteer to get karaoke going at a wedding.

To David, who did the laundry and dishes and made the kids' lunches when I was on deadline. I love you and joi sia! Alice and Sophie, thank you for not touching Mommy's computer.

Finally, a big thank-you to the readers, librarians, booksellers, bloggers, and content creators who support my writing. I literally couldn't do any of this without you.

About The Author

JULIE TIEU is a Chinese American writer, born and raised in Southern California. When she is not writing, she is reading, on the hunt for delicious eats, or dreaming about her next travel adventure. She lives in the Los Angeles area with her high school crush husband and two energetic daughters.

READ MORE BY
JULIE TIEU

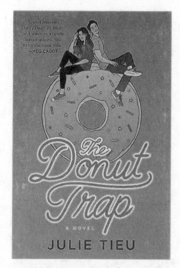

"Donut miss this tasty treat! Julie Tieu is going on my auto-buy list. Her writing is as fresh and warm as a newly baked glazed. You need this book now."
—Meg Cabot, author of the *Little Bridge Island* and *Princess Diaries* series

Julie Tieu sparkles in this debut romantic comedy, which is charmingly reminiscent of the TV show *Kim's Convenience* and *Frankly in Love* by David Yoon, about a young woman who feels caught in the life her parents have made for her until she falls in love and finds a way out of the donut trap.

"Endearing, unabashedly tropey... Cadence and Matt's very different, but equally loving, family backgrounds only enhance their romance. This breezy outing is sure to please."
—*Publishers Weekly*

Julie Tieu, an exciting new and diverse voice in contemporary romance, returns with a hilarious and sexy new novel about colleagues who decide to take their relationship outside the office.